I0760388

HOUSE OF DUSK, HOUSE OF DAWN

THE HOUSE OF CRIMSON & CLOVER VOLUME XII

SARAH M. CRADIT

Cover Design by Sarah M. Cradit
Editing by Lawrence Editing

First Edition
ISBN: 1976466199
ISBN-13: 978-1976466199

Publisher Contact:
sarah@sarahmcradit.com
www.sarahmcradit.com

ALSO BY SARAH M. CRADIT

KINGDOM OF THE WHITE SEA

Kingdom of the White Sea Trilogy

The Kingless Crown

The Broken Realm

The Hidden Kingdom

The Book of All Things

The Raven and the Rush

The Sylvan and the Sand

The Altruist and the Assassin

The Melody and the Master

The Claw and the Crowned

THE SAGA OF CRIMSON & CLOVER

The House of Crimson and Clover Series

The Storm and the Darkness

Shattered

The Illusions of Eventide

Bound

Midnight Dynasty

Asunder

Empire of Shadows

Myths of Midwinter

The Hinterland Veil

The Secrets Amongst the Cypress

Within the Garden of Twilight

House of Dusk, House of Dawn

Midnight Dynasty Series

A Tempest of Discovery

A Storm of Revelations

A Torrent of Deceit

The Seven Series

1970

1972

1973

1974

1975

1976

1980

Vampires of the Merovingi Series

The Island

and more

The Dusk Trilogy

St. Charles at Dusk: The Story of Oz and Adrienne

Flourish: The Story of Anne Fontaine

Banshee: The Story of Giselle Deschanel

Crimson & Clover Stories

Surrender: The Story of Oz and Ana

Shame: The Story of Jonathan St. Andrews

Fire & Ice: The Story of Remy & Fleur

Dark Blessing: The Landry Triplets

Pandora's Box: The Story of Jasper & Pandora

The Menagerie: Oriana's Den of Iniquities

A Band of Heather: The Story of Colleen and Noah

The Ephemeral: The Story of Autumn & Gabriel

Bayou's Edge: The Landry Triplets

For more information, and exciting bonus material, visit www.sarahmcradit.com

FOREWORD

Here we are, at the end of everything.

Or, at least, *The House of Crimson & Clover* series.

When I began this journey, with a star-crossed love story called *St. Charles at Dusk,* I envisioned and built an entire world to support that single tale. I'm surprised I didn't know back then how it would turn into not only a series but an entire world... a saga. Rich family histories (particularly when those families are witches) have always been a favorite read of mine, and, like most authors, I write the books I want to read.

Imagine my surprise (and delight!) when so many of you wanted to read them as well. Writers write because storytelling and word-spinning are organic pieces of who we are as human beings, but there's a wholly new kind of magic attached to the moments when someone who is not us says, "I want more."

You wanted more, and the series blossomed. Imagination is like an unpeeled onion, and as the story unfolded, more stories revealed themselves. At some point, I began to see we were cresting the mountain, so to speak, on the storylines driving *The House of Crimson & Clover*. Yet even as we neared this end point, it was clear to me that there was more—a lot more—story to be told. I had toyed with the idea of spinoff series concepts, but it wasn't until I made the decision to tie up *The House of Crimson & Clover* that the new ideas took on fresh life and clear formation. Thus, *The Saga of Crimson & Clover,* the world in which this series and future series are contained, was born.

Endings are always bittersweet. I've devoted many years of my life to *The House of Crimson & Clover*. But these particular stories have reached their natural conclusion, and I hope you will be as satisfied with where I left each of our heroes, heroines, and villains as I am. For some, their stories end here (for now). For others, they will live on and take on new adventures in the series to come.

Presently, there are three additional series in this world. *Vampires of the Merovingi* is aa historical fantasy look into the de Blanchefort vampires and their origins. *The Seven* follows Colleen and her siblings through the most critical years of their youth in the '70s, and the events that shaped the family into who they are now. And *Midnight Dynasty* picks up, for some of the characters, where this series leaves off.

So, Dear Reader, as you begin with the end of the current journey, I leave you with the promise of new stories, new adventures, and a world I will likely be writing in until I draw my final breath.

Thank you for being here.

You can find a complete list of content warnings on my website: sarahmcradit.com

For every reader who has taken this journey alongside me, encouraging me, pushing me to find the words and giving me the inspiration to take this all the way to the finish.

"In the end is my beginning."

Mary, Queen of Scots

THE EMPRESS

PART ONE
THE BATTLE FOR FARJHEM

1
TRISTAN

Tristan gave one last searching glance at the monolithic glacier towering above them, a frozen wall stretching clear to the sky. Though inanimate, the iced fortification pulsed with the life of what lay beyond. The steam of pure cold rising from the ice was as clear a reminder as ever that he was as far from home as the earth allowed.

Anders was not wrong: the magic cloaking Farjhem was infallible. Marveling at this sheet of ice so massive it was seemingly unscalable, one would never guess it foreshadowed an entire world beyond. Only the subtle undercurrent of beating power rising with the steam betrayed this glacier was more than it seemed.

Harriett bundled in tighter. Her mind was as silent as her mouth and Tristan did nothing to challenge that. Even if he had felt talkative, he had nothing to say. The danger they headed into was immeasurable next to anything they'd done in their lives so far. Words would be as inadequate as they were useless at this juncture.

Tarek nodded at Anders. "Are we going to admire the view or get this done?"

The words snapped Anders back to his regimented self. "Follow me." He started off into the mounds of snow, but halted, turning to face them. His shouted response was hardly a whisper among the interminable blanket of eternal winter. "Say nothing when we get inside. Not until I've determined we are alone."

He trekked forth without awaiting a response. Tristan, Harriett, and Tarek dutifully followed.

TRISTAN WAS IN THE SEVENTH GRADE WHEN THE FIRST *HARRY POTTER* book released. He'd clamored and begged his mother to stand in line with him outside the Garden District Book shop, hours before it opened, sweating in the late summer heat. A boy wizard is sent to a magical boarding school, where he learns cool spells, makes lifelong friends, and triumphs over evil sorcerers? What's not to love?

He never told Elizabeth, not after the first book, or the second, or even the fourth, that he knew deep in his marrow his own life would have turned out for the better had he been sent away to learn more about who he was instead of spending his youth minding the emotional state of his mother.

Now, he would give anything to go back to those old days, to ease her from a panic attack, or reassure her of his love. He would take all the bad and uncomfortable just to have her back.

Both Elizabeth and Connor were on his mind as the stalwart group moved achingly through the blinding snow. He focused on lifting one boot with great effort and thrusting it back down with powerful inertia. Over and over. They were not going far, but a yard was a mile in snow this deep. *Mind your body temperature,* his mother cooed from the back of his mind somewhere. *If you begin to sweat, you must slow down. It won't do to have the sweat freeze against your skin.* His father had words for him as well. *Don't think about how far you have to go, son. Instead, think of how far you've come.*

Tristan slammed to a stop when he hit a wall. No, not a wall, Tarek. The snow muffled Tarek's grumbles. Harriett fell against his back as she caught up to the traffic accident.

"We're here!" Anders yelled.

Where? Tristan wanted to ask. The view hadn't changed in an agonizing long while. Snow and ice as far as his gaze could span. White upon white upon more white.

Anders looked up, along the ice shelf, toward the sky. With a brief glance back, he nodded and moved forward. He disappeared into the glacier.

Harriett gasped behind him. Tristan felt the same shock. But Tarek didn't falter in his lagged steps, and then, he too disappeared. They were both gone, with no instruction and no explanation. Just... gone.

It's like that book of yours, Tristan. You know. The one about the wizard.

Harry Potter, *Mom. And it's not just one book.*

Yes, whatever it's called. I remember you telling me the little wizard walked right into a wall and it took him somewhere magical. In my day, we called an experience like that a 'good trip.'

Platform 9 ¾. Not LSD. No one cares about your drug stories, Mom.

Well, whatever, Tristan. You know what to do.

Yes, he knew what to do.

He reached for Harriett's gloved hand in the blizzard and squeezed through the thick fabric.

Tristan closed his eyes as he approached the glacier and took a leap of faith.

. . .

THERE WAS NOTHING AT ALL TO IT. NO FLIP-FLOPPING OF HIS UNSTEADY stomach, no strange gust of wind. Arriving through Farjhem's secret, forgotten entrance was as easy as walking through any regular old door in Tristan's world.

The consistency of the air changed dramatically in an instant. The choking, bitter cold of outside was replaced by a new but equally repressive must that filled their lungs and produced immediate bouts of coughing from all but Anders. The creature had no pressure points, Tristan thought. His construction was pure blood and steel.

Plumes of dust fell from the dark sky. Anders' refusal to bring in light meant Tristan was left to guess at the contents of the sediment, and his mind immediately went to the crumbling, ancient bones of his Empyrean ancestors.

A shudder passed through him. Harriett shook her head.

Don't tell me you didn't think the same thing. He broke their shared silence.

If I had but one last wish, Tristan, it would be to visit all the places your imagination goes to and see the world through your eyes.

Tristan didn't know how to respond to that, and meanwhile, Anders had progressed forward and disappeared from his limited view. He struggled to catch up, and Harriett fell into pace behind him.

He had so many questions. He should have asked more before the start of the mission, should have quelled his swiftly beating heart and budding adrenaline and stopped long enough to understand the practicalities. How long was the tunnel once inside? How big was the Blacksmith shop? What the heck was the crap that would fall on them from the sky like old death?

And how would they know when the rest of the Brotherhood's army made it into Farjhem and put their plan into motion? Anders and Tarek intimated *they* would know, but would they share?

Ahead, Anders' heavy steps stilled. Tarek as well came to a stop, and soon, Tristan could see why. They had entered a clearing that seemed to be some kind of room, if you could call it that. More like an enclave, and a somewhat tidier version of the dark and dusty cave they'd just emerged from.

The room had some natural light, though Tristan could not determine the source. All around them, extraordinary steel languished in rotting wooden cases. Sword upon sword, the likes of which Tristan had only seen in movies and read in books. But these weren't decent props; before him lay a graveyard of perhaps the most impressive sword collection existing upon the earth.

Moths and spiders ate away at the corners of the Blacksmith shop. Two massive steel anvils flanked a cobwebbed forge whose better days were long behind it. Termites, or some other parasite, had long consumed most of the wood in the room, and the cases listed to this side or that, barely held aloft by their foundations. Some had long ago given up the ghost and lay in tattered heaps on the dirt floor, their steel contents in a messy pile. Weapons that would sell for more than his father's car in a free trade market just *lying* there, as if they no longer had a purpose in this world.

Tristan had a strong urge to ask more about the place, but his better sense—which was a new, surprising part of himself he was only beginning to come into—kicked in before he could make the error. The time for his questions had passed, and that time may never come again. He was not a child anymore, expecting placating by all the adults cultivating his natural curiosities. The dependencies of adult intervention in his life were his greatest struggles in achieving grown-up independence. Now, for the first time in his life, he made the switch from child to adult without much effort.

He looked at Anders. Anders closed his eyes. Listened. For

what, Tristan didn't know, and once again, knew better than to ask.

When his eyes flashed open, Anders had a peace about him that calmed Tristan enough for him to release his long-held breath.

"We are alone. For now." Anders' voice reached barely above a careful whisper. "I do not expect this will last long. I have nothing else to tell you, Tristan and Tarek, that you don't already know. The clock here will tick faster than any you've ever encountered. Harriett and I will pace the perimeter for as long as we need to, or until our safety has been breached. Are you ready?"

Tarek nodded. Tristan paused long enough for Anders to say,

"You have no choice. The clock starts now. Be swift!"

Tristan felt the quick, soft squeeze of Harriett's hand, her one brief reassurance before she disappeared to help Anders. He looked to his left at Tarek, but the creature's lids were closed, the eyes beneath them fluttering like the onset of R.E.M. sleep.

Tristan drew in one final breath, cleared his mind, and his eyes, too, closed.

Aleksandr. Show yourself.

2
AGRIPIN

From Farsengel to the throne room at the palace. Agripin would have heartily approved of the change in scenery, swapping prison for opulence, under just about any other circumstance. Except, in their present reality, the prison was their only blanket of safety. As long as they were there, they were not headed for their execution, or, possibly, standing on the very spot of the event. The throne room under his soulless sister Oriana was no longer a place for joy and celebration. It was now the centerpiece for her short but bloodthirsty reign of terror.

Guards lined every inch of the perimeter. In their crimson uniforms, pressed up against the shock of lily white walls Oriana had ordered painted under her rule, they appeared to be elaborate elements of the scenery more than a threat. But Agripin harbored no illusions as to why they were here. Not to protect Agripin and Aleksandr, but to prevent them from trying to flee.

All the chairs were removed from the vast throne room, except the throne itself. The absence of furniture had the effect of lengthening the room into an abyss of white and crimson marble —Oriana would have removed the crimson from the flooring,

Agripin was certain, had the marble not been centuries old and the materials so difficult to bring into Farjhem—that stretched on farther than Agripin had remembered.

He himself had sat upon that throne, however briefly. He could do it now if he wanted. The guards were unlikely to stop him. They weren't likely to stop him from doing anything, really, except escaping, and he had no illusions of *that* with the magic bindings they'd applied before the heavy doors closed with a resounding boom.

Agripin suspected the guards were lulled into a sense of security by the magic trussing him and Aleksandr, but he knew something they apparently did not. Bindings only bound so much magic on a mystic. His abilities were only muted, not extinguished. Agripin hypothesized the same was true for the tall, quiet, so-called Savior of the Realm, who leaned in introspective silence against the dais.

Agripin could not help but be amazed by Aleksandr, who seemed to be taking the fact of his imminent execution with the strength of one bearing a spine of crucible steel. He betrayed no emotion when the guards dragged them from Farsengel, and had said or done nothing since to indicate his distress. He *must* be terrified, Agripin thought. Although he had the face of a grown man, he had barely walked the earth for a year. He was an infant in many ways that mattered... a babe lost in the wilderness, without the loving protection of his mother or father.

Or *was* he terrified? Since meeting Aleksandr, Agripin had come to learn the boy met none of his pre-conceived ideas. He was no child, and certainly not naïve, not in the ways most would define the word. Aleksandr had said to Agripin that he wasn't afraid to die, and he saw none of the untested bravado of the very young in his eyes. Reflected back rather was the calm resolution of the very old. He was an enigma, one potentially very worth deciphering. Agripin worried there wasn't time to solve this mystery before their lives became forfeit to Emyr.

"You're very brave, Halfling," Agripin ventured. His pacing stopped as he approached Aleksandr.

Aleksandr squinted as he chanced a look up, ever briefly. "What would you know about bravery?"

Agripin overlooked the slight. He had, after all, ordered the execution of Aleksandr's father. A few verbal jabs would hardly even the score. "You get that from all three of your parents. They all know their own bravery, and I've witnessed it in each of them. Your mother draws her strength from a fire deep within her. Your first father, Finn, from the water stretching across the earth. And Aidrik from the air around him."

"What is that, poetry?" Aleksandr pulled his legs to his chest and dropped his head on his knees. "Or do you always get reflective when your head is about to roll?"

"You are right to infer my head has been poised to roll more than once," Agripin joked, though the fun fell short and neither of them laughed. "Your mother and fathers are some of the best creatures I've ever known. Perhaps I *am* reflective. Perhaps I'm only offering you an honest perspective and kind words. Which would you rather believe?"

"I don't believe anything that comes out of your mouth," Aleksandr groused, his words muffled against his grubby jeans.

Agripin continued, not for Aleksandr, but for himself. He had always pushed forth in action, sometimes without much strategic forethought, and as a prince of the realm, things had always worked out. But the execution of Aidrik, he could see now, was not one of his finest moments. It might be his darkest. "I regret what happened to your father," he confessed. "At the time, I convinced myself and others my decision to throw him on the sword was to save us all. I see now it was only to save my own hide."

Aleksandr tilted his head to the side against his knees. One eye peered up. “You only see that now?”

“Have you never made a mistake? Never erred in your own judgment?”

Aleksandr smirked, but it disappeared in a cloud of thoughts Agripin couldn’t read. He wondered if Aleksandr was questioning his own decision to trust someone who had pretended to be his friend and then led him to his fate in Farjhem.

“I mean the words. I need not your belief in me to say them,” Agripin pressed on. His boots clicked against the solid marble as he resumed his pacing. He had no real desire to move, only the knowledge he might not have the luxury much longer. “I was jealous of Aidrik the Wise. He was the son my father wished I could be. I knew it then. I know it now. It matters not at present, and perhaps it should not have mattered then. Aidrik was a friend and brethren, and I would have killed for him. But I confess it now—to you, whether you’ll hear it or nay, for there is no one else to hear it—I felt a sharp satisfaction in ending his life. In this truth rests the darkest corner of my soul. We all have one, you know. Some of us only manage to avoid it longer.”

“You say you regret killing him, then you say you loved it?” Aleksandr rolled his head away. “Confessing you’re a monster doesn’t make you less of one.”

“Did I say I was less of a monster? Or only a clearer one as I paint the whole of myself before you?”

Aleksandr said nothing.

“Despite what I’ve confessed about my darkness leading me into that terrible decision, I regret it. I do. In my dreams, I stole away from Farjhem with your parents, forsaking my realm for my loyalties. In the beginning, I misread your human parents’ peculiarities as weaknesses. I saw them as less than what I was, and I derided them for this. But as I grew to know them, and later, when they were gone and I continued to unravel who they were, I understood their strength—their combined strength, in addition to their unique individual strengths—was greater than any I had ever known. In my prejudice, I overlooked something marvelous. I regret that as well."

Aleksandr waved one arm around the room without looking up. "There are hundreds of people here who might care more than I do."

"Yet none who deserve these words more than you."

"What I deserve is some peace before I die."

"You're still resolved to let them kill you."

Aleksandr laughed. "You keep saying stuff like that, but you haven't offered a single idea for how the hell to get us out of this mess. So yes, monster, I'm coming to terms with my death because I'd rather not die trembling in fear."

"You? The son of Anasofiya of the Darkness? Of Finnegan the Brave? Of Aidrik the Wise?"

"Mock me all you want, we're both ending this day the same way."

The massive double doors at the other end of the throne room yawned open with a cavernous belch. Agripin whipped his gaze in that direction.

It was not Oriana, though, nor the executioner. Cyler rushed across the marble, his robe a crimson wave flying behind him, one long contiguous swish across the flooring. The guards broke their silence, mumbling in confusion as the interloper drew closer to the prisoners.

"Oriana means to kill you both," Cyler said in haste.

"Why, the whole world must know this by now!" Agripin said with a booming laugh.

Cyler didn't crack a smile. "Publicly, Aggie. She means to murder Aleksandr before the crowd to silence any further insurgencies in Farjhem. And you."

"Publicly. Privately." Agripin waved his hands around. "Dead is dead."

Cyler's frustration rose in his cheeks. "You didn't train me to lie down like a beaten dog before my enemies."

A flurry of activity rose near the door as new guards flooded into the room. Cyler gave a single glance back and then returned his eyes to his old master. "You trained me to remember that nothing is over until it is."

The guards swarmed Cyler, asserting he didn't belong, wasn't authorized. Word hadn't reached Oriana of Cyler's treasonous release of Maxima or he'd be in chains. Cyler shook them off and obediently followed, but cast a long glance over his shoulder as he exited.

Do something, his eyes beseeched.

But what? Agripin wondered as the doors closed on them. And why would Cyler look to him for a solution when he was the prisoner? What could he possibly do?

But while the answer remained elusive, the question nagged at him from every corner of his mind.

Agripin's greatest trait—and he would tell anyone this, over whiskey, over warfare, with his sword at their throat—was his resourcefulness. He was often disloyal, self-serving, and short-sighted, but these things had never proved fatal due to his unusual ingenuity.

And could it be... as he thought of his confessions... his true depth of remorse... that his greatest trait could also lead to his atonement?

Agripin turned from the boy and set his sights on a plan.

3
NERYS

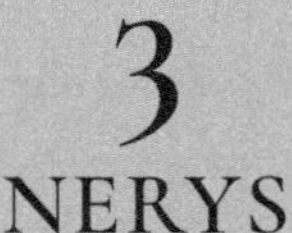

It was Nerys' idea to enter Farjhem first, before the rest of the Dragon Brotherhood. They didn't like her plan. The idea was too risky, they said, throwing her out like a decoy when she was so valuable. Her life meant more than this.

And how am I even a drop more valuable than any of you? Any of us?

Nerys received no response. To speak aloud the arguments against these questions would be to admit their cause was not as noble as they liked to believe. These were the tenuous threads holding their movement together, separating themselves from those on the side of the enemy.

Nerys waited until the precise moment she felt Anders and the others disappear beyond the magic barrier of Farjhem. Their entrance might or might not signal guards, but as soon as Nerys stepped through herself, the focus would shift squarely to the bold duchess striding across the ancient lands of her ancestors.

As predicted, they detected her no sooner than her feet landed on the soft grass of the Valley of Meditation. Of course, Nerys hadn't slinked into her homeland using a side or secret entrance. She arrived the way any respectable Empyrean would, entering mere feet before the guard station that opened onto the dirt road to the palace.

The roaring current of the River Farvann stilled her soul, even as a rush of guards came at her. With her rogue braids and leather tunic, she didn't belong here, at least not to them and their adherent sensibilities.

One of the younger ones, a cherubic fledgling with a mane of hair as red as his robe, puffed his chest as he prepared to launch his interrogation, excited at the opportunity for action after what had undoubtedly been an entire service of peace. She heard his impending questions in her head as if he'd already said them. *Do you have the authorization to enter Farjhem? Who provided the authorization? What is your business here? Show me your Mark!*

But an elder recognized her even quicker than she anticipated. He pressed his hand to the fledgling's chest and stepped forward, dropping into a reverent bow. "Duchess. It has been far too long."

"Rise," she said gently. "We are all equals in the eyes of Emyr."

The guard's eyes widened as if she had just committed great blasphemy, but he remembered himself and smiled. "The empress did not advise us of your arrival. You know I must ask you..."

"And I shall tell you," Nerys replied, "that my sister, Oriana, does not expect me, nor shall she be particularly grateful to see me."

The other guards shuffled in unease, awaiting the one with authority to guide them on what this meant and how they should handle it.

"Duchess..."

"I won't cause trouble for you," Nerys soothed. She stretched a hand toward his arm and smiled. "In fact, I insist you escort me to the Royal Palace. Without binding would be my preference, but it is not my way to impede your tradition, or put you in position for reprimand later."

The guard dropped his eyes, and a great flush appeared in his soft, round cheeks. "I would never... but I have your word? You will ascend in peace?"

Nerys leveled a look on him, kind but with the reproach of a mother. "If my word is needed, then you have it."

He looked suitably contrite as he gestured toward the path that ran alongside the Farvann. "We will walk five paces behind you. That is all I can afford."

"And I thank you for affording me that," Nerys replied and started toward the path, toward the hill, toward her sister.

Toward a plan she was not as confident in as she had led her peers to believe.

THE TREK THROUGH THE VALLEY AND UP THE LONG SLOPE OF THE GLACIER leading to all important and official structures of Farjhem came and went without much fanfare until they were past the Market beyond Towne Center. Nerys might have passed without detection on her own, but flanked by a dozen guards meant all eyes instinctively drew toward whatever caused such substantial attention. Empyreans employed within the realm of Farjhem—scholars, merchants, tradesmen, and all others who kept the land thriving without the need for outside influence—shopped for breads and jams, for textiles and earthenware. Those who had chosen a life in Farjhem were among the most devout, and thereby, very old. Old enough to remember the last time Duchess Nerys held court.

One scholar, Scholar Mya if Nerys' memory served, let her basket sag down her arm, dangling precariously from her wrist as her mouth gaped in shock. Shocked to see her, Nerys wondered, or to see her enter with such an escort? A silversmith Nerys remembered as one of her father Aeron's favorites lowered both arms to his sides in slow reverence and bowed his head. Nerys prayed no one working for Oriana witnessed this, or the man would pay later.

Nerys allowed herself a light nod in appreciation, enough to thank him but hopefully not enough to draw the attention of the guards his way. Others followed suit, emboldened by the silversmith, so Nerys pulled her eyes back to the path, unwilling to see good Empyreans punished for her decision to return uninvited.

She straightened her spine and threw back her braids. She also tried to heave away her growing fears, which festered even more with the panicked looks of her brethren.

Nerys was forced to admit she did not have enough information to have assessed the situation so thoroughly and confidently. She believed she knew her sister, but she had never seen Oriana rule from a throne larger than The Menagerie. She had never seen Oriana mired in desperation and struggling to rule a land that didn't want her. Nerys was counting on Oriana recognizing the people loved Nerys too much for her to be expendable, but what if Oriana was past such considerations?

As they ascended the glacier, the grade of the passage slowed their pace. Soaring above them, Senetat Sanctuary, only a crescent from afar, moved into full view. Towering spires of crimson and gold wound clear into the sky, with the domes at the base glinting from the last of the day's sun. Nerys had never supported the governing body of Emyr, but she longed for the days when there was at least concern to keep up appearances. Now it was a circus of thieves and vagabonds whose only qualifications were continued attendance at The Menagerie.

They pushed past the Sanctuary and farther up the hill. The air was crisper the higher they drew northward. Nerys had forgotten how icy her homeland could be and, despite

Empyreans being born of fire, she was no longer used to it. But she betrayed no outward signs of her discomfort and trekked on.

The running water of Farjhem's many waterfalls kept her mind company on the long, quiet walk. The guards, especially the most senior one behind the decision to allow her to walk unfettered, looked ready to engage her in questions, but never did. Whether it was because their respect for her ran too deep, or their fear of Oriana did, Nerys could only speculate.

At last the golden gates yawned open, and the palace lay before them. Nerys turned to her gaolers and smiled. "I know my way from here. Thank you for the escort."

Their discomfort in letting her go on alone was written clearly across all their faces, but at last the senior guard nodded. He sent another on ahead to deliver the news to Grand Empress Oriana, and then nodded at Nerys.

"We will be at the doors."

She regarded him with patient understanding. His meaning was clear: we will allow you your dignity, but your entrance will be a one-way trip unless Oriana deems otherwise. Our hands are bound on this.

"If the fortune of Emyr smiles upon us today," Nerys replied, one eye to the palace and the troubles she had invited upon herself, "then you and I will next meet under much more favorable circumstances."

"You are either very brave or exceptionally foolish for coming here," Oriana charged.

"What if I'm neither?" Nerys dared not approach her sister, not out of any great fear, but more the risk her heart might soften at the sight of her own blood. She couldn't afford to forget Oriana was their adversary. "I only wish to talk."

"You've come a long way for that." Oriana huffed as she

turned to face her sister. "Or have you? I don't know *where* you've been all these years."

"Most Empyreans roam when they reach maturity," Nerys said. "My leaving was not unexpected."

"Most Empyreans are not of royal blood."

"And what did that matter for me, the third born? Agripin was always the next in line to our father and then came you in the event our brother met with some unfortunate accident. That never left room for me, least not in any official capacity." Nerys had said the words at face value, but as she heard them replay in her head, she realized the important truth behind them. She had never experienced any resentment toward her siblings for their elevated stations, but only now had she understood how this fact had shaped her life. For better or worse, Nerys had lived for herself.

Oriana's heels clicked across the marble as she approached. She bent her hand at the wrist and swatted Nerys' braid, wound with leaves and other forest detritus. "Rebellion doesn't suit you, sister. When have you last bathed?"

"This evening past," Nerys answered, unfazed. "When have you last stepped foot outside Farjhem to see how the rest of the world lives?"

Oriana flashed a proud, haughty smile. "Never. And I never will."

"Father did. Father knew it was important to rule with the world in mind, not our tiny homeland."

"Father was foolish, and the Senetat had him killed for it."

"Father understood most of us live outside Farjhem, not within. He had his faults, but he ruled far longer than most of his predecessors, and this didn't happen by chance."

Oriana crossed her arms over her chest. "*Father* is why the rebels were allowed to flourish in the first place. His treasonous ideals about personal freedom have led to more Empyreans living outside our tracking system than within, and how does that lend to solid leading?"

"You are describing a leadership that only thrives when the leader controls his subjects." Nerys sighed. She shouldn't argue with her sister over something she could never change, but her passion was too great. "Emyr did not create us in the belief any one of us was greater than another. Good leaders govern so that their people may thrive. Great leaders can do it without encroaching on others' lives more than they need to."

She shook her head. The sound shimmered in the air with her hair full of jewels. "You know nothing, Nerys, and never have."

Nerys felt her face flush dark red as the blood rushed forward. "You are killing your own kind! Murdering them, Oriana! If you think even *one* of those lives is expendable, is not as great as your own—"

Oriana's hand snaked out and slapped her across the cheek before Nerys could move from her path. "You are a fool, Nerys, who has never, not once, had to lead anyone but herself. Spend a day governing our people and then tell me you would do better."

"I don't *need* to spend a day as empress to know I would do better," Nerys hissed. "Because no cause on earth would compel me to order the murder of my people! Innocent people! And now... now you have set your sights on destroying the hope of a prophecy that, if fulfilled, would grant peace to all Empyreans. A leader who loved her people would do anything in her power to see it done, and instead, you are determined to see it unraveled. You cannot stand before me and pretend you love Emyr or his creations while setting out toward their destruction."

Oriana's eyes narrowed. Her shadowed lids sparkled. "You won't stop me," she said. Her heavily powdered face looked shocking and unnatural as she drew closer to Nerys, noses nearly touching. "You can't entice me with lovely words about redemption, or seeking to better myself. I am not Agripin, preening for compliments filled with pandering half-truths. I know who I am, Nerys. I know who I am not. And if your Brotherhood was hungry for a better leader than me, they should not have set out to destroy Farjhem and leave me no choice but to take my place at the helm!"

With those words, Nerys confirmed her deepest suspicions about her sister: Oriana had not seized power out of hunger to rule, as some charged, but because there was no one else to do it. Oriana was not wrong about the Brotherhood. They had not planned well enough when they sent Agripin to Farjhem, and the result was the mess they now had before them.

This was a key reason why Nerys had never, until recently when she felt there was no other choice, aligned with any group. The rebels were *more* right than the Senetat in many ways, but they were not above reproach. Sometimes the path to goodness was wrought with collateral damage, and Nerys struggled with that more than the Brotherhood leaders who justified the carnage—physical and otherwise—as means to a peaceful end.

"Why not put our brother back on the throne?" Nerys asked, though even she did not think this option was still viable.

Oriana cackled. "Why not set ourselves on fire for sport?"

"You don't want to lead our people," Nerys said. "I understand. I never wanted to, either, though there was never much risk of it falling to me to begin with. So why not find another?"

"Who? Tell me, Nerys, who would be suitable? Agripin's loyalties change by the hour. You... well, if we are not outright enemies, we are at the very least adversaries. There is no one else of our blood, and the only other way to take this throne is by right of conquest, which would mean my death. Tell me, which of those choices sees me thrive?"

Nerys desperately wished she had a satisfying answer for her sister, but this was the underlying problem all along since Oriana had taken the throne. Oriana wanted only for the status quo —*her* status quo—to be maintained. Agripin's defection and subsequent fleeing of Farjhem ripped her from a place of comfort to a place of vengeance. She couldn't trust him to leave her in peace, and she couldn't trust Nerys not to have her tried for her crimes against their people. And Nerys could not promise that either of those things wouldn't come to fruition.

At least she had kept her sister occupied long enough to allow the Brotherhood to slip into Farjhem. And they were in now… she could feel them. So many of them! Trygve, Birger, Astrid, all the others. Their hearts beat in her own veins and gave her hope, purpose.

Oriana's choices lay at the tip of a double-edged sword, and Nerys would never sway her with words.

What she needed now was time.

"I *will* kill the boy," Oriana declared, cutting a swath through the long silence. She shuffled to the other end of the room, to the table housing her many bottles of wine. She poured a glass of something dark burgundy. She didn't offer one to Nerys. A long-swirling rumor had it that Oriana's wine was poisoned, and that she had built up her own resistance over the years. "I know that's why you're here. It's the only reason you would risk your neck when you know coming here means your death as well."

Nerys felt the curve of her bow at her hip. The guards around the room stirred but didn't move to strike. "You won't kill me, Oriana."

"How can you be so confident?"

Nerys gestured toward the assembled Crimson Guard. She watched them throughout her exchange with Oriana and observed the way they looked at each woman. They served Oriana from a place of dark fear, from a lack of another leader to lead them. Nerys did not necessarily want the job, but she knew who they would follow if it came to a choice. "Because, deep down you know that if you gave the order on my life, every last individual still in Farjhem, including those guards, including your hand-picked Senetat, would take yours instead."

Oriana's blood red lips parted. The gloves were off.

Come, my brothers and sisters. Quickly!

4
AIDRIK

Jonathan drove the rental car. The others were not in any presence of mind for more than gazing out the window in tormented reflection. Aidrik suspected Jonathan wasn't faring much better, but the stoic man never betrayed any emotion.

Aidrik might have offered to take the task for himself. He kept his enduring level head even with the world falling around him. Aidrik and cars were not on familiar terms, however. He believed they were convenient, but also an indulgent creation that brought Emyr's creations too far from their roots to be a boon. He had not spent enough time operating a motor vehicle to be confident he was the right choice now. And if their drive from Trondheim, Norway, was thwarted by something as banal as a traffic stop, he did not possess the appropriate paperwork to prove he had the right to be at the wheel.

Imagine, he thought, that their mission could fail on such a human technicality.

Finnegan sat beside his brother in the passenger seat, one elbow propped against the plastic door panel. He rested his face against his hand, and his eyes hadn't left the passing countryside. His fist drummed a persistent pattern against the middle console, which had to drive Jonathan nuts, but he said nothing.

Aidrik observed Finnegan struggle to maintain vital control. He retreated somewhere even Aidrik could not reach him. He stopped trying. His brother needed to be wherever he was if it afforded him the strength for the task ahead.

Jacob had joined Aidrik in the backseat. He mimicked Finnegan's quiet consideration but wore his anguish more visibly. Aidrik felt the Child of Man's fears for his wife ripple from him in palpable waves. That Jacob had nearly lost Amelia more than once sat at the front of his mind, laid bare in his vulnerable grief. Aidrik tried not to read his thoughts, but in his experience, the stronger the emotion, the louder it announced itself. Jacob's emotions were screaming.

Aleksandr was alive. Aidrik knew it, just as Finnegan knew it, in the intrinsic way a limb understands blood still flows through its veins. This feeling only lived in each single moment, with the knowledge everything could change in the next.

They had less than an hour to go, but it may as well have been a lifetime knowing what even a second could bring.

Jonathan rolled his hands over the wheel, tightening. Loosening. Tightening. The color returned to his knuckles and then disappeared again. Jonathan hadn't had the benefit of a year's training like his brother, Finnegan. He didn't yet know the means to block his thoughts, and perhaps didn't know he needed to. They were exposed to Aidrik, and where he felt some remorse in reading Jacob's, the same could not be said for Jonathan, who had caused great distress for Anasofiya. If Aidrik considered fate as a road, Jonathan set her on the highway leading her to the agonies she'd lived through in the past year.

No sooner had he seen through the mind of Jonathan St. Andrews did he wish to be free of it. This was a tortured soul unlike any other. His regrets twisted in the yawning darkness within, and they were ugly things, with teeth and poisoned tongues.

Now he also understood the man's intentions. Jonathan came along on this dangerous voyage with the intention of offering his life in exchange for his nephew's, and finally, be rid of his shadowy passengers.

Aidrik didn't welcome the empathy rising within him for the creature. He switched off his thoughts, and thus, Jonathan's, for the time being.

Finnegan sighed against the window. His breath fogged the glass and the snowy landscape beyond disappeared. Aidrik had not spent much time considering his own feelings, but his great love for Finnegan was one of the few times in his long life he had surprised himself. When he thought of Finnegan, he often still saw the young Child of Man who had, wide-eyed and innocent, asked to touch his sword. He could have never foreseen that man to one day be his equal.

Now he knew, as he watched his brother rap his knuckles on the plastic, as he watched him draw long breaths and release them with forced control, that he loved Finnegan as much as he loved Anasofiya. He was as much bound to his brother as he was to her. His willingness to share her with Finnegan had been a matter of grudging practicality when all along the fates had determined that Finnegan was also a significant part of his redemption. Of his soul.

Finnegan's realization of this connection came as a physical display in the dining room days before. That it should come on the eve of a battle that could result in one or both of their deaths was a cruelty startling even to Aidrik. But it solidified for him what he knew he must do.

It was likely they would all die today. But Aidrik, who had cheated death once, would not deign to do it twice. He didn't know if his revival was meant to be permanent or merely a tool intended for a single purpose, but he would rise to the occasion.

He would return his gift of resurrection to save Finnegan and Aleksandr, and send them home to Anasofiya. Jonathan, if so determined, might join him in the afterlife.

Anasofiya and Finnegan would have a life after today, and Aidrik would find a way to give it to them.

"HALT," AIDRIK DECLARED. ALL THREE MEN JUMPED AT THE SUDDEN break in silence you could cut with Ulfberht. "We leave the vehicle here."

"We're in the middle of nowhere," Jonathan said. The windshield wipers smeared snow to the edges of the window. He squinted through the walls of white all around them.

"As is Farjhem," Aidrik said without offering further explanation.

"I don't see anything resembling... anything," Jonathan argued. But even as he challenged Aidrik, he turned off the car and slipped on his gloves.

Jacob zipped his jacket and tucked his short hair into his knit cap. He flexed his hands to settle them into his thick gloves. "Right, then. Blind trust? Check. Invisible kingdom? Check. Ancient wizard who communicates only in vague, foreboding ways? Check."

He reached for the door, but Aidrik clapped a hand over his. "I do not know what we will find in Farjhem. Nora tells us of war, but we cannot know if we arrive on the eve of battle, amidst it, or in the wake of its carnage. I cannot sense what lies ahead."

"Doesn't matter," Finnegan muttered. "Aleksandr is alive. The rest is noise."

"The rest could become the difference between his life and his death," Aidrik countered. "I have no means to communicate with the Brotherhood. No inkling of their plans. I cannot guarantee the safety of *any* of us." He turned to Jacob. "Your wife and child await you at home. None will judge if you choose safety over danger." Then to Jonathan. "And you. This is not your battle."

"It's my only battle," Jonathan said softly.

"Not going anywhere, Merlin," Jacob added. "Not even if you bind me to the car with a complicated knot that I will then have to use my wits to—"

Aidrik silenced him with a hard look, despite his itch to smile. Jacob's use of humor as armor was unique, but it was not without value.

"We hear you," Finnegan said after a long, heavy pause. "And we put our faith with you, brother."

Aidrik looked ahead at a glacier in the distance. To the untrained eye, the land mass disappeared into the sea of more of the same.

Aidrik saw his homeland.

Aidrik felt his son.

5
HARRIETT

Harriett Broussard had always been a peculiar child, with peculiar ideas. She'd heard this very word used to describe her, by her own family, more times than she had the patience or capacity to count. She'd been called worse, too, but when one counted among their siblings Estella Broussard, one could expect regular doses of unkindness.

But, unlike most peculiar children, Harriett didn't particularly mind being thought of as different. To be like everyone else wasn't especially interesting, and she often thought the one single injustice of her life—to the outsider looking in, there had been a great many, but Harriett, being peculiar, did not see the world through those same eyes—had been that she hadn't had the fortune to be born at a time where being different was something to be celebrated.

New Orleans, of course, was a city filled with the peculiar, but her family ran in the circles that embraced the familiar and the ancient. The dusty reliability of old money and unflappable traditions, and of falling in line when the moment called upon you for service.

Harriett was not the only Broussard child not to fall in line. Leander constructed his life and façade to the world as everything *except* what his parents expected. Estella came closer to what her parents desired, using her beauty to great advantage, but fell short in many other ways.

When Harriett realized her words were only used against her, and never to any benefit, she stopped using them altogether. Many attributed her persistent years of silence to the abuses wrought upon her by her older sister, Estella, and there was no use in explaining the truth. The truth was peculiar, in a world where explanations must make sense. Estella's cruelty spoke a language her parents understood. Harriett's deeper connection with the world did not.

Harriett's decision to speak again was also not, as some suspected, because of Tristan's unique ability to heal her of any past wounds. There had been nothing wrong with Harriett, so there was nothing to heal. Rather, Harriett finally discovered in her small world a soul capable of, and more than willing to, hearing her words and learning who she was.

Because, where Harriett was peculiar, Tristan was special.

Tristan saw himself through the lens of others around him. He saw within him his eternal youth, his naiveté, and wide-eyed curiosity that was the opposite of the wisdom he wished he possessed. He saw a sad kid who had lost everything and was unable to pull himself up by his bootstraps.

Like Harriett, who was incurably misunderstood by the world, Tristan was perpetually anxious and worn down by the push and pull of others' expectations. But Harriett, unlike Tristan, did not desire to please everyone's behavior. More, she was almost certain she never would.

She might have, had she made different choices leading her to a different outcome.

But Harriett knew when she left New Orleans with Tristan

that she was exactly where she was supposed to be, where she was always meant to be, and precisely how that would end.

Harriett Broussard was not afraid.

ANDERS PACED BETWEEN THE TWO ENTRANCES TO THE BLACKSMITH Shop, deep in the recesses of Farjhem. One was where they emerged from the outside world, and the other led up a winding path ending near the Scholar's Temple. It was hard for Harriett to imagine the magical world beyond the path, but she didn't need to. Anders told Harriett the walk from the temple to the disarrayed shop took about ten minutes, at a fair clip. From the temple to the palace, another twenty. To start at the Blacksmith shop and end in the Valley of Meditation would take roughly thirty. But there were guards all over Farjhem, not only at the palace and the gates, so they should assume the nearest threat was ten minutes away.

Harriett saw him doing these calculations, his lips soundlessly moving as he paced between the entrances. His patrolling grew increasingly frenetic with each passing moment. She hoped Tristan didn't open his eyes because that agitation would undoubtedly pass straight to him. Especially since neither of them had seen their mentor so close to losing his cool.

Tarek groaned where he knelt and shifted his weight to the back of his feet. "I'm sensing many, and the number grows by the moment."

"Brotherhood," Harriett whispered but stopped short of capping the realization with a smile. Yes, they were in, but how many lived in Farjhem before the infiltration? How many served Oriana? Empyreans of Farjhem were kept intentionally in the dark about the "rebels." According to Anders, most believed they were dangerous mercenaries without conscience. The propaganda spread about any who had dared to rise against the

Senetat ran deep and strong, and would take more than a smile and rousing speech to change. Birger and the others were hopeful, but Harriett, a peculiar girl in a non-peculiar world, was a realist.

Whatever their chances out *there,* the Brotherhood was no help to those secluded in the old shop, waiting to succeed or die.

Anders paced and paced.

Harriett didn't share Tristan's gift of breaching telepathic blocks, but throughout her life, as she gave up speech, she learned to listen better. She trusted this sense the most, and what it told her was this: they were out of time. Anders would announce this soon, once his own senses caught up. The guards had started down the path and would be here soon.

She said nothing. They had one goal, and only one. *Come on, Tristan.*

"I haven't picked up Oriana, but I did find Nerys, and she appears to be with her from the thoughts I hear," Tarek announced. He tilted his head. A whistle passed through his teeth. "Yes. They are together."

Three minutes. At most. Harriett held her breath and turned from the others. It wouldn't do to have Anders read the truth in her eyes and cancel the mission prematurely. Two minutes and she would call Stian with her mind. Two minutes would be a risk, but unless Tarek and Tristan could do it in one...

Anders stopped. His mouth parted as he strained to listen at the mouth of the door leading into Farjhem. Harriett tried to get his attention, to stop him from saying the words and interrupting the focus, but she couldn't get to him in time. "I hear something."

Two minutes.

"Footsteps," he pressed. "Many of them."

Harriett's heart surged. It beat so hard she felt her eyeballs pulse with the intensity. They were so close... if Tarek had found Oriana, then Aleksandr had to be next.

Thirty seconds... thirty seconds and she had to call Stian or risk everything.

"Aleksandr," Tristan whispered. He toppled back onto the dusty floor. "I found him, and he's alive."

Anders rushed to him and clapped his hands on both shoulders. Tristan winced as his mentor's fingers dug in. "Where? We need a where, Tristan!"

"I..." Tristan's tightly closed eyes released trickles of tears. "There's too much interference. He's not close, but he's not *that* far, but how far..."

"Focus harder than you've ever focused before, because we have to go, *now.*"

One minute.

While Anders pressed Tristan for more, Harriett turned her mind to Stian. When she registered his response and could breathe again, she let her eyes fall on Tristan. Her beautiful prince, her paladin.

You were meant for great things, my darling. And I promise you, you will get the chance.

Harriett closed her eyes and looked away, counting down the final seconds of her life.

6

ASTRID

Astrid had, for many nights over many years, dreamed she was back in her homeland.

She was one of only a couple dozen Empyreans born under the watchful eye of Farjhem and later freed to join the Dragon Brotherhood. Birger, her love, was the one who freed her.

The day he came to Farjhem, Astrid hadn't known anything about anything, though she believed herself, as youth are wont to believe, in possession of the wisdom of the ancients. Back then, Birger's mark still burned proudly on his bicep, despite his secret, terrifying knowledge that every day he let it remain seared to his flesh was a day his life could be forfeit to the Senetat should they discover he had aligned with the rebels. But Birger's mission had not yet ended. He'd heard tell of several fledglings who dared question the authority of the Scholars and whose curiosity might lead to their end. He'd arrived to sequester them from Farjhem and usher them to the safety of the Brotherhood.

Their escape from Farjhem very nearly cost all six of them

their lives. The guards arrested Birger as they cleared the passage, but the five fledglings fought the guards bravely. At the time, it was exhilarating to the young, sheltered Astrid, but she now understood how close she and Birger, and the others, had been to losing their lives. They escaped with the guards in hot pursuit, and they ran on foot, faster than any of them had ever run before, until they reached a warded safe house where other Brotherhood awaited.

Astrid had watched from the doorway as Birger drew his sword, facing down ten Crimson Guards. His biceps rippled with the weight of his sword, but also his exhilaration. Later, he would confess, also fear. Astrid fell in love with Birger in that moment, and she knew she would follow him anywhere he led.

That night, she helped him cut the Mark from his arm, fearful as her hand shook that the Senetat would end him before she could complete the work of separating him from their dark magic. When she finished, relieved, exhausted, he gently took the knife from her hands and pressed it to her flesh to return the favor.

Over the years, she evolved from the wide-eyed youth in love with her mentor to an equal, and beyond, to lead him at times. Many saw Birger as the leader of reason, but it was Astrid he often turned to for wisdom. Astrid whom he deferred to when they faced a critical decision, as they had when deciding whether to storm Farjhem and risk everything.

Astrid, he'd confessed the night before by moonlight, hand brushing lightly over the trace of the scar where her Mark had once burned. *What does it say of me that my greatest reservation with our plan is knowing it may result in the loss of you?*

We are warriors, Birger, she had soothed. She shared his fears, but also possessed the intrinsic understanding that what he needed was reassurance, not agreement. *But the Senetat is responsible for making us warriors. We are so close now. The Senetat as we know it was destroyed, but our victory doesn't end there. We have one final obstacle. We must return Farjhem to her people and lift the shadowed veil of the Prophecy, and then we can shift our sights from fighting to living.*

My greatest strength lies in my love for you, but I fear, also, this to be my greatest weakness.

Astrid whispered the next words against his lips, *We cannot win a war if we have nothing to fight for. Nothing worth dying for.*

With her boots sinking into the damp grass of Farjhem, Astrid felt the presence of both Birgers with her; the confident elder who strode into her life and changed it for all time. The fallible leader who fell asleep in her lap the night before his greatest battle. The first she had never asked for but needed just the same. The latter gave her the courage to take the next step, and then another. Whether her strides drew her closer to victory or doom, only Emyr knew.

ASTRID HAD TWELVE OF HER SOLDIERS IN TOW. YIVA, THE SHE-WOLF OF Thailand, flanked her with at least four times as many marching five paces behind. As they moved through the valley, Empyreans popped out of their homes to survey the disturbance. Guards appeared and began to unsheathe their steel, but were quickly silenced by the growing number of Brotherhood entering from all sides.

Astrid saw a swarm far in the distance, to the west, and knew it was Birger, Trygve, and their followers. Her heart constricted, and she said a short prayer to Emyr for her mate's safety. She wanted him at her side, but they agreed they could spread the risk by taking separate flanks. They had to think of Eydis, their only daughter, who was not ready enough for the world to lose both parents.

To her right, Thorvald and his impressive Spanish army

flooded in the east entrance. Skadi and Jorun and their soldiers pulled up the rear; their biggest contingent yet, and they were headed directly for the palace, collecting allies or enemies on their way.

Astrid detected a flurry of activity at the market. Some took up arms and others gathered their wares in retreat. Astrid raised a hand and closed her eyes. She detected their fear; fear of Oriana, of how easily she dispensed with her subjects. She sensed also a deep love of who they were, and of their maker, Emyr.

These were not her enemies.

"Come with us," she cried out. "Help us retake Farjhem for the people! We have too long allowed others to decide the course of our lives. Today that changes!"

Astrid didn't pause to await responses or arguments. They had no time for it. As she moved on, she felt their numbers slowly swell behind her. That it had taken only a few words spoke to their quiet desperation for change.

Numbers only matter until they don't. Astrid didn't let her relief relax her. *We could have a million and Aleksandr may still die.*

The spires of the palace at the crest of the east glacier rose into the cloudy sky. Crimson and gold twined high, shouting glory to the heavens, crying against the injustices committed within. Yiva tensed at her side and Astrid cast her a sidelong look, sharing her own anxiety in a brief betrayal of emotion.

"Scryers," Yiva hissed. Her lip curled in a feral snarl.

"Yes," Astrid acknowledged. All across the valley, the Brotherhood collected more to their cause and made their way up the valley, toward the path that would take them all to the royal palace. But Yiva's point landed with Astrid, who knew something about the Scryers many did not: they were not chosen for their soothsaying powers, but because they were the Empyreans born with the rarest of abilities. Necromancers, etheric summoners, mystics. One of them alone was potentially more powerful than the entire quorum the Brotherhood brought with them. All of them together could stop them in their tracks.

To beseech them was a gamble, but to ignore them altogether could prove to be the biggest oversight of their entire lives.

ASTRID HAD ONLY ONCE BEFORE IN HER LIFE STEPPED FOOT IN THE Scryers' Temple, where the great soothsayers of Farjhem existed to protect the royal family and their land from chaos. The Scholars brought all fledglings there to instill in them a sense of fear and awe. One visit had been enough to commit the dome to memory, for she had never until then, or after, seen its equal.

The single circular room of the broad building was a sea and sky of the mapped heavens as outlined in the Tablets of Emyr. They had taken the words of Emyr and built the world of Him.

The Scryers had all been born with the gift of foresight, but they also claimed to call on Emyr for further wisdom. Their visions were gospel to all, both the good and the bad.

As Astrid, Yiva, and their followers stepped into the dome, they were surrounded by moons and stars, by light and dark. Planets followed a set trajectory, occasionally passing in the night, and suns lit the far side with dancing lights simulating the ocean tides. Scryers lay in a wide circle along the edges of the room, calling upon their own gifts and those granted by Their Father.

Scryer Johan rose and stepped into the center of the circle. Astrid dared not look at Yiva. Any sign of fear in her sister might shatter her confidence.

"We have awaited you," Scryer Johan said in the soft, undaunted tones of one who had never had a reason or occasion to develop their voice. "We foresaw this."

Yiva grunted. "We are not in chains," she observed.

Johan tilted his head as he regarded her. "Would you like to be?"

Astrid stepped forward. "If you saw this, why has the empress not ordered our arrest? Why wasn't she more prepared?"

Johan's unblemished flesh spread into a short, tight smile. "The empress does not know."

"You didn't tell her." Astrid sagged under the weight of releasing her relief back into the world. "Why?"

"You ask this, Astrid," Johan said, "yet you have the answer already, for it lies within you. It does not take a scryer to understand the outcomes of our paths are not so very different."

"Why wouldn't you tell us? Why leave us wondering about where you allied yourself?"

"The end was the same," Johan said, with a touch of sadness. "You were always meant to come here. To stand before me asking this question. We cannot affect the future, we can only scry it."

"Spherical nonsense," Yiva barked.

"Time is spherical. Time is also fluid," Johan replied, unruffled. "To seek you out a year ago, a hundred years ago, would be to find you in a time you were not yet prepared for the task. You are ready now, and so you are here. And you now know we will not stand in your way. You are free to go on, and you will go on, as that is the future Emyr has shown us."

Astrid reached a hand and laid it upon his shoulder. "Tell me, Scryer Johan. What happens next? What happens when we reach Oriana?"

Johan looked at his feet. "To tell you would go against our creed, and that is a betrayal we cannot make. Information is power, dear Astrid, and I cannot give you a power that you did not enter with. What will be, will be."

"Is there nothing else you can tell us?"

"Only what you already know in your heart: thrive together, perish apart."

Yiva tossed her hair and launched into more animalistic disdain. Astrid didn't feel so terribly different from her friend, but she didn't leave the Scryers Temple without hope.

If Scryer Johan and the others had foreseen their arrival, then they were meant to take this path. For better or worse, the Brotherhood's future was always intended to bring them to Farjhem, at this time, at this place, in these circumstances.

What she could not predict, and refused to try for the sake of herself and those bravely following her lead, was whether or not they were destined to be here to lead their people to a new and brighter era, or if they were destined for their cause to die in the land of Their Father.

Astrid looked at all those assembled behind her. She drew a breath and released it with her words. "We need to alert Birger, Thorvald, and the others: we make for the palace immediately."

"Thrive together, perish apart," Yiva mumbled.

7
TRISTAN

"On a hill... uh... not a hill..." Tristan mopped the moisture from his face with the back of his hand. The damp room was freezing, but he couldn't stop sweating. Now he *heard* the guards Anders warned were coming. Their heavy footfalls against dust; the low hum of their hurried, excited voices.

"Tristan, find him, now!" Anders cried.

"Glacier." The weight of his vision knocked the air from his chest. "Tapestries on the walls. A big chair. Lots of red." Where was Harriett?

"The palace. He's in the palace." Anders released a whistling sigh and ripped Tristan to his feet. "Go! Run!"

Tristan turned to look for Harriett but was shoved forward in a blur of motion. Dust flew in the commotion and choked him, blinded him. He tried to call her name, but his throat was bone dry, and Anders shoved him into perpetual movement, down the way they came in... down the tunnel.

Harriett, are you behind me?

Nothing.

"*Move!*" Anders screamed. Tristan had only a fleeting moment to register how unusual it was to see Anders this worked up, before he tripped and fell into Tarek. In one fluid move, Anders and Tarek had him on his feet again, each taking an arm. He heard the guards now with much greater precision. Walls no longer separated them from their aggressors.

Harriett, come on, this isn't the time to be silent. I need to know you're back there!

The dusty, narrow corridor felt dustier, narrower on their return. Every inch turned to twenty as the guards closed the gap. *Run! Go!* Tristan absorbed Anders' chants like they were coming from somewhere far, far away, but he did as commanded, caught in the rush of adrenaline-charged fear. When he didn't think he could move any faster, the momentum of Tarek ahead of him and Anders behind him carried him along.

The guards cried for them to halt. They were almost close enough, and in their direct line of sight, to stop them with powerful magic. Tristan swallowed down the acrid, metallic saliva burning his mouth and pushed his will down through his muscles, moving faster than he'd moved in his entire life.

Tarek moaned in guttural relief. Tristan raised his head to see a portail had appeared in the distance ahead. He, too, cried out and pushed harder despite the fire in his lungs and the cramping in his thighs as his legs threatened to buckle.

Dust plumed from behind him. The rush of guards drew closer. He turned his head again for a glimpse of Harriett, but Anders was hot on his heels.

Tarek was the first to the portail, and he dove through without pause, disappearing in an instant. Tristan stopped when he reached the glowing orb. He spun around. He wasn't going in without Harriett's hand in his.

The air left him when he turned and registered the blur of activity only feet away.

Anders, too, paused. His head dropped to the side as he beseeched Harriett, who no longer moved forward but *away* from them. Away, *not* in the direction of the portail and their escape.

"Harriett!" Tristan screamed, drawing forth a sound that began deep in his belly, each syllable raw and powerful. "*Ha-rri-ett!*"

Harriett pitched forward with the weight of the assault as the guards swarmed over her.

"We have to close the portail *now*!" Tarek yelled.

Anders flashed a miserable look at Tristan over his shoulder and backed slowly away from Harriett and the assailing guards. Tristan launched himself in their direction but was jerked back when two strong arms pulled him the other way, toward the portail. *Through* the portail.

"We will find her, Tristan," Anders' faraway voice called, twisted by the vortex of being stretched through time.

The last thing Tristan saw before leaving the cave was Anders' desolate, horrified face, the horrifying knowledge of what Harriett had done for them reflected in it.

The last thing Tristan heard as he straddled the precipice between worlds was,

Thank you for loving me.

8
ALEKSANDR

Aleksandr wished Agripin would stop his pacing. He couldn't ask, because then the abominable creature would know his behavior was affecting him, and if Aleksandr was going to die today, he wasn't going to do it with Agripin's arrogant smile confirming he'd gotten under his skin.

Their conversation in the empty throne room—more specifically, Agripin's random, nonsensical confessions and Aleksandr's scattered, annoyed replies—left Aleksandr even more confused as to the genuine nature of the beast who had murdered his father. Was Agripin losing his mind on the eve of his death? He wouldn't be the first in history. Or was there any substance to his claims of regret?

Aleksandr didn't want to spend the time to think about this any more than he wanted to think about his mother's face when she received the news. Or his father's. Or Fiona's. Of all his regrets, his greatest was the grief he would leave with his loved ones. The whole thing had been avoidable, had he only listened to his instincts about Sebastian instead of ignoring them in favor of humoring his desperation for friendship.

Speak of the devil and he appears, thought Aleksandr as Sebastian suddenly burst into the room. Unlike with Cyler, the guards didn't look ready to accost him. That meant he was here with permission, and only one person could have granted it.

"The traitor, I presume," Agripin announced. His pacing mercifully ceased. "Did my sister send you in to inflict greater torture?"

Sebastian had the wild, scattered look of an animal assessing the inadvertent danger it had fallen into. He gaped at Agripin and shook his head wildly before turning it on Aleksandr. "How are you?"

Aleksandr spread his arms to his sides. They tickled the empty dais behind him. He didn't stand. "Fantastic, Sebastian. Couldn't be better. Having the time of my life."

"Aleksei..."

"Get out," Agripin boomed with all the protective passion of an angry father. "You are not welcome in our presence."

Some of the old, arrogant Sebastian returned. His lip curled. "No?" He snickered at Agripin's Roman centurion armor. "What are you gonna do about it, Custer?"

"Caesar," Aleksandr murmured with a weary sigh.

"Underestimate me to your misfortune," Agripin said evenly. "I'm marked for death, so nothing I do will worsen my sentence. I may lack the power or quickness to dispatch every guard in this room, but you?" He laughed. "A moment's work, at best. You would be in pieces before help was halfway across the chamber."

Sebastian huffed. He shifted his feet, vacillating between his confident stance and a place of growing unsureness. He looked at Aleksandr. "You must hate me."

Aleksandr's mouth dropped open. The childish audacity of Sebastian astounded him, even now. He wanted to scream. He wanted to throw his old friend across the room and watch him sail into the marble. He wanted to laugh. But he did none of those things. Sebastian wasn't worth whatever energy he had left in his final moments. "I feel sorry for you. Whatever devil you sold your soul to isn't the kind that rewards disloyalty. What do you think will happen to you when I'm gone? When your only leverage is gone?"

"She said my reward was killing you."

"Congratulations?"

"You're not afraid?" Sebastian knelt lower, so they faced one another. "I'm not making that up. She said I was the one who gets to kill you."

"Afraid? Of you?" Aleksandr's head spun with his anger, but it was directed not at Sebastian and his betrayal, but at himself. His naiveté brought him here. He had no one but himself to blame. "I might have been intimidated by you once. Even in awe of you and your cool car and how *easy* everything was for you. But you're spineless, Sebastian. You have no courage or any mettle of any kind whatsoever. You *raped* Fiona. What kind of man has to force himself on a woman to feel in control? And what kind of man needs to pretend to be another man to get it?" Aleksandr's heart was ready to jump out of his chest as he sprang to his feet. He continued, spittle flying from his mouth as the words leapt forth. "And what does it say that you had to trick me to trap me? Insecure much, Sebastian? Maybe you knew deep down I was stronger than you, and you were afraid that seeing it would be like looking in the biggest and worst goddamn mirror of your life."

Aleksandr stepped forward, larger than life, cheeks aflame. He threw his arms wide, beat his chest, then opened them again like a bird preparing for flight. Sebastian stumbled back. "Well, here I am! You want to kill me? You have *permission* from your mommy? *Then do it*!"

"Aleksandr, are you mad, provoking him?" Agripin hissed. He moved to position himself between the two boys, but Aleksandr shot him a hard look, and he stopped, poised in anticipation.

Sebastian's face flushed dark red. He wasn't the same man who had stood at the dock and tried to bully Aleksandr into swimming across the lake. Whatever upper hand he once possessed had fled, despite that he was the only one in the room who was not a prisoner. Yet, he *was* a prisoner and seemed to slowly be coming to that realization as he stood before Aleksandr, changing, shifting between who he thought he was and who he could have been.

"I can't kill you here," Sebastian said. The fire died from his words. The emptiness of them tempered Aleksandr's heat. "She wants it to be a public execution."

"Don't look so down, Sebastian. You've always loved an audience," Aleksandr spat.

Sebastian looked at his feet. He moved his gaze around the room, searching for something, perhaps words, perhaps strength. Perhaps his soul. Aleksandr didn't care. The sight of his old friend looking lost after what he had done brought forth within him a reaction so unexpected that even he couldn't explain it.

Aleksandr began to laugh.

Both despicable creatures in the room snapped their necks toward the sound least expected on the eve of an execution. Aleksandr's laughter increased, taking over from his belly all the way to his throat.

"This is *funny* to you?" Sebastian sounded as horrified as Aleksandr should feel.

Aleksandr doubled over from the power of whatever consumed him. His side burned, and tears rolled down his cheeks, but he couldn't stop. He couldn't make himself stop. He didn't want to.

Sebastian reached for him, but Aleksandr swerved. "How the hell are you laughing at a time like this?"

Aleksandr's laughter slowed to soft, happy moans. He swiped at his eyes and pulled himself erect. "You really don't know, do you?"

Sebastian lifted his palms in confusion.

"You were so busy living up your own ass, in love with yourself, that you never bothered to wonder about me," Aleksandr said. He'd resumed control of himself, but small titters rippled through him, and the smile stayed on his face. "Who I am. What I can do."

"What does that mean? What you can do?"

"You've always misjudged me. You saw me as less than you. You liked that about me, didn't you? That you thought you were better than me?" Aleksandr pulled in a deep breath through his nose and released it through his mouth. "You're not a very smart villain, are you?"

Sebastian's jaw hung open. Aleksandr wondered if he was afraid of him now, or surprised by how crazy he was acting, and then realized he no longer had any desire to know what Sebastian Gehring was thinking. He would die not giving a good goddamn what Sebastian was thinking.

"I didn't know they were going to kill you," Sebastian mumbled.

This time, Aleksandr choked back the rumbling laughter threatening. "Right, because people always ask you to kidnap someone against their will and smuggle them out of the country so they can throw them a surprise party. You're weak, Sebastian. Weak in mind and weak in soul, and that's something you're going to have to live with, or reconcile with your god, or Oriana, or whoever it is you serve, if you even serve anyone other than yourself. But don't look for your absolution in me. The only thing I have for you is your reflection."

Sebastian's hands trembled at his sides. In another world, another set of circumstances, Aleksandr's tender heart might have melted at the sight of a man who had gotten himself into something he couldn't unwind. But he had already given so much of himself to his betrayer. He couldn't offer him anything more.

The massive doors croaked open. They all turned toward the sound.

A guard—an important one, by the extra fanfare on his robes—appeared with a retinue of lesser guards.

"You are all expected in the square," he announced. On command, the guards flanking him strode across the room with efficient purpose. Aleksandr steeled himself, drawing strength from the genetics offered to him by all three parents. "We are reapplying your bindings. Cooperate, and they will not hurt. Struggle, and you will find them unbearable."

Aleksandr obediently held out his hands before the guards even arrived. Agripin shook his head in exasperation.

Yes, monster. I'm full of surprises.

Sebastian disappeared into the sea of red cloaks. As they were bound, Agripin caught Aleksandr's eye. He looked itching to say something.

They were led, pushed toward the doors. In the chaos of noise around them, Agripin finally ventured to speak, dropping his voice into a whisper.

"Be brave, Aleksandr, but not foolish."

Aleksandr rolled his eyes. How cruel of fate to give him his father's killer as his final confidante in life. Agripin's presence had become almost a comfort, even if he would never admit this to himself or the creature at the end of the sentiment.

"If you won't heed my words, heed the ones within you. You alone know what you can do, and you alone can stop this."

"That's your great plan? Me?" he hissed in reply.

"You walk to your execution, but you do not have to die today."

Aleksandr's chest tightened at even the flicker of hope existing in the words, but when he went to ask Agripin where these thoughts were coming from, the creature had already been pushed forward into the crowd.

9
TRISTAN

Tristan thrashed and howled. He scratched, spat, screamed, and clawed for the ebbing orb that shrunk smaller, smaller, until the portail disappeared altogether.

"Harriett!" He pressed the name from his lungs, expelling the syllables into the universe with the last of his hope she might still follow them through. Tarek held him in place, and he may as well be chained to a wall for all his weakness in comparison with the Empyrean's iron strength. Even as Tristan's tears spilled onto Tarek's straining forearms, Tarek didn't lessen his grip. Instead, he pressed his mouth to the crown of Tristan's head.

"We will find her. It's not over. We will find her," Tarek whispered as the last of Tristan's strength left him. He went limp in Tarek's arms. Exhausted. Depleted.

Anders hovered nearby. He stared at the wall of the cave with a look that terrified Tristan. Anders, the man with the plan, had the dazed, shell-shocked expression of one who was eager for war until he experienced the lines of battle.

"Now what?" Tristan sobbed. "You did this. Anders. You did

this, you did this!" He wanted to thrash and howl, to scratch and spit and scream. He had nothing left in him. Tarek had even lessened his hold and left only a firm hand on his upper arm, more ceremony than function.

Anders pivoted. The hollowness in his eyes gutted Tristan. "I don't know what happened, Tristan... I don't know what she was doing. She was behind me; *right behind me...* she didn't have to..."

Tristan wilted in Tarek's arms. The soft scent of Harriett's strawberry shampoo appeared from his memory, and he could suddenly smell nothing else. The fuzzy blond down from her arms tickled his cheek. The sound of her voice in his head, more bright and beautiful than anything she allowed out loud, whispered to him to be strong. *My paladin.*

How can I be strong when you were my strength? I was nothing before I met you. I'd lost everything. You gave it all back.

No response came, neither real nor imagined. In his stabbing grief, he could no longer even draw from the memories of her wisdom. *Harriett, why? Why? You could have made it. Why did you do it?*

"No," Tarek said. "Harriett saw what the rest of us did not. Without a diversion, we would not have made it through."

"We did! Three of us got through just fine," Tristan cried. "They weren't that close, or we wouldn't be here. They could have used magic. This doesn't make any sense! Anders, why didn't you stop her?"

"Anders isn't to blame," Tarek replied. "You didn't see what I saw when I pulled you through. Harriett gave herself over to them because they were right on top of Anders and you. It was over, Tristan. We're fortunate any of us made it out."

"I also wondered why they didn't use magic sooner," Anders said. His voice scratched. "Harriett must have sensed... with her gift of foresight, maybe, I don't know how, but she must have known the moment they would... but when she fell into their arms, they were surprised long enough for us to escape."

"And you let her do it. You *let* her save your ass." Tristan found new life and sprang forward, but Tarek was swifter and subdued him just as quickly.

Anders bowed his head. His chest heaved in and out with dense breaths. "If Harriett had told me her plan, I would have taken her place."

"How easy that must be for you to say now, when you're safe, and she's..." Tristan couldn't finish the words. He was afraid to. They caught in his throat, choking him. He had to believe there was still hope in finding her, and that when Tarek said they would, they would.

Harriett, Harriett, Harriett, Harriett, Harriett.

Why? Why? Why?

He knew why. He had known before Tarek and Anders pieced it together. She believed her life was less valuable than Tristan's and made that decision for them both.

His anguish escalated to anger. How dare she make that choice on her own? It wasn't hers to make! She never even gave Tristan the opportunity to weigh in, and instead went on about how they probably wouldn't make it out alive, making him believe they would breathe their last breaths together, hand in hand, fears checked at the connection of their skin and their shared strength. Had it all been a lie? A diversion? Did she know all along what she meant to do?

Fuck you, Harriett. Fuck you, fuck you, fuck you, fuck you.

"I'm sorry, Tristan." Anders pressed his lips tight. The glossiness in his eyes was a phenomenon Tristan would have bet his entire Deschanel inheritance was impossible. Instead of comforting or vindicating him, it tore his guts out. "We will find her, at any cost."

Stian stepped into the light. “Let me be of service once more. Where can I send you?”

“Outside the north entrance,” Anders said. He pulled his shoulders back and his face underwent a visible change. He was the old Anders again. Controlled. Restored to purpose. “We can hike down from the Scryers Temple to Farsengel.”

Tarek nodded. He released Tristan. “Aye. She’s either in Farsengel, or she’s—”

Anders shook his head. “Wherever she is, we will find her. *I* sent the halflings in. *I* own their fate. *I* will see them both out of Farjhem, and safely.”

THEY TREKKED DOWN THE GLACIER. IF TRISTAN THOUGHT THE TUNDRA outside Farjhem was cold, it was an oasis compared to the biting, bone-deep chill of this strange, magical land.

All around them, spires of gold and red towered into the heavens, swirling down to gleaming domes of very official-looking buildings. One was the palace, no doubt, where the heathen Oriana held court. The wicked Senetat probably occupied another. The rest were looming reminders that the power of Farjhem rested along the ridge of the glacier, and not in the idyllic valley below.

Tristan didn’t have the presence of mind to take in the awesomeness of what he saw. That, to most of the world, this land didn’t even *exist,* let alone all the creatures birthed from the fires of its earth.

Tristan’s life had changed entirely in a single year. The boy he began the year as was a college dropout who found twisted solace in the arms of a married woman. Afraid to die, even more afraid to live. The man he was now hardly recognized that boy, but in his current helplessness, he remembered the sleepless nights of eyes burning with tears and shame eating at his heart.

The man he was now trekked through a magical, foreign land, unafraid to die because he had lived.

A figure leaped into their path. They all drew into defensive stance. Anders identified the intruder first.

"Maxima," he said. All three relaxed. "I could have killed you."

"I just returned from Farsengel. Aleksandr isn't there anymore," she said, rushing her words. Her eyes darted around in fear. "He's not there anymore, did you hear me?"

"Yes, we knew that, thanks to Tristan," Anders replied. He didn't rise to her pique of excitement, and Tristan felt glad for it. He loathed Anders—he needed someone to blame, and it was between him and Harriett, back and forth, back and forth—but he needed him at his best.

"You..." Maxima gawped at him. "Where is he, then?"

"The palace."

"Then why are you heading toward Farsengel?"

Anders looked annoyed. "We lost one of our own in the Blacksmith Shop trying to retrieve this information. We're going after her."

Maxima shook her head, incredulous. "Where are your priorities, Anders? If Aleksandr dies, all is lost. Everything we have fought for! All wars have casualties, and it isn't like you to stray from your course for some soldier of Emyr who knew what she was getting herself into, as we all did."

"Look, bitch—" Tristan felt the pinch of Tarek's hand on his arm, stopping him.

Tarek stepped forward. "You showing up here was fortuitous. Go, tell the others about Aleksandr. Leave us to our own mission, which has shifted. We will rejoin you when our unit is whole again."

Words formed in Maxima's gaping mouth, but none made it to fruition. She righted herself. "You'll find two guards temporarily incapacitated. Not for long. But you should know the cells of Farsengel are empty."

"There are many cells in Farsengel," Anders said. "I have to assume you didn't check them all."

"No, yet..." Maxima sighed. "Thank you for the information. Be safe." She disappeared down the path.

The trio continued on.

Harriett. Answer me. Ignoring me is torture, and you know this. You know this. You know this. I'm dying inside, and if you're dying on the outside, I need to know, I have to know. Stop protecting me, stop making decisions for me.

Harriett. Harriett. Harriett!

The entrance to Farsengel announced itself with an eerie silence. Flags flapped in the wind, their sharp snaps the only sound. No guards patrolled the area, and they identified no outward sign of danger, despite the acute sensation it was especially near. If this was a video game, Tristan thought, this was a save point, because just beyond was the boss fight. *Time to get our mana back, pop a health pot, and take that bio break.*

"She said the guards were down, but I don't trust the magic to hold long," Tarek said. "And someone may have ordered more." He glanced at Tristan as if he was about to suggest he stay behind, or hide, but he didn't. This was the difference between the adults in Tristan's life back home, and the ones he had at his side now. Here, he was an equal, if not in ability, then at least the capacity to face danger as one.

Anders led. He slowed his heavy gait into the soft strides of a ballerina, each step laced with caution. Three of them against Farjhem wasn't a battle, it was a bloodbath. The line between life and death could be crossed with no more than a blink.

I'm not afraid, Harriett. Not for myself. If I have to die to save you,

I will, but I guess you were thinking the same thing earlier, too. But you know if you die, I die too, right?

Harriett?

They stepped into a vast dungeon unlike anything Tristan had seen in any video game he'd played, and he thought maybe he'd played them all. So much of his life wasted, his father would say, though he'd never felt more himself than when he could escape into a world not his own.

Just as he was now.

The center was a hollow circle, and around the edges of the circle lay the doors to hundreds, maybe thousands of cells. "We divide them up," Anders said. His manner reflected the futility of the task, but he was determined, and Tristan had no doubt Anders would search every last cell himself.

It wouldn't be necessary.

"She's not here," Tristan said, and there wasn't even a sliver of doubt in his proclamation.

Tarek nodded. "No, they must have taken her straight there."

"Where?" Tristan asked.

Anders and Tarek exchanged a heavy look. "To Oriana," Anders said.

Tristan didn't need to employ his special trick of breaching a block to read what had passed between Anders and Tarek.

If she was with Oriana, there wouldn't be a trial. She wasn't a valuable prisoner like Aleksandr, or any of the Brotherhood leaders.

Harriett was an interloper, an expendable soldier taken to the new empress to face her swift sentence.

10

NERYS

The Brotherhood drew closer, but their approach was agonizingly sluggish. Securing support along the way was integral to the plan, but waiting for them to arrive was bamboo under the nails; a good stretch on the rack. And Oriana had called for Aleksandr and Agripin. *To end this*, she had said, though she had no inkling of the hell she invited if she carried out her intention.

"There's still time to correct your course," Nerys said to her sister. She no longer held onto the hope she could sway Oriana with words alone, but she refused to stop trying. Talking bought time. "There are other ways."

Oriana swung her head around at the sound of Nerys' voice. Red wine stained her lips and dribbled down her pale chin. An Empyrean vampire.

"There's still time for you to leave and save me a third execution," Oriana snapped back, though the bite had faded. The power struggle surrounding who wielded the most favor in this land had been silently resolved already, but Oriana would have her words. And, if Nerys couldn't find a way to stop her, she would have more blood on her hands.

"We could end this day without a single execution, and it would be a good day."

Oriana rolled her eyes, then skimmed them around the guards lining the walls. "Where is Cyler?" she barked. "I believe this is the third time I've asked this question today! Does no one listen to me?"

They all shuffled and exchanged looks. None answered.

"Oriana, why did you not surround yourself with strong strategists?" Nerys asked this question with genuine curiosity. "Instead of rewarding your patrons of The Menagerie? You could have given them other roles to show your favor, but what you needed most was a council of experienced statesmen."

"You ask questions to taunt me, not because you desire answers."

"I ask because an august council would advise you that there is no hurry in executing the boy. None! Once you play that hand, it is done. There is no bringing him back if you determine later he was more useful alive."

"You answered your own question." Oriana poured another glass of wine. She watched the door in growing anxiousness, through hawkish eyes. "I have no use of a council full of hesitations. We act. It is in our basest of natures, and I believe, I have always believed, we are most ourselves when we respond from instinct rather than debate an issue into oblivion."

Nerys could dispute this point into the ground, but the effort would be lost on Oriana, whose growth was stunted by her desire to live within her base nature.

They were interrupted by a new intrusion. A flurry of guards appeared and, behind them, Agripin. And another... the boy. Aleksandr.

She had sworn once to protect him, and here he was, exposed and in the greatest danger of his short life.

Another boy lagged behind, an unremarkable Child of Man she didn't recognize. But his flushed face and contrition in his eyes revealed his identity as the traitor who brought Aleksandr to Farjhem.

When the turncoat Child of Man stepped into the light, a strange shimmering sound filled the air behind Oriana. Nerys turned to look and at first could not completely comprehend what she was seeing.

The form materializing lacked the solidity of a living, breathing creature. All of her flickered in and out, as if she had been projected into the air using defective technology. Nerys had seen many spirits in her long days, but none struggling so hard to stay tethered to the physical realm.

This was no simple spirit. This, she realized, was a malevolent apparition employing some form of dark magic to stay present in the world. The way she faded and returned to form, over and over, reminded Nerys of a high wind pressing against a delicate flower.

What did she have to do with any of this?

"Sebastian, my child." The words emanated from the spirit, but Nerys heard them in her head, not aloud. *Beware, the myths of midwinter.* "Are you ready for the gracious reward our benefactor has offered you?"

Sebastian's eyes studied the marble floor. "Yes, Mother."

"Good. The time is upon us."

"I say when the time is upon us," Oriana barked. "Guards, escort the prisoners outside the gathering area! Send criers through the valley. All are welcome!" She turned to Nerys. "We will see, sister, how they still favor you when they see what I do to those who do not favor *me*."

• • •

THEY STEPPED INTO THE SUN. GUARDS TASKED WITH SPREADING THE news ran ahead to their mission, but a crowd had already assembled. More made their way up the long hill, meandering toward the gathering area.

Nerys' pulse quickened. The Brotherhood had put this in motion, but there was no way to know the minds of the growing onlookers. Were they friend or foe? Did they themselves know the answer? Most of Farjhem had long been sheltered from the atrocities just up the hill, beyond the valley. One of the Senetat's —and royal family's—greatest feats had always been managing to keep those physically closest the furthest from the truth.

"What is this?" Oriana demanded of her head bodyguard.

He started to raise his shoulders in a shrug when two new guards appeared from the gap in the crowd. Their faces flushed bright.

"Empress," one panted. He doubled over to catch his breath, and the other continued for him.

"We've been breached. Rebels are here."

"They're everywhere!" the first one rejoined. "All entrances... everywhere. We tried to stop them, but we were overrun. We returned to the palace for reinforcements."

Oriana's wine glass slipped from between her fingers. The crystal shattered at her feet in a vibrant puddle. "Rebels," she repeated. The color in her face drained away with her wine. "You're sure? Rebels?"

As she said the words, she turned slowly toward Nerys and the whole of her unanswered questions began to fuse into a painful truth. Nerys watched this metamorphosis in her sister without joy. Her heart wished it hadn't come to this. She wished Oriana could have remained the lord of her kingdom underground, and that the problem of the Senetat and the bastardization of Emyr could have been resolved without the need for war.

Nerys didn't know how to reconcile her natural pacifism

with her endorsement of the sacking of Farjhem. She questioned whether she ever would.

"Yes, Empress. Hundreds. More, maybe. We didn't have the resources to tally them." He stared at his leader in a terrified daze. "How can there be so many? I thought the royal house destroyed their forces?"

"You fool, that's what the old Senetat wanted you to believe," Oriana snapped. "Go, get your reinforcements!"

Agripin threw back his head and laughed. "Allow me to speculate on the catalyst behind our growing number of visitors."

Oriana spun on him. "You think they're aligned with your precious Brotherhood, do you? You think they would give up *this*"—she gestured around the land—"for a life on the run, in hiding?"

"They won't be in hiding anymore," Nerys said, finding her voice. "They only had to because the power running Farjhem pushed them into caves and corners."

"Not me!" Oriana cried.

"Not at first," Nerys agreed. "But you slaughtered our own kind to make a point to the Brotherhood. That point is made. You had a chance, sister, to take the yoke of leadership and make a new and better way. You chose instead to reign in terror."

Dozens now gathered thirty feet away. Standing. Waiting. Their expressions were eager, but otherwise blank, betraying no clear evidence of their alignment.

Oriana scrutinized them. She drew her conclusions as she passed her eyes over a crowd now doubled in size from moments ago and still growing.

She turned to face the prisoners and those guards still doing her bidding. "Forget the ceremony. Prepare the prisoners for execution."

"Oriana, you can still redeem yourself," Nerys pressed. None of her friends were at the palace yet, and she didn't know what to make of their absence. She didn't know if those who had come to watch would try and stop Oriana, or join her in the needless slaughter. "You can still do the right thing by our people!"

Oriana's smile spread slowly, cutting a sharp line through her beautiful, delicate features. "Oh, Nerys. That's exactly what I plan to do."

11
ASTRID

Astrid left her flank of the resistance in a cave a short walk from the palace. *If I am not back when the sun falls over the southern grove, go on without me, but I must get word to our other arms. We approach Oriana together, and cautiously. All other side plans are folly.*

Astrid, don't be a fool. You'll be taken captive. The others know to meet us at the palace. Nothing more to it. Yiva said more than she had the whole venture.

You heard the Scryer. Thrive together, perish apart. We have to approach Oriana as one.

Others chimed in. They mimicked Yiva's concerns. She was foolish, throwing herself out as a target by wandering alone. Maybe she was a fool, but she didn't believe in using others as armor to protect herself. She was a leader only by occasion and willingness, not by worth, and could strengthen them all by sharing the Scryer's words.

The words she heard in the Scryers Temple haunted her, though they had only lived with her a short time. She was less confident about their path now than she'd ever been, and she wouldn't sacrifice any who had given up their everything to come to Farjhem. Not one head. They either ascended to the palace as single, united Dragon Brotherhood, or they regrouped and aborted mission. There was no real leader of the Brotherhood, but she had enough clout for her declaration to carry weight.

Every life was valuable. Not only for the years lived, but for the infinite not yet lived. She couldn't endorse friendly fire or needed sacrifice to attain their goal. She wouldn't allow even one single Empyrean to die. Not again. Not anymore.

At her shoulder, a small sparrow chirped. Astrid smiled at her familiar. Nodded. *Yes. If I should fall, the burden of sharing the news falls to you, Mina. Birger knows your language, as you are an extension of me. You will fly to him, my treasure?*

Mina chirped her response in a language Astrid knew as well as she knew her own heart.

Yes, she undertook great risk to venture into the heart of Farjhem alone, but if the end of her life came to pass, no other lives needed to be lost with her. Birger and the others *must* know they were on the right course. The Scryer's words may be the difference between courage and fear in their darkest moments. Mina would find Birger and share her message.

She had one more, for her daughter, Eydis. She prayed to Emyr that Eydis' young, impulsive heart was open to receive the words.

Astrid stepped out from a thicket of trees. The second she hit open land, a strong arm clipped her across the chest and knocked her stumbling back into the forest.

She choked away the sudden theft of her breath, and in a single, swift move, went for her bow. Her assailant stepped before her, arms in surrender. Astrid's fingers twitched against the base of the arrow fletching.

"Cyler?" She eased back the tension but didn't return the arrow to its quiver. "What are you doing?"

"I could ask you the same, Astrid. Are you trying to get yourself killed? If the answer is yes, by all means, continue."

Astrid dropped her arms to her sides but kept her arrow strung in the bow. "How are you in Farjhem and still alive? After freeing Maxima, I would think you'd be far away by now."

"I should be," he agreed. His eyes narrowed, but he trained them on the horizon. Toward the palace. "I will be. I had things to tend to before I left my homeland, because, unless you and your merry traitors are successful, I doubt I'll ever be back."

"If they find you, they will kill you. You must know that."

"I'm no fool," Cyler said with a snort. "Or I am, but not the way you think." His hand fell to his sword hilt. He showed no intention of unsheathing the weapon. Astrid read this subconscious move as his means of drawing strength in a moment colored with so much uncertainty. "Here's the truth, if you want it. I thought I could save him, even now. If I could offer the right words, he might find himself clear of this mess as he always did with any other."

"Agripin?" Astrid didn't know why she asked when the answer was clear. The key to unlocking Cyler had always lain within his love for his master. "Do you think he would want to see you die here today, Cyler? Do you not know how deeply he loves you?"

Cyler's eyes dropped to the grass he'd run his boots across in agitation moments before. "He loves only himself. Somehow, that never stopped my love from growing greater than myself. Everything I've done... everything, all of it... was for him. I studied him as a fledgling and lived for the moment he would even rest his eyes on me. When he took me into his service, nothing else mattered. What was personal happiness when the Grand Duke Agripin had chosen you?"

Astrid took a risk and put away her bow. Birger would have chided her, but if she could not trust her own instinct, then she had greater problems.

She had to leave. To find Birger and Thorvald, and finish this, or abandon it, but the invisible hourglass underlying the whole operation from the moment Nerys ventured bravely forth alone into their homeland was nearly out of sand.

At the same time, Astrid couldn't find it within her to leave without offering Cyler words that might give him comfort in his many, many days ahead without Agripin.

Her hand came to rest on Cyler's flamed cheek. He recoiled in a short jump, but allowed the gesture. His pain, years and years of it, passed into her and she knew, finally, the infinite sadness of Cyler. He may have been an accidental ally of the Brotherhood, and even an adversary sometimes, but he lived rigidly by his code of service, and in this, he was a good creature. A Child of Emyr in one of the purest ways one could be. True. Brave. He veiled his unflinching selflessness in callous words and defensive tactics, but Cyler's heart was not so hard to find.

"He loves you," Astrid said softly. "All creatures are capable of different kinds of love, Cyler, and Agripin's is flawed, but it has always only been yours."

Cyler's tears burned her hand, but she kept it against his flesh. He would loathe himself for his lapse in strength later, but while the connection lasted, she would give him the words he needed. "Go, Cyler. You have served your duke, then your emperor, and always Emyr. It is now time to serve yourself."

"Why are you being kind to me?" His voice rasped in the cold air. He wouldn't meet her eyes. "I have never been a friend to the Brotherhood."

"Your kinship, if you prefer to call it that, is what may have saved us. Your decision to free Maxima is why we are here now. The only reason we are here now. Now, go, before the choice is no longer yours. If I can save Agripin, I will. But you are free of your bond to him, Cyler. Go."

Cyler nodded against her palm, a hesitant, slow move she barely felt.

"Move an inch and I'll gut you like a moose."

Astrid tensed into fighting position. Cyler's eyes widened and then squinted with a wince. The assailant passed into view: Thorvald. With his sword pointed at the center of Cyler's back.

She laughed in relief. "Thorvald, stand down. Cyler isn't our enemy."

Thorvald's sword didn't waver. "He serves Oriana."

"We sent him there," Astrid retorted. She kept her tone reasonable. Thorvald was a composed warrior until his bloodlust was stoked and it was often no simple task to cool him. She had witnessed him cut down friend and foe alike without serious thought. "With Agripin. Remember?"

"He chose to stay once his task of delivering Agripin to the infidel was complete."

Cyler's old grin returned. "You think she was going to let me just walk back out? Have you met her?"

Thorvald's jaw flexed. "I say again, he serves Oriana, Astrid."

"Without him, Maxima would have been executed!"

"A moment of clarity does not make a pattern of loyalty."

Astrid sighed. She let her eyes rest on Cyler a moment and turned them back to Thorvald. "Then let us agree that we may never see eye to eye on this and move forward. As fortune would have it, I was out looking for you when I came upon Cyler. We must find Birger and put the last of our plan into motion. We are nearly out of time."

"And move forward we will," Thorvald replied. He shoved his

sword tip into Cyler's back and the younger Empyrean howled as the skin broke. "He is coming with us."

"With us? Why?" Astrid's braids flung back behind her shoulders as her head shook. "No, Thorvald, he needs to leave Farjhem *now* before he's captured and executed for treason. And we have more important tasks at hand than arguing about it."

"This isn't an argument. I've decided. Cyler has no value to us outside Farjhem. Here, he may provide us leverage."

"Leverage?" Astrid's blood boiled. Thorvald had been her friend and ally for over a thousand years, but when his mind was set, only spilled blood could sway him. She was not prepared to fight. They couldn't allow such a distraction on such an important day.

"Oriana has someone we want. We now have someone she wants," Thorvald replied, and his reasonableness stoked her anger higher.

Cyler's laugh rang with sadness. "You vastly overestimate her value of me."

"Forgive me if your word is suspect," Thorvald answered. He looked at Astrid. "Birger and his flank are already on the route to the palace. He may already be there. Let's go."

Thorvald shoved his new prisoner into movement. Cyler made a choking sound but stumbled into motion. Astrid followed with a sickness rising within her, which grew fouler at the spreading bloom of blood on the back of Cyler's jerkin.

Who are we if we turn on one another? If we use one another for gain? How are we any better than Oriana, or the Senetat if we believe our own cause and our own lives matter more?

Astrid again thought of Scryer Johan's words and wondered if the ambiguity in his prophecy had more to do with their own unpredictability than the adversaries awaiting them.

. . .

THORVALD'S STEPS FALTERED. WHEN ASTRID SAW WHAT MUST HAVE come into his vision, she stopped altogether.

"What do you think is happening?" Astrid asked. She didn't peel her eyes from the mass of crowd gathered at the palace steps. Friend, foe… from a distance, she couldn't tell. She strained for recognition, but the gathering area was a blur of motion.

"An execution is the only explanation," Cyler answered. What little fight he'd had when Thorvald assailed him fled on the short journey, reduced to defeat and acquiescence. "Judging from the restlessness of the crowd, I gather it hasn't happened yet."

Astrid turned to look at Cyler, and the waning light in his eyes hit her harder than she was prepared for. Why didn't she fight more? Thorvald might have backed down. He respected her.

But he wouldn't have, and one of the three would not have made it out of the encounter alive. When this was all over, Astrid determined she would personally escort Cyler to safety anywhere in the world. For now, the best she could offer was limited protection against Thorvald's as-yet-not-shared plan.

Thorvald grunted. "Then you may yet be of use." He kicked Cyler forward, and Astrid shot him a flustered look.

"He's not our prisoner, Thorvald. Stop treating him like an animal."

"Explain to me how this dogged blind follower of a demigod isn't an animal."

"What were you doing out here anyway, alone?" Astrid couldn't keep her eyes from the gathered throngs. Somewhere in the blur were Nerys, Oriana… and Aleksandr.

"Searching for you. My people are already in the square. Birger and his people are in the square." His eyes narrowed. "What were *you* doing out here alone?"

"Searching for you!" She didn't like this. Not at all. Thorvald's machismo terrorism—bold, even for him—and the onset of infighting. If they couldn't trust one another, then they had nothing. Even if they succeeded here, they still had to rebuild, and *this* was not helping.

"Conversing with a known adversary," Thorvald corrected. His expression softened when he saw hers so horrified. "Come, Astrid. This is nearly done. Most of those gathered came with us or were swayed by us. We are among friends."

Something wasn't right, if those were all allies. "Why, then, are they standing there, letting Aleksandr's life dangle in risk? Don't tell me they're waiting for us?"

"I cannot answer for others," Thorvald said. "But you and I are decisive, Astrid. We have always been. Shall we end this?"

THEY ENTERED THE SQUARE FROM A GAP IN THE FOREST PATH. Empyreans stood shoulder to shoulder. Thorvald was forced to sheath his sword in the thick crowd, but Cyler made no move to run. Astrid's heart sank again at seeing the fight leave the born warrior. She promised herself she would make up for her failure to help him later, that she could fix what had fundamentally changed in him when he decided to surrender instead of fight. He was not the first warrior she had witnessed lose their fight.

Thorvald pushed Cyler ahead and they wound through, sandwiched between body after body. Astrid searched and discovered familiar faces, but no Birger. None of his men. Were they across the plaza? Hanging back? Thorvald said they were here already, but perhaps Birger had told him they were en route and took a detour.

Astrid smelled the fear among those standing. Waiting. She understood then how no one came forward to rescue Aleksandr. So few had ever witnessed any great horror. Deep within them, they believed in the goodness of Emyr's creations and that belief meant they could not comprehend Oriana carrying out her promised terrors. Even the Brotherhood, created *because* of such terrors, suffered from most of their members having only experienced the terrible deeds of the Senetat through storytelling.

Thorvald was right. *They* had to act.

Astrid was so lost in her evaluation of the crowd she didn't realize they'd arrived at the steps until Thorvald abruptly stopped.

Oriana's wild hair rippled in waves down her white gown. She stood no more than ten feet ahead, above them, perched at the crest of the stairs with a grin betraying her confidence she still had the upper hand.

Did she? Astrid was not prone to second-guessing herself, but something about the whole situation felt... off. More than it should. She did not at all like that smile.

"Thorvald and Astrid. Yes, I know your faces, same as you know mine. We are of the same god, are we not?" Oriana's pitched voice had all the pleasantness of an eager hostess. "I am so pleased you could join the festivities!"

"We come to make an exchange," Thorvald said. He shoved Cyler forward.

The sensation of impending doom spread further through Astrid, settling into the ends of her limbs.

What had they done?

"Ahh, Vakkar," Oriana cooed. She clucked her tongue and shared a look with the younger Empyrean that Astrid could not read and later wished she had not seen. "Words fail me. Come closer."

"He remains until you send down the heir."

"The heir remains until I've had a closer look at my soldier."

Astrid forced herself to look at Aleksandr, who stood a pace ahead of Agripin. He was surrounded by powerful mages who awaited a signal—Oriana's insurance against the rebels swarming the stage, and an answer, at last, as to why they didn't.

She last saw Aleksandr when she and Birger delivered him to Louisiana for safekeeping. That was mere months ago, but the young creature awaiting his execution had aged a thousand cycles in that time. His shoulders pulled back and he showed no signs of fear; nothing could be read from his face that offered power to others. He looked ready to give Oriana his life, but refused to offer her anything more.

I see now. I see how this halfling can be the heir. Emyr, forgive me for not understanding how the child he was could become the man he is now, but I see it so clearly.

Thorvald nudged Cyler. "A step. Two. No more."

Cyler dropped his eyes to the clay stairs. His entire body sighed as he ascended the first step. With the second, Astrid saw him shrug off the last of his fear.

All at once she understood what was happening, what was about to happen, but the realization came too late.

The moment played out in a series of flashes.

Oriana's light nod to the guards behind her.

How they stepped forward and raised their arms.

Cyler's head lifting. His eyes closing.

Understanding.

Accepting.

Astrid screamed, but the sound reverberated in her head alone, and when her mouth finally found voice, Cyler's crumpled form lay in a heap across the stairs.

"No!" she cried. She thought of her promises, how hollow they felt as she made them, how she had missed this, caused this, failed to prevent this. "Oriana, why?"

Oriana kicked at Cyler's lifeless arm. "Why not?"

12
AIDRIK

They didn't stop moving from the second their feet landed on the soil of Farjhem.

Where there should have been guards, they found only the quiet serenity of the valley and the river bisecting the emerald land. The utter stillness of the entrance unsettled Aidrik, for it came with no immediate answers.

"Look." Jacob pointed ahead.

Aidrik lifted his gaze and beheld, for the first time since his rebirth, the glacier hill housing the epicenter of power in his homeland. Even now, when Aidrik was no longer enchanted with the pomp and ceremony of the royal family or the purported nobility of the Senetat, the image stole his breath. Beauty was still beauty.

He then saw what Jacob referenced: the reason there were no guards at the entrance was that most of Farjhem gathered at the palace. From their vantage point, thousands of bodies bled together in a series of colorful dots, impossible to make out faces or alliances. Aidrik prayed the Brotherhood and Quinlans filled their numbers.

"What do you make of it?" Finn asked the question, but Aidrik saw his mind churning on the answer already.

"Not enough information," Aidrik answered. His eyes traveled around the valley. Chimneys pumping out the smoke of dying embers and open doors belied the quickness in which Empyreans left their homes. Not a planned departure, but one of alarm. Excitement. Immediacy.

"Something feels off. I can't put my finger on it," Jonathan offered. He choked out a clipped laugh. "Hell, I don't know what I'm saying. I'm not like the rest of you."

"Do not dismiss your instinct," Aidrik replied. "Your brother may be the draoi, but you both descend from powerful magi." His eyes closed. He knew better than to trust his foresight, as it was an erratic gift that led more to madness than comprehension. "You sense a disruption to the tranquility."

"A disturbance in the force," Jacob whispered. He didn't smile. "We're going up there, right? With the rest of them?"

"Does anyone have a map?" Jonathan asked.

"Aleksandr is there," Finn said. He adjusted Ulfberht at his side. His mouth formed a tight line across his face. "I can feel him."

"Aye," Aidrik said. "We must discover who else is."

THEIR PACE BEGAN WITH A SPRINT. BY THE TIME THEY MADE IT HALFWAY up the glacier mountain path, they had slowed to a jog.

The travelers stopped briefly at the market to see what they could learn. Dozens of stalls lay abandoned, with tools and wares settled haphazardly.

They prepared to move on when a bread maker stepped from the shadows.

"Tell us," Aidrik said, further explanation unnecessary with only one topic worth discussing in Farjhem on this day.

"Two thousand years," the baker said. He looked toward the valley, not the hill. "I have never questioned an execution. But no trial? No crime announced by the criers? I cannot participate. Father Emyr cries to see his people treat each other so."

Finnegan's breathing quickened.

"The others who have joined," Aidrik replied, "do they believe as you? Or do they go to revel in the act?"

The baker tilted his head. He tightened his robe. "Both? I cannot say. To speak of what happens upon the hill now is to risk finding yourself in Farsengel. Ah, you wonder why I gave you my voice? I know who you are, Aidrik the Wise. I have served you the breads of my fathers more than once in my lifetime. It is the sister of *your* old friend responsible for the horrors that changed our homeland into a world no better than the one Children of Men ruin. I wish to believe most of my brethren share my values, but war teaches us that when the true nature of another is revealed, it may be darker than we suspect."

"Yes, Agripin's sister did this," Aidrik said. "But it is my son she desires to murder. Be well, baker."

"And you," the baker replied. "Oh, aye!" he called out when Aidrik and the others continued on. "The others? Are they with you, then?"

"Others?"

"The rebels. Runeans, word says. They were through here nigh an hour ago, less perhaps."

"How many?"

"More than the four of you. Less than the whole of us."

"Helpful," Jonathan muttered with a groan.

Finnegan edged forward. "Aidrik, let's go. A hundred or a thousand, doesn't matter. It's where we're going."

"If any of you have a mark, I suggest now is the time to remove it," the baker bellowed as they returned to the path.

"We do not," Aidrik replied over his shoulder. "And if the day ends well, none will ever bear one again."

THEY COMPLETED THE REST OF THEIR SHORT JOURNEY IN A SILENCE colored only by heavy breaths of exertion. Jacob, his face having turned from red to purple, looked ready to drop to the ground, but he pushed on ahead of the others. Jonathan pulled up the rear, leaving enough room between himself and his brother, but creating a barrier in case of a surprise attack.

Aidrik had no trouble opening a telepathic connection with Jonathan, who had never been trained to block from others.

You came here to die.

Jonathan's steps faltered at the intrusion. He stopped and looked around.

Keep moving. I am in your head.

But how?

You know how. You have never experienced it yourself until now, but you have been around others who have. Enough to accept.

Wouldn't it be easier to speak?

If we speak, the others will hear.

Jonathan sighed out loud. No one noticed among the exhausted panting spread through the group. *What do we have to say that the others shouldn't hear?*

You came here to die. Finnegan does not know.

I came here to help.

You have already decided. You will die if it saves Aleksandr.

We all feel that way. Isn't that why we're here?

You will die to save any of us. You feel your life holds no value. You believe your actions leave you beyond repentance.

Jonathan was silent for several paces. The grade of the hill steepened and they strained to maintain a jog. *So you know what I did. To Ana.*

Aye. I have always known. Are you wondering why you still draw breath?

Actually, yes.

That vengeance is not mine to exact. It is Anasofiya's. It has always been hers alone. Her choice was forgiveness.

Aidrik could almost feel the burning behind Jonathan's eyes; the jagged breath drawn in the crisp air.

I don't feel I need to explain myself, but since you asked, and since we all might die within the hour, I will tell you. It isn't only what I did to Ana that keeps me up at night. There was another, years before her, and I loved her, and I failed her. I failed Finn. I failed Ana. And I failed myself. If my last action in life can be not to fail my nephew, then I will die better than I lived.

Child of Man logic. One action does not erase others. It does not need to.

I have to live with everything I've done, so what you think means less than how I feel.

To live with your sins is preferable to dying with them. Your death would cripple your brother. Aleksandr needs his uncle. Anne, your mate, awaits your return. You come here to provide the ultimate sacrifice. I am here to inform you this will not be needed.

You know something we don't?

If a sacrifice is needed, Jonathan St. Andrews, it will be mine.

Finnegan and Jacob stopped in tandem as they crested the last steep switchback on the hill. At the summit, the edges of the palace crowd were almost close enough to reach out and touch.

"Well, we're here," Jacob announced. The lack of necessity in his words almost elicited a smile from Aidrik, but there was little joy to be found in what lay ahead.

A sea of robes and armor. A mix of the free Brotherhood and the Empyreans who had never left their homeland. Friend and foe, though the latter may be friendlier than they thought.

And ahead, at the top of the broad stairs, their son, shackled in magic and body alike.

"Aleksei," Finnegan whispered. His knees buckled.

Jacob reached over wordlessly to right him.

Jonathan appeared along Aidrik. *You don't get to choose for me, old man. If sacrificing myself can help my brother and his family, not even you and your crazy, weird magic can stop me.*

13
TRISTAN

Tristan saw her. He wasn't close enough to touch her flesh, but he still imagined stretching his arm across the long space between them and pulling her to safety. To his chest, where he could hold her again and speak the things in his heart that had been so hard for him to say.

Harriett! he cried out from within. All his energy went into moving forward, so he had little left for his own voice. He watched her being dragged from the shadows to the edge of the stairs. Beyond them, more Empyreans than he could ever count, gathered.

Doing nothing.

"Why are they still? Why is Oriana not the one in chains?" Tarek hissed to Anders. The crowd teemed with hundreds of their own, but they, too, did nothing.

"It takes no more than a split second to end a life," Anders replied. He guided them to a gap in the gathering at the peripheral of the palace steps. He articulated no plan but didn't stop moving toward where both Aleksandr and Harriett's lives hung in tender balance. "If they miscalculate an attack, all the prisoners could be struck down before they reach the top of the steps."

Tarek grunted in response. Tristan didn't like that answer, either. Where did that leave them? Was this no better than a siege?

"What do we do?" Tristan tugged at Anders' arm like a confused child. He was glad he couldn't see himself, just as he had been glad there was no video of how he handled the loss of his sister, Danielle, or the news of his mother's suicide. Tristan retreated into himself and became again the needy babe looking to elders for guidance.

Anders shrugged Tristan off but patted his arm as he returned it to his side.

"What do we *do*?" Tristan whined. A series of animalistic cries sounded inside him, and he feared he might release them at any moment. He couldn't look at Harriett again, bound and pushed to her knees, or he would tilt back his head and sound all his pains to the sky like a feral wolf. "Anders, you're the one who always knows! You have to know!"

Anders pulled him to the side, beyond eyesight of the palace steps. He lowered his head to Tristan, close enough to feel the brush of his clammy skin. His mentor's breath was acrid with the strong scent of his fear. "I need you to calm yourself, Tristan."

"Calm myself? *Calm myself? Calm myself?*" Tristan sounded a series of short, pained laughs. The sweat from his fear prickled across the surface of his dirty face.

Anders gripped his arm tighter. "We don't have time for this. I can't think. This is my fault, and I will fix this, but I can't if you're twitching and moaning behind me."

Tarek stepped into the shade of the tree where they huddled. "Later, we can talk about this, Tristan. For now, let Anders lead. We have no time."

Tristan slumped against the cool stone of the palace, panting. He prayed to a God he wasn't sure he believed in after all that had happened to him, bargaining. Why did it have to be Harriett? He closed his eyes and imagined it had instead been Anders who fell back into the rush of oncoming guards, that Harriett had slipped through the portail at the final moment. He didn't feel bad about wishing this. He was past all point of a conscience or humility, and he wouldn't get either back until Harriett was safe.

But she wasn't safe. She was in very, very grave danger.

Great, keening aches rippled through Tristan. He couldn't breathe... spots formed before his eyes and his vision doubled before swimming into a blur of color.

Tarek slapped him. "We are going. Now."

Anders had already left. Tarek followed, and Tristan sucked in a hard breath and told himself he, too, must go or he had no business calling himself a man.

Anders wound through the crowd and ascended the bottom two steps. They sidled up behind him, and Tristan realized they could not be closer to the prisoners unless they stood at their side. Tristan saw every snarl in the knotted mats in Harriett's messy hair, pulled back from her face in the fist of one of the guards. Tears and snot cut through a thick layer of dust on her face, forming trails of mud, but her eyes... her eyes were wild and brave, daring them with a fearlessness Tristan had never known himself.

Behind Harriett, the other prisoners stood. Aleksandr and another... Agripin, he decided, given what Maxima had relayed. But there was another, crumpled at the center of the stairs. None approached him. Tristan noticed Astrid crying silent tears.

"Ahh, Cyler," Anders said with a heavy sadness. He bowed his head. "Another casualty of this war."

"May he be the last," Tarek joined.

"A rebel!" a shrill voice cried and cut through Tristan's daze.

He swung to look in the direction of the sound and saw the most magnificent creature.

He did not admire her for long. He knew exactly who she was.

"See her! See her clearly! This agent of treason. This harlot of the crumbling resistance," Oriana exclaimed. She tore the dangling Harriett from the guard's hand and held her aloft in her straining, jeweled hands. Harriett's eyes closed in a brief recognition of her pain, but she didn't cry out. "How easy it was for our guards to stop this rebellion. All of you, look upon her and know this could be *your* fate."

Tristan's breaths came so fast the spots returned to his eyes. "Anders, I don't like this. I don't like this at all."

Anders put a hand on Tristan's chest and ascended another step. Oriana didn't turn, but it wouldn't take much more before she noticed some of those gathered were emerging toward her.

"Release her, Oriana." Thorvald's voice this time.

Tristan strained to see him, but the crowd was too thick. Tristan's heart surged. Thorvald was a badass. If anyone could save Harriett, it was Thorvald.

"Grand Empress Oriana," she corrected.

"You have made your point."

"You will know when my point is made, Thorvald of Spain."

"Anders..." Tristan licked his lips. Bit his tongue. Anything to not distract his mentor from what he needed to do. He swallowed and tried to pull in a deeper breath, but the effort was no use. He was drawn further into the center of his panic attack, and it was pointless to continue to fight it.

"I will take her place," Astrid announced, stepping past Thorvald. Gasps rippled through the crowd. More hope rippled through Tristan.

"No need. I'll have your head soon, Astrid of Erin," sang the empress.

Tristan pressed his hands into fists and flexed them, repeating, fearful he might lose consciousness at any moment if he didn't willfully prevent it.

Harriett! I'm here. I'm here, Harriett, and it's going to be okay. Anders has a plan and—

Tristan. My paladin. Your family needs you.

Harriett! My God, I love you, I'm here, I love you, I'm so sorry I let you—

Do you hear me? Your family needs you, Tristan. All you've experienced has been preparation and training for this service. You were always meant to serve this family. To save them. Your mother, she must have known this, too. You must move on. You must promise me this.

What are you talking about? I'm not moving on anywhere. We're here to save you, Harriett. Everything is going to be okay now.

Look away, my love.

What? No. What do you mean, look away? Anders is coming and—

I love you, Tristan. And if you love me, you will look away and you will remember my words.

Harriett, come on—

Tristan's heart seized. The world screeched in bright light and then went utterly and irrevocably silent. The silence in his head boomed like the heavy staccato of approaching war drums. He stopped breathing altogether when he heard Astrid's soothing voice cry out into the sky. Next to him, Anders moaned and fell to his knees.

Anders. That was the end, the second Tristan knew whatever hope he had brought with him to the palace had been the whimsy of a child.

This moment would never seem real. But nothing in his life had ever been more real, or held more weight.

Harriett's body arced into the air as the magic of Oriana's

minions passed through her, a current of wild electric death. Her arms flew to her sides. Her hair waved in the charged air. Pain only passed across her face briefly, and then a soft peace spread through her, starting with her eyes and then dancing across her cheeks as her soul was mercifully ripped from its torture and put to rest.

In Tristan's horror-stricken mind, Harriett hovered in the air like a suspended, fallen angel, arms draped toward the ground, dress flowing around her.

None of this happened. The abruptness in which Harriett's body slammed into the clay ground struck him like a sword to the chest.

Two strong arms encircled Tristan. Then four. Somewhere in the back of his mind, he knew they belonged to Anders and Tarek, but they were elsewhere, and he was elsewhere, and nothing was real anymore. Not the flesh on his bones, nor the air flowing through his lungs and out his parted mouth.

Harriett...

Harriett no longer existed, so Harriett did not respond. A voice—his mother's maybe, but she wasn't real, either, nothing was—whispered that Harriett would always live in his heart, but that was bullshit. Complete and utter bullshit, because she was gone, gone, gone! She was alive one moment and now she wasn't, and nothing was real or would be ever again.

Tristan was dragged from the stairs. His feet gave up desire for purchase and were pulled through the dirt and grass as strong arms dragged him from the chaos, from Harriett, who should be in his arms right now. He wanted to crush her lifeless form to his and breathe his own breath into her lungs, rip his heart from his own chest and thrust it into hers with the powerful violence of his love.

The ground rushed up, but it was only his protectors lowering them to a spot under a tree. He could no longer see the stage. Harriett had disappeared from his view, and he howled for her. Threw back his head and howled his pain into the cold Farjhem air as the two creatures held him.

"Haunt me," he pleaded through what was left of his breath. He had no tears. Tears meant he was still a man with flesh on his bones and blood flowing through his veins. "Harriett, do you hear me? Haunt me, torture me, love me!"

"I am so sorry, Tristan. Emyr, help me, I never meant for this." Anders crushed his limp form and Tarek held them both in poignant silence.

Tristan closed his eyes and Harriett mercifully appeared. But it was not *his* Harriett—not yet, not at the juncture in this memory—and somehow that was still okay, because it was the day he'd met her. She hadn't spoken in years, but when he met her eyes, years of unspoken words passed between them.

Will you save me? those eyes asked.

Yes, he answered. Later, he would amend that to, *It was you who saved me.*

And then I let you slip away from me because this time I missed the words unspoken.

Tristan took himself back to that day, slipping away from the moment that was too real to be real, and never would be real, as nothing else ever would be again. He needed to go to where Harriett was still haunting him in her hospital gown, and he was that troubled kid who had never known love.

14
ORIANA

Oriana had wasted so much time. Sparring with her sister, with Thorvald and Astrid, with those who did not understand her and had no desire to. And now, all the Brotherhood had gathered and Oriana, Grand Empress of Farjhem, daughter of the great Aeron, Mistress of The Menagerie, allowed herself the single flicker of fear that her wasted time may have cost her the upper hand.

To restore the balance of power, she must do what she had promised to do. To show her people she would not be swayed, or crossed. To remove all hope from the pestilent Brotherhood, who would then slip in the bowels of the obsolete where they belonged. Where they had always belonged.

Oriana also lamented her decision to deal with Margarethe, the way one lamented the decision to wear wool undergarments. The meddling spirit lorded in the background like a queen in the wings of her own palace. She would be rudely surpraised at how little patience Oriana had for those who deigned to trifle beyond their station.

The crowd—*her* crowd, for she refused to see them as

anything but, even the rebels, even those who would rise against her—awaited in shocked silence. She earned this shock and would use it to her advantage in the coming moments. Yes, she had killed Cyler, but he brought this fate upon himself. She'd given him more chances than any other creature in her service, and that fondness turned to weakness. Had he left Farjhem, she would not have wasted her time hunting him. He had chosen his end by staying.

The other death, that of the halfling rebel, was more forgettable. That the Brotherhood valued her so much was the real quandary taking up space in Oriana's precious mind.

Oriana thrust her wine glass into the hands of a guard. The dark liquid stained his white gloves as he struggled to attention, his flushed face a demonstration of his fear of displeasing her.

Lucky for him, she had bigger matters at hand.

She snapped her fingers at the slack-jawed Child of Man, Sebastian. "You. It's time."

"Oriana..." Nerys started, but Oriana nodded at the guards to subdue her. Nerys put up no struggle, and Oriana took that as a sign her sister, and others, rightfully feared Oriana still had the upper hand... still had the ultimate power in deciding Aleksandr's fate.

Sebastian looked up. His eyes widened to the extent Oriana thought the eyeballs might pop from their mortal sockets. The rest of him hung limp and ineffective. Another pang of disgust ripped through her, same as it had with Margarethe. She was better than this. In the future, she would not rely on such drivel to help her achieve her aims.

"Time?"

"Time, yes, time!"

Sebastian shot a look in his "mother's" direction, but Oriana stepped into his view. "It is time for you to accept payment for your alliance and delivery of the prisoner. Have you decided your method of execution?" She sneered as she ran her eyes over him, from head to toe. "I assume you prefer a banal weapon, like a sword, since your illusions won't even break the skin."

The sniveling Child of Man shuffled where he stood but didn't answer. The steam of anger rose from deep within her, but she would give him a chance. He had brought her the greatest prize, and, for that, she would put aside her annoyance. For now.

"Sebastian. Darling. Do as the empress asks so we may collect our reward and be on our way," Margarethe prodded, as if she was asking him to do the dishes.

"Don't look at her. Look at me!" Oriana cried.

Sebastian snapped his head up, revealing a trembling jaw and a face as white as her dress.

Weakness. He was all limitation, no grit. And he was of no use to her.

"Ease up on him, sister," Agripin called. "He hasn't had his nap today."

"Oriana, let him be." Birger's strong voice wafted off the crowd. From the fringe, she saw he now flanked Astrid on one side, with Thorvald still taking up reign on the other. "Let them all be. You're outnumbered, and if you do this, your life and freedom will be forfeit."

Oriana didn't bother to turn. She wouldn't give him the satisfaction of a formal audience. "When I take the life of your heir, your strength drains into the nether." She wrapped her hands around Sebastian's jaw, jerking it from side to side. "Answer me, or I rip the teeth from your sniveling mouth."

"You won't touch my son!" Margarethe cried.

"Know your place, harpy!"

"Hey, sorry, me over here," Aleksandr said, casual, strange, lacking any sign of the concern that should, by all accounts, be written on him from head to toe. She wanted to rip *his* teeth out. Maybe then he would understand his life was hers. "This is getting a little boring. So, if Sebastian lacks the... um... *desire* to kill me, can we just assign it to someone else and get on with it?"

"Emyr help us," Agripin hissed.

"He's right. I... can't." Sebastian's voice, though a whisper, cut through the banter. "I can't do it."

Oriana returned her attention to him. "Cannot or will not?"

"I don't know. I guess both, maybe." He turned away from Oriana—away! The gall!—and looked at Aleksandr.

"I'm sorry, Aleksei. Everything you said about me was right. We both had a weird childhood, and I don't know, I thought maybe it marked me as different, and I didn't want to be different. I wanted to be known for something other than being a freak, and when my mo—when Margarethe told me I could be something more, I believed her."

"Child, you know not what you say," said Margarethe. "All I have promised you is within our reach, so close even I can feel it. You know your mother always knows best."

Tears poured from Sebastian's eyes. He trained them on Margarethe briefly. "You're not my mother. Katja is my mother."

"You should say that to Katja," Aleksandr said. "She deserves to hear it."

Sebastian's sad smile infuriated Oriana. "I'm never going to see her again, Aleksei. We both know that."

"You have ten seconds to choose your weapon," Oriana warned. She has no patience to indulge his weepy confessions or insipid human family drama. She''d counted minutes since the last time she noted time was running out.

Sebastian shook his head. "Aleksei, forgive me."

"Nine."

The first crack appeared in Aleksandr's smooth countenance. "Sebastian..."

"Seven."

"Sebastian, you *can* do this. We are so close... so very close to all we talked about. To everything we have worked for," Margarethe prodded. Without a physical form, her words rang benign as she hovered in the corner like a bad cobweb. "There's only this one last thing, and then the world is ours."

Oriana was ready to shut the spirit up for good, but that was lower on her priority list. She rolled her eyes. "Three."

"I'm sorry I wasn't a better friend to you and a better man," Sebastian wept. His head dropped to his chest in a form of surrender, and Oriana remembered why she never employed Children of Men except as slaves to Empyreans.

"Sebastian, you know not what you say!" shrieked the trifling banshee.

Oriana turned briefly to her sister. "You ask me why I elevate thugs and sellswords? Because others only disappoint me and I end up having to do everything myself."

Oriana whipped her hand around. In one move, she had the sword from a guard's hilt, and in the next, she ran it across the soft white milky neck of the whimpering human disappointment.

Everyone around her, from the crowd to those gathered around her on the palace steps, went silent in horror. Sebastian flailed around on the stone as blood evacuated his body in violent, arcing spurts. Oriana rolled her head to the side and inspected her work with bland curiosity. She may have cut too deep. His neck flapped at the cut and she wondered if it would fall clean off before the rest of his life drained away.

After what felt like the longest moments of her grueling day, the useless Child of Man finally collapsed. He twitched twice more before going still.

Margarethe shrieked in an agony that Oriana wished she could turn into gelatin and eat for dessert.

Aleksandr was the first to find his voice. "What's *wrong* with you? He's not the one you wanted. I'm who you want, and you have me! How unfulfilling is your life that you have killed *three* people today who aren't even on the menu? Hello, I'm standing right here, lady. Your hesitation makes me think maybe you don't have a clue what you're doing."

Agripin stepped forward but was yanked back by his bonds. "What Aleksandr means to say—"

"I just said what I meant to say," Aleksandr cut in. "How long has it been since she said she wanted to execute me? Hours?" His voice was as confident as it had been throughout his confinement, but his eyes didn't leave the corpse of his friend, and she sensed in him an unsteadiness that he fought hard to keep from the rest of them.

"A decision you can still take back," Agripin said to his sister. "You once valued my head for strategy. I could be useful to you yet. I can aid you through the alternatives."

"If you surrender Aleksandr unharmed, we will promise safe passage for you as well," Thorvald said. He ascended a step. "Our true battle was fought and won. The Senetat is no more. You hang onto a crippled world that is no more. You are a master of survival. You must see the merit in what we offer."

Oriana could not let the halfling or the others get to her. She guessed Aleksandr's prodding was meant to drive doubt in her, but she had only moments ago lectured her sister on trusting her base instincts, and she would not prove to be a hypocrite now.

As for Thorvald and the others... their words only incensed her further. Their promise was as solid to her as the human blood pooling around her heels. Their vows were fluid, taking shape with the opportunity of the moment.

If Oriana surrendered her advantage, she was as good as dead.

Agripin and Aleksandr. She must eliminate them both, but each meant something different to her current standing. The Brotherhood had concerns only for the halfling heir, and only held their peace temporarily for fear of how quickly she might dispatch the child if provoked. But all of Farjhem awaited *something* that would spur them into action. They were muted from all they had seen and needed a turn of events to show them where their alliances lay.

Aleksandr may be more valuable to her in the long term, but Agripin's death would give her the immediate advantage that may turn her people back to her side and help ensure the Brotherhood was not able to assail her once Aleksandr's execution was complete.

Oriana turned toward the crowd. She choked down her shock at the sheer number of Empyreans standing, waiting. In all her years, she had never seen so many of them in one place. Not even close. Quinlans, too—had they ever been in Farjhem before? She didn't know. Didn't need to.

All were gathered because of her. It was time to decide why.

"Now that we have dispatched ourselves of two traitors and a weakling, it is time to commence with the executions you have all come to see."

Nerys squirmed in her bonds. The Brotherhood leaders tensed in readiness.

"Many of you still hold a great love for my brother, the Grand Duke Agripin, who served a very short tenure as the Grand Emperor of Farjhem. To protect you and your love, we have not shared with you the full list of his crimes, but I shall run through them now so you can understand the great pain driving me to order his execution now."

The crowd's energy revitalized, but it was dark, disturbed. She was right to start carefully, for it was clear she had underestimated their love.

She faced her brother. Agripin looked blankly back.

"Grand Duke Agripin, son of Aeron, I sentence you to death for the following crimes:

"Conspiring in the death of our father, Grand Emperor Aeron, to assume your own gain.

"For—"

"I did no such thing, and you know this." Agripin lifted his chin. "You know this, Oriana, and yet you lie to our people. Those guilty are already dispatched. The Senetat chose to turn on him."

Oriana ignored him. "For conspiring with the Dragon Brotherhood, also known as Runeans, also known as rebels against the teachings of Emyr, to take the throne of Farjhem and act as the puppet of their aims."

Agripin laughed. He looked out at the sea of friend and foe alike, beseeching them with a desperation in his eyes. "I have only ever served Emyr, Farjhem, and myself. To even insinuate that I would take orders from *anyone* is treasonous itself!"

"For mating with a halfling abomination who was created by a rebel without authorization and against all rules we hold sacred."

He snorted. "I never laid with Anasofiya. I wouldn't be standing here if I'd even tried."

"For making her your empress and blighting the very throne that connects us to Our Father."

Agripin raised his eyes and grinned. "I did do that."

"For these crimes, and crimes we cannot possibly know about, you are sentenced to die in the old way of Our Father. I have chosen five powerful conjurers who will send the full command of their gifts surging through you, cutting your cord with Emyr. Your pain will be brief, but your eternity of damnation will sting far worse."

Her brother's smile faded. "Oriana, truly, you cannot kill one of royal blood. Even you know this."

"Treason surpasses royalty. Even you know this." She spun, turning her back on her brother. Facing the crowd once again.

Now, they were less agitated, but she could not read the

emotion replacing the restlessness. Did they support her decision to exact the laws of the land against Agripin? Did they doubt her commitment to it?

Oriana turned her thoughts to Emyr. She had never been especially devout, but their god did not require the same devotion as the one Children of Men dropped to their knees to praise.

Hear me now. I will take these lives. And I will succeed. I will thrive. And you will help me do it, or see this land of your creation turn to famine and flame.

She faced her prisoners. Aleksandr wore a bemused look, one she could not wait to see ripped from his face.

But Agripin... she could not meet his stare.

All his pomp and arrogance had drained away. Disbelief colored his cheeks, and his eyes, as he saw she really meant to do it. As he drew in the realization that he was now in the final moments of his long, storied life.

And she couldn't find the strength, the courage, the... whatever it was she knew she should possess but did not, to face him. She prided herself on a clear lack of sentiment in her constitution, but Agripin, for all his faults, was her kin. They had sparred over the years, but was this not the way of siblings? She was seconds away from giving the order to end his life, to elevating herself as the undisputed elder once the deed was done.

If she did not take Agripin's life, the people would eventually rise and place him back on the throne. He was the rightful heir, and she, the hardly tolerated usurper. To leave him alive would mean looking over her shoulder the rest of the days, and she could not envision any joy in a future with that much uncertainty.

"Oriana... sister. If you take my life, something within you dies as well. Something that even Emyr cannot give back to you."

I am either a creature of resolve or I am a creature of nothing. This decides the matter.

Oriana nodded at the five guards. She had the sharp urge to close her eyes, but if she could not watch the results of her mandates, then she had no business making them. If she was to lead Farjhem, she could betray no weakness.

Not even to herself.

The guards stood in position like a firing squad. Agripin's defeated look would haunt her for the rest of her days, but it was better than a real live ghost threatening her life and realm.

Oriana raised her hand. *Ready.* With a short breath, she dropped it. *Now.*

She diverted her attention to the guards only briefly, but it was long enough to miss the mayhem that had everyone both on stage and gathered in the crowd stirred to frenzy.

When Oriana returned her gaze to execution, it was not her brother lying in a crumpled heap on the stone.

It was Aleksandr.

"He... he jumped out... I..." Agripin stumbled through his words as he knelt at the side of the dead halfling. "Oh, Aleksandr... you foolish, foolish child..." He buried his face against his chest, against the melted wool of his scorched sweater.

Oriana couldn't move. She couldn't breathe.

It was not that the halfling had died, it was this other thing... this loss of control... this knowledge she could give the orders but even that had not been enough. And now her most powerful leverage was gone, and she had not yet considered what her next step should be.

At that moment, the entire world turned to chaos.

15
ALEKSANDR

Aleksandr heard the pronouncements on Agripin's crimes along with the thousands gathered. All along, the unfolding events seemed like amateur fighters flexing their wimpy muscles in hopes they might trick the spectators into thinking they knew what the hell they were doing. And while he had no doubt it would end in his own death, whether they knew what they were doing or not, he wasn't prepared for the feeling of *officialness* that came from hearing Agripin's crimes and sentence read.

Oriana really was going to kill her brother, and Aleksandr didn't know if that made her crazy or a genius, but it left him with a feeling far from vindication.

And he *should* be vindicated, right? Agripin had ordered the death of Aidrik, not for any great crime, but to save himself. In the end, everything fell apart anyway. Only when presented with the inevitability of his mortality had Agripin bothered to express any regret. How could his words be taken as anything more than a gallows confession?

Agripin had told Aleksandr, when they were locked together

in that tiny cell, that Aidrik was still alive, but that didn't make any sense at all. Anasofiya watched him die, and she would never lie about something that important. Beyond that, Aleksandr had *felt* the moment Aidrik gave up his ghost to Emyr, all the way from the bayou of Louisiana. The sensation shocked him straight out of a dead sleep. No one had to tell Aleksandr his second father was gone. He *knew*.

Never matter that he began to feel his father again, catching a rogue thought or sensation, like a phantom limb. Aleksandr suspected this was his way of coming to terms with the imminent end of his own life, and he couldn't trust anything his mind sent him. He once read a book about the wonders of the human brain, how it knew more than it allowed the conscious self to realize. The brain protected you by employing dopamine and serotonin, or amnesia for the very worst moments. When it detected the end of your life, the brain sought to comfort you and divert your attention to something less traumatic.

Aleksandr *did* feel Aidrik now, but that was his second life calling him, the one he would find beyond the disconnection of his soul from his body, after the execution completed its dirty business. When he found his way to his second life, Aidrik would be there, waiting... and others, like poor Harriett, and even Sebastian. Maybe even that unfortunate lackey of Agripin's, Cyler, whose lifeless body collected flies on the stones next to Sebastian's. Agripin clearly tried to maintain his bravado, but Aleksandr caught the creature gazing at Cyler's figure with heavy, dark pain.

Aleksandr understood. His grief for Sebastian was colored with acute betrayal and so much confusion, but the pain was nonetheless real.

He couldn't believe how many had come to see him die. He recognized some of them, but most of the faces blended together, into a mosaic of color and anxious movement. Those he most wanted to see were not among them, but he drew comfort from knowing his loved ones were not here to see what was about to happen to him.

Aleksandr wondered quietly, vaguely, what would happen to the Prophecy when he died. Would Amelia's daughter wander aimless and lost without a mate? Would she have a normal life? And the family... would they continue to suffer in the wake of his failure to save them?

The pragmatic voice of Aidrik provided him wisdom from somewhere within him.

You are one man. The world cannot hinge upon the shoulders of one man.

Aleksandr drew from that same sagacity to find closure on his own life. Fiona's dark eyes and soft, apple cheeks appeared. *She will love again.* His mother's vague but intense love, and his father's quiet intensity. *They will find the needed strength to move past this, in each other.*

Aleksandr released the competing voices screaming at him that Fiona was his greatest love... his soul mate, his once-in-a-lifetime... that his parents would wilt away if he died... that he, Aleksandr, still had so much life left, and living to do.

The words, true or not, were useless to him now. In that dark cell of Farsengel, he began to change into the man he would be in the final moments of his life. His fears slipped into the small stone cracks. His hopes took on new life as memories, not indications of the future. Aleksandr no longer really knew who he was, beyond that he was not afraid to die anymore.

And he would, once Agripin was dealt with.

At Aleksandr's side, the creature went rigid. He'd shrugged off his loose-limbed arrogance as fear stretched itself through his veins, to toes and fingers, from elbow to knee. The loss of his confidence rendered him stiff as a cadaver, as if his body was preparing him for the moments ahead.

Oriana continued running down the list of crimes she'd charged to her brother. Her smug voice intoned across the crowd, who stood rooted to the cold ground as if frozen. Aleksandr tried to clear his mind and make his peace, but he could not stop thinking about Oriana, and her words, and the creature moments from his death. The creature who *deserved* death.

Deserving or not, it was wrong. All wrong. All of it. Agripin's crimes required an answer, but it was not on this ridiculous stage to satisfy his sister's need for an audience. No one, not one single onlooker, stepped forward to speak for him, or to stop it. They had all watched as Oriana cut down first Cyler, then Harriett and Sebastian. He supposed he knew why. Aleksandr had mages standing siege around him, waiting for the kill order if anyone tried to defy Oriana. Which was wrong, all wrong, because that presumed Aleksandr's life was more valuable than Cyler's, Harriett's, Sebastian's, Agripin's.

"No," he whispered. Agripin flinched, observing him from the corner of his gaze.

Aleksandr didn't think of Fiona. He did not think of his mother, or either of his fathers. Not his family. Not his memories, happy or otherwise. His mind was clear, but focused, as he drew from a power he had only used once before and waited, waited for the right moment to use it.

I told you, Sebastian, that there were things you didn't know about me. Things I could do. Are you watching now, from wherever you are?

Oriana raised her hand.

Lowered it.

Aleksandr leapt in front of Agripin at the same moment the guards released their magic at the accused. Yet as his body soared in slow advance toward the spot the magic was directed, prepared to engage his ability to stop time and prevent the execution of his enemy, Aleksandr caught something from the edge of his vision that shook his focus.

He saw his fathers.

Both of them.

Yes, there was Finn, and there was... Aidrik. Aidrik, real, in the flesh, not dead. Very much alive.

Aidrik!

And in this split-second break in concentration, Aleksandr's attempt to stop time fired a second too late. He heard nothing, except the collective gasp that passed across the thousands. But he felt everything.

A wall of scorching fire hit him and tore through his skin, into the soft tissues and organs vital to his survival, ripping apart his veins from the arteries. Everything was fire and light, brightness and exquisite, consuming pain.

Aleksandr surrendered to the white-hot assault. His mind, which he had only earlier accused of working against him, became a blank slate of mercy as the life force drained away.

16
FINNEGAN

What have you done?

The pitched call of these words sounded all around him in fevered cries. Hundreds, thousands of Empyreans screeched them in guttural demand, first out of sync amidst the chaos and then in perfect congruence. *Oriana! What. Have. You. Done?*

Finn commenced the mad rush to the top of the steps where Aleksandr had collapsed. His compatriots were right behind him, and then the rest of the gatherers followed suit, as if they had only been waiting for a catalyst to stir into action. Finn inadvertently led the scene from a stunned and grieving father reaching for his son to a group swelling with incredulous anger.

He and his friends were crushed in the bulge of many bodies trying to fit into the much narrower span of the stairs. He may as well have been pushing through a wall of tar for all the progress he made, but he didn't falter. He muscled his way through, fighting one battle at a time, each step feeling as if he were pulled farther away, instead of brought closer, to where his son had fallen.

Fallen.

No, he would not believe it, not yet. Aleksandr was strong, stronger than any of them knew, and he would not have thrown himself before a cabal of magic without a plan. Certainly not for Agripin.

He has your blind kindness. Don't be so sure.

Finn kept his eyes forward. He couldn't look at Aidrik. The truth would be read clear in Aidrik's eyes, and if that truth clashed with Finn's hope, he would lose control of everything, and he couldn't let that happen. Not until there was nothing left for him to maintain control for. He must stay strong and focused, as he had when he discovered Aleksandr missing. Strength and focus were the only pillars protecting him from a collapse into complete madness, and once he descended there, he did not know if he was capable of emerging again.

"Hurry the feck on, ye gobshites!" a voice cried, and it was a moment before Finn recognized the perfect Irish brogue of an angry Jacob Donnelly.

In a vague moment of clarity, Finn recognized that he could not have asked for better companions to rescue his son. His best friend. His evigbond. His brother. He couldn't have done this alone; it would be nice to believe himself capable of forging ahead bravely, but they were stronger together, and he couldn't have forced them to stay home with any degree of persuasion.

Finn said a brief, silent prayer that their sacrifice would not be a final one.

Aidrik appeared at his side. "There are resurrection shamans with him. Astrid's tribe. Four. But it is not... it is not..."

"Don't say another word," Finn replied through his clenched jaw. His muscles locked as the crowd grew denser and the sensation of tar turned to cement. "Not one."

"Finnegan, you must prepare—"

"*Not one, Aidrik, goddammit!*"

Some of the Brotherhood, better positioned than they had been, breached the top of the stairs. Those not tending to Aleksandr assailed Oriana and her guards. She flailed in the bonds. Finn hoped they didn't kill her before he could lay his own hands on her.

He glimpsed his brother off in the distance. Jon had broken off from their quartet at some point and attempted another way forward. He reached the top step and landed only a few feet from where Finn saw his son's lifeless—*no, not lifeless, just at rest*—hand lying palm up against the cold stone. Agripin perched nearby, wailing at the sky.

Finn heaved to a shocking halt as the Empyreans ahead of him planted their feet in tandem, forming an instant wall. He opened his mouth to scream when, amidst the yawning moans of shock, he began to see what had given them sudden pause.

He saw it, but he didn't know what to make of it.

When Finn was a child, five or six, he had an experience that he had never been able to explain well to anyone. Not his parents, not his teachers, not Jon. He'd stood in the doorway of his father's operating room at the house—his rogue father, who, in the absence of a hospital on their small island, harbored the contraband equipment needed to do emergency surgeries himself, in his own home—and a woman stared back at him. He knew this woman... or *had* known her, because she was no longer among the living. She had died in their house the night before, in that very room where she lingered in a bloody, patterned hospital gown.

At the time, Finn lacked the vocabulary to describe the differences between the living Mrs. Caldwell and the ghost of her. She didn't flicker like the spirits in his favorite movies. He couldn't see straight through her at all. Her feet rested firmly on the ground; she didn't hover above it. She looked as solid as Finn would if he glanced at himself in a mirror, but she also looked...

flat. Later, the word that would come to him was one-dimensional, but even that wasn't right, because she had plenty of dimension to her, but lacked something else, something vital. The substance of flesh, of blood pumping through veins and feeding life force to organs. She had lacked *realness.*

Now, a grown man in a magical world, fighting for the life of his son, Finn saw her again. But this was not Mrs. Caldwell.

The whispers around him provided a possible answer. *Morrigan. Goddess.*

Even Finn, in all his demanding panic, was rendered motionless at the sight of her. He felt frozen to the cold earth beneath his feet and couldn't will himself forward even a single step.

"Jesus, Mary, and Joseph," Jacob whispered.

That Finn could hear him so clearly was testament to the quiet settling over the people.

Finn's mouth was a field of cotton. His lips parted, but the potential of words remained trapped behind his tongue.

Morrigan loomed larger than life, like Freya peering down from majestic Valhalla. She glided through the air before the stunned crowd, though she seemed oblivious to anyone or anything except Aleksandr.

She knelt at Aleksandr's side, and even in her lowered state, she towered into the air. An unutterable sadness lived in her face, as if she bore the grief for all the world. She wiped away invisible tears and turned to the crowd.

Her voice rang sharp and true, carrying across the gentle breeze. It met no resistance. The crowd absorbed her in shared awe. "I alone straddle the realms of life and death. I alone control the fates. I did not ask for this gift, just as none of you asked for the gifts your god granted you. When the Goddess Danu granted me this power, she did not ask if I wanted it, or how I would use it. Yet she must have known."

Morrigan rose. The effect of her form unraveling into its full height startled everyone gathered. "The Empyreans and the Quinlans cannot exist without harmony. And yet, you are both failingly human in the ways that matter most. When the time arrived to prove your unity, The Empyreans broke their blood pact and this action propelled both races into a long period of strife that even Danu could not mend. Yet I found the gift she gave me, to control the fates, was not without usefulness. I could have mended your fortunes without the trouble of a Prophecy, but history would have fallen into the same cycle. You needed a reason to unite again and remain united. You required a common goal, one that demanded your cohesion and sacrifice, for anything less would be transitory like the pact previously severed. And thus I gave you one, with the Prophecy. And here we are."

Morrigan cast a tragic look at Aleksandr. "Now I see before me the greatest sacrifice of all. The young man you all placed your hope in chose a different path, one not predicted by any of us. He surrendered everything to do what he felt was right and just. To save the life of a creature who had taken so much from him. He gave his own life in exchange for the life of one who did not deserve such a sacrifice."

Jacob slipped his hand through Finn's. Finn held his breath. The rest of him was tethered to the ground like the roots of a tree. His thoughts were not his own.

Morrigan surveyed the silent crowd. "I see also, the races coming together for the first time in millennia. United, in a battle you were far from certain of winning. Knowing the risks, taking them anyway. I watched from afar as Empyrean protected Quinlan, and Quinlan shielded Empyrean. I am witnessing an altruism that did not exist when the pact was broken. While the Prophecy may have spurred you into these intersecting paths, what I see now is not grudging partnership, but true alliance, united for what's right, and against the injustices of what is wrong."

Morrigan pivoted away from the crowd. She again knelt at the side of Aleksandr. She gently nudged away those huddled around him—the resurrection shamans, Finn thought, but also Agripin, who had to be ripped away like a scab on a wound—and hovered her hands above his still form.

No one said a word. No one breathed aloud. An eagle soaring ahead cut a brief shriek through the silence, but then it was gone and there was nothing but the loudness of pure quiet.

Aleksandr pitched forward. He coughed and gasped for breath, rocking in place as the goddess passed her magic through to him, filling him once again with life.

Tears poured down Finn's face. His heart stuttered and a great lump lodged in his throat. Jacob gasped at his side, and then he was crying, too.

Morrigan extended a hand to Aleksandr and pulled him to his feet. Next to her, he appeared no more than a small child, and the uncomplicated look he gave as he peered up at her made this even more the case.

"Aleksandr," she purred. She bent to kiss the top of his head. "You humbled me with your bravery. With your pure selflessness and love for mankind. For that, I give you this gift: The Prophecy is no more. Your life is your own, my son, for you to live it as you choose, with whom you choose. Your path is yours."

"I..." Aleksandr's throat scratched. He swallowed and found his voice. Finn strained to hear. "I don't understand."

Morrigan smiled. "And yet, of all those here today, I believe you understand the most, Aleksandr Nicolas St. Andrews Deschanel."

"What about Moira?"

"Moira's requirement as the heir expired with my revocation of the Prophecy. She will be born as any child is born, and will grow as other children grow. And yet she, and you, and the parents of you both, will live forever. For, while I have rescinded the requirements of the Prophecy, I leave with you the blessings."

"Immortal?" Aleksandr nearly whispered the word.

"You may fall from a sword, but you will never fall from disease. You will cease to age. The fruits of this world are yours to enjoy. This is the gift I give you and your loved ones, Aleksandr. The gift of the Empyreans, who stand before you, united, ready to give up their own immortality to save you."

Agripin hobbled forward. He prostrated himself before Aleksandr, shaking with tears. "I am your bondservant, Halfling. I am yours to command. My life is yours."

Aleksandr shook his head. "Get up." When Agripin did not, he sighed. "Agripin, stand *up*."

Agripin rose, no longer the arrogant, commanding man who had ruled over Finn, Ana, and Aidrik's lives in Farjhem. No longer the cowardly tyrant who ordered Aidrik's death. Finn loathed himself for the sympathy he now evoked, but then he let that emotion dissolve into the nether, for this was not a day to remember the pain, but to embrace the joy. He wanted to rush forward to his son, but he knew, as Aidrik knew, as Jacob knew, as Jonathan knew, that this moment would come.

"I don't want anything from you," Aleksandr said. "You don't owe me anything."

"I owe you my life."

"Then... I don't know... go do something useful with it for a change. Go bury your boyfriend and help the Brotherhood rebuild your homeland. You're looking to me for answers, but I didn't save your life because I wanted you to do good things with it. I saved your life because I knew I wouldn't be myself anymore if I watched them kill you and did nothing to stop it."

Morrigan offered a hand to Aleksandr. His palm fit into the tips of her fingers. "Peace is yours to enjoy, or to destroy. I am no longer the architect of your fate, or the soothsayer providing the path. The Prophecy is no more. I pray your choices take you down the road ahead together, in unity, but I will no more tell you how to get there. Your lives are your own."

Morrigan disappeared. Aleksandr whipped his neck toward the spot where she had stood, as Empyreans and Quinlans in the crowd mumbled their confusion.

Finnegan found his legs again, and they held true as they took him through the break in the crowd, up the stairs, and in the direction of his only son.

17
NERYS

The Brotherhood asked Nerys what she wanted done with her sister.

How could she answer that? Nerys spent her life advocating for peace, and yet she knew, had absolutely no doubt, Oriana must answer for her crimes. They did not roll away with Aleksandr's miraculous resurrection. The shaman had been unable to return life to Cyler, Harriett, or Sebastian, and the goddess had not offered. And what of the dozens of her own Oriana had ordered killed, simply to prove the point of her strength?

But Nerys could not order Oriana's death, as many others in the Brotherhood would have her do. Amidst the dazed chaos was a new regime taking form, and it could not begin, as the last had ended, with bloodshed.

"Sister, I banish you to the realm of The Menagerie. You and all who closely followed your word," Nerys declared. She could physically *feel* Thorvald's displeasure from the other end of the portico, but she didn't require his approval, and this was not his decision to make. "The doors will be sealed. There is no emerging from that world, not anymore."

Oriana cackled. She hung slack in the bonds, having given up on fighting. "*This* is your punishment, sister? An eternity in the only place I have ever loved? You'll remember one day that it was *me* who first labeled you weak!"

"Weakness is taking the path easiest in the moment but harder on the soul," Nerys countered. "It seems that you, in your desire to critique my decision, haven't considered it with any foresight. What you love about The Menagerie is not only the exotic escape it provides, but the variety in clientele. The richness in refreshments. When I declare this door sealed, it will not ever open again from either side. Not from the outside, nor the inside. Your squabbles may become wars. Friend, over time, foe. There will be no more importing of fine wines or meat from outside Farjhem. What is there now is all there will be. Your fruit trees and bread ovens will have to be enough to sustain you. For the magic sealing this door cannot be opened once laid."

Nerys' courage failed her here. She could not witness the fire die from her sister's indignant eyes. She had never enjoyed Oriana's hubris, but nor could she enjoy her fall.

She waved her hand at the guards. Her sister's screeching insults burned her ears, but there was nothing left to be said.

"You went easy. Too easy," Thorvald accused. He now stood at her side. "What message does it send, that the new leaders are weaker than the old?"

"What message would it send if we were no different?" Nerys sighed.

"Her castle will become her prison. Even I see the poetry in this punishment," Birger said with a short laugh. "And all those who followed her, who preferred The Menagerie when they had the freedom to come and go? I predict a revolt within the year, and the end will be the same."

Nerys craned to search for Stian. As if on command, he appeared, stoic, ready. "Stian, I have an ask of you."

"I already know your ask. I fulfill it willingly." Stian disappeared into the bowels of the palace, following the screaming Oriana to her forever home, which he would seal in place for all time.

"There is one more piece of nasty business," Nerys said with a frown. She turned toward a slight bend in the air. She could not see the spirit, but she felt it, and there were others among her who communed with the dead, despite Margarethe's meager attempt at hiding.

"Necromancers!" she cried over the mayhem. "I call on you now to banish this creature into the nether! She must not be allowed to return, not even if called back by the strongest magic. She had her time, and then stole more, costing many lives. No more."

Margarethe didn't have time to protest. The dark magic she employed to keep her tethered to the world of the living was severed in an instant.

In this decision, Nerys felt no conflict. They were all granted but one life and this ghoul had stolen many more than her rightful share.

A great weariness stole over the duchess. She pressed her shoulder blades into a pillar and let the stone bear her weight for a moment.

Years—millennia—they had waited, plotted, planned, and prayed for the return to a time of peace. In a short afternoon, all had come to a head. One moment she was unsure if she or her friends would emerge from the land alive, and now it was...

... over. It was simply, over.

The Senetat, no more. Oriana, the last thread of an old regime, defeated. The Prophecy, fulfilled, even if not in the way promised.

Farjhem was theirs.

Farjhem was Emyr's.

Farjhem meant, in the most literal sense of the word, Father's Home.

Farjhem was, finally, *home.*

Birger's whisper in her ear brought her back around. "It is time. If we don't give them a leader now, they will seek one out. We have come too far to let such a decision rest on chance."

Nerys nodded.

18
ALEKSANDR

Aleksandr had seen enough in his short, turbulent life to know the re-appearance of Aidrik was not to be questioned or taken for granted. He gave himself a single moment to be shocked and then accepted it and allowed himself joy.

So, the monster wasn't lying.

The once young, but now ancient Aleksandr thought this as both his fathers crushed him to their breast, fawned over him, cried, and laughed. He had never had so many hands on his face.

Agripin stayed on the front of his mind while the back of it responded accordingly to the love heaped on him by his fathers, uncle, and Jacob. He should be enjoying this moment—he wanted to, he did—but a numbness spread across his soul. He didn't know where it came from, exactly. Maybe from the experience of dying and being brought back, or maybe something simpler than that, like shock. But this sensation, whatever the cause, divided him in two. On one end he was a stoic, cautious, deadened young man, and on the other, a passable actor guided into the emotion of the moment.

Agripin didn't lie to me. It doesn't absolve him of his many other crimes, but in what he believed to be his final moments, he told the truth, and it matters.

Agripin had tried to offer his services to Aleksandr three times. He didn't refuse him out of any great honor, or disgust at the idea of having a bondservant. He heard whispers of some from the Brotherhood suggesting Aleksandr was *too good, too pure* to take Agripin up on his offer, but that presumption was far too generous. He said no because he couldn't bear a tether to the parts of his past that had caused him the most pain. His refusal was as selfish as Agripin's offer was noble.

Aleksandr was impressed at how well he continued to engage with his loved ones as they peppered him with questions and love. He wished all of him could be with them in this moment, but there was a reason for this detachment and he needed to follow it through to the answer.

Around him, the world dissembled and reassembled into something newer... better? The Brotherhood and Empyreans of Farjhem debated the future of their ancient city, and names for the royalty to take them into the next era were bantered around. Aleksandr knew who it would be. His power of foresight had only strengthened with his resurrection, and he already saw this process play out. But he watched with fascination anyway.

Uncle Jacob had broken off to comfort Tristan. Aleksandr's heart fell—the one in both halves of him, not just one—at the memory of Harriett surrendering herself to her fate. Harriett had always been so nice to him. To everyone. And it was more than fair to say she had saved Tristan as much as he had saved her.

"Maybe they can keep trying. The shamans... why did they stop trying? Why did they—" Tristan blubbered this to the sky, the stars, anyone listening.

Jacob wrapped his arms around Tristan from behind and rested his head against his. "Sometimes magic is magic and sometimes it's nothing," he said. "They tried. All of them tried. Ana told me once that there's only a small window of time, and once it closes... it doesn't re-open."

Jacob's kindness is what we should all strive for. His wife is pregnant and sick back home, and he's here shouldering the emotional burden for everyone else.

Tristan rambled his grief into incoherent short sentences, and Jacob stopped him with something useful: a request for help. "We need to get Sebastian home for a proper Catholic burial, wouldn't you say?" he asked the blubbering Tristan, who stared at him, clearly confused. "How about you help me with that, and I'll help you with Harriett?"

"Why.... why would you want to help Sebastian? After what he did?"

"Because his mother is family, and she deserves to have a place to mourn her child and know a piece of him is there to mourn," Jacob said. His voice dropped to barely above a whisper. "Katja deserved better than what she got."

Tristan dropped his head to his chest and sobbed. His body shook hard enough to shrug Jacob off. He didn't try to hold him again, but he stayed close. "Jasper deserves that, too, but there's nothing anyone can do to make Harriett look like her again."

Jacob nodded. "Aye."

"We can't take her back to her family like that."

"No," Jacob agreed.

"So, what do we do?"

"Well, Tristan, we tell them the truth. That Harriett died honorably and her body rests in the home of our genetic ancestors, which I suppose is sort of like an American soldier being buried in Arlington Cemetery, you know? And if we're lucky, they'll see the honor in it, but even if they don't, we will know we spared them from the worst of it."

"I'll never have that myself," Tristan whispered.

Jacob pivoted himself in front of the younger man. "Hey. You saw something, and you know something, that they will never see or know. You knew Harriett better than any of them. This is the good and the bad of it, and no one can take either from you. But when we get home, you and I, we will plan something for Harriett. Something private just for you, and for her. The sendoff we couldn't give her here, or there." He put his palm against Tristan's heart. "Some people put a lot of stock in wakes and tombs, but we know better, don't we? Our loved ones live in here." His hand traveled to Tristan's shoulder. "You're not alone, Tristan. Her leaving you didn't make that the case. You'll never be alone."

Aleksandr softly sighed and pulled his attention from the two of them. The other half of himself heard Finn make a joke about something that happened on their journey. Uncle Jon laughed. Aidrik pretended it wasn't funny. Aleksandr laughed and laughed, as they would have expected.

The stoic side of Aleksandr again turned away from his reunion.

The government of Farjhem was in happy chaos. The Senetat, forever dissolved. Oriana and her minions locked away. No remnants existed from the dysfunctional empire, and those still spread about the world would eventually discover their purpose changed. They might scatter to the wind. They might fight. But they would not ever be in power again.

Or at least, thought Aleksandr, not until the next revolution. History was a perfect circle.

The last hour was a futile attempt to convince Birger and Astrid to be the next Grand Emperor and Empress, but Aleksandr could have told them that it was a waste of opinions. There must be other clairvoyant mystics thinking the same thing, but, like him, they quietly let the day play out. This was democracy at work, and most were eager to see things done well.

It will be Nerys and Trygve. Nerys, for her royal blood and the way they love her and believe in her. Trygve because he is one of the ancients, and to combine his blood with hers represents the life all those most connected to Emyr have always believed in.

Aleksandr again turned away. It would be another hour before that came to pass, and he didn't have the patience for debate and rhetoric when he already knew the outcome.

Nearby, Jacob asked a handful of Empyreans to help him with Sebastian. They gathered around and prepared to lift him with all the delicacy of moving old furniture. Jacob scolded them all for the rough handling, as if it mattered anymore, but that was Jacob, and Aleksandr loved him for it, just as everyone loved Jacob.

Sebastian, though... Aleksandr couldn't peel his eyes from his friend. Even now, he could not find another word for him. They both had their demons, Sebastian's had just been louder and more convincing.

You never had a chance. No one else will ever give you that latitude, except maybe your mother, but I know who you were deep down, Sebastian. It wasn't your fault some crazy, ancient ghost picked you. You weren't who they're going to say you were.

Aleksandr's mouth pulled into a tight line as he watched them carry his friend away. Had the resurrection shamans even tried with him? Or had he been deemed unworthy of a second chance?

"Aleksei, what's wrong?" His father Finn's voice pulled at him, reconnecting both his halves. Now he was theirs and only theirs. But he was no less disconnected.

Aleksandr then, suddenly, understood why he had been so unable to give himself over emotionally to the reunion with those who loved him best.

He loved them no less. Maybe he even loved them more, and in ways they would never understand because they had never lived a life anything like his.

But he was not theirs anymore, and they were not his.

Had it taken death to clear this notion through his mind? Rebirth? Or had he known it, always, or at least from the moment he yielded himself to love under the old oaks in the forest beyond Killianshire?

Aleksandr could not go home. Not to their home. His home was elsewhere now. He couldn't be the Deschanel heir. He couldn't be the child his parents still wished he was, and he couldn't pretend their life was enough for him.

He would give his life again to protect them, but his soul was not his to give anymore.

"I." He rolled his tongue around in his mouth, wetting the dryness.

"Aleksei? What is it?"

There was a world around him to watch, but what mattered most was getting the words right for the world just before him. "I love you, Far. And Mora. And you, Aidrik. And you, Uncle Jon. And Uncle Jacob and Aunt—"

Finn's sigh was full of all the happiness and sadness Aleksandr hadn't let himself feel. "Son. Stop. We didn't come here to drag you home and force you into your old life. We came to save your life so you could make the decision yourself."

"You heard the goddess," Jon said, wearing a look that said he didn't have to like what he saw to admit he saw it. "Your life is yours, Aleksei. Yours and only yours."

"But..."

"But? What a foolish word," Aidrik said. "Children of Men's need to extend a message beyond a natural end is the cause for much suffering and sorrow."

They all stared at him in a way he was likely used to by now.

Aidrik shrugged. Aleksandr smiled. The old wanderer had left his impact on them, but they had also left human touches on him as well.

"Will Mora hate me?"

"Silly boy." Finn laughed. "If anyone will understand your decision best, it's your mother. She spent her life trying to conform to what others felt was 'normal' for her, only to realize she wasn't ever going to find it until she gave up and let life happen."

"How did you know that I was not... not coming home with you?"

The three men exchanged looks. "Because you're my son, Aleksei," Finn answered first. "What's in your eyes was once in mine, when I gave up everything to follow your mother to a place I'd never been."

"Once your father makes up his mind, it's done. There's no changing it. You wouldn't believe how hard I tried to get him to stop pursuing Ana," Jon said with a light smile.

"He was afraid things would change," Finn said. "It had always been Jon and me against the world. What we had was comfortable. Maybe even happy, when there wasn't anything else to measure it against. But when I met Ana, the world around me changed forever. I didn't know I was living in a world of sepia until she came and colored it in."

"Poetic," Jon teased.

"I don't even know if Fiona wants me," Aleksandr said. He ached for the split in his head that kept his emotions working under the guise of logic. He didn't want to feel this. He didn't want the ache of his father's loving understanding, or Aidrik's ancient wisdom.

"Pfft," Finn said. "If you believed that, you wouldn't be looking at us the way you are now."

"How am I looking at you?"

"Like you're afraid of hurting us, or letting us down." Finn pressed his hand to Aleksandr's cheek. "You're not. You could never."

"What about Uncle Nicolas? Do you think he'll be mad if I don't want to be the heir anymore?"

"You bear no responsibility if the Child of Man is too inadequate to bring his own issue forth into this world," Aidrik said.

They all laughed.

"Far, will you tell Mora—"

Finn shook his head. "No. Whatever you have to tell her, you can tell her yourself, Aleksei. When you come home for Christmas in a couple weeks. Because if you think I'm going to let you move out and *not* see you at every major holiday, you've got another thing coming."

The tears living in Aleksandr's chest since the moment of his rebirth rose into a swelling wave behind his eyes, and the relief he felt in allowing them to spill was a greater catharsis than he had ever known.

His two fathers and his uncle swallowed him into a hug, and, this time, he let himself feel the love they offered.

19
TRISTAN

Tristan watched the Empyreans divide up their government and decide the future fate of the realm. He didn't want to be here. Not where Harriett had died. But he didn't want to be anywhere else, because she wouldn't be there. At least here, he had a sense of closeness to a place where she recently had blood pulsing through her veins and a heart beating in her chest.

In any case, could he just walk out? Was it that easy? He thought it probably was, now that the cancer had been cut from the land, but where would he go? He was in the far northern reaches of Norway, in the middle of their coldest season. He had no car. Taxi service probably stopped a few minutes out of Trondheim, and that was over an hour by car, never mind what it might take to walk in several feet of snow. He might be able to persuade Stian to open a portail... there was that. But he didn't see him in the sea of faces, and anyway, where would he go? Home? To a place where every last person sharing his blood would want to know everything, and he would have to tell all of them, over and over, how Harriett died, how Sebastian died?

No, thanks.

So, he waited. And watched. Back and forth the debates raged, and through it all, Nerys demurred. She wasn't a politician; she wasn't meant for this. Blah, blah, blah, thought Tristan. She was going to do it and everyone knew it, but she had to go through her show of denials first.

Tristan bowed his head. Anyone else watching wouldn't have assessed the situation with such nihilism. They'd see a creature with a tremendous heart and care for her people, fearful of making a decision with potential to harm them further.

He wasn't himself, unless this new, pessimistic man *was* himself now.

Of course, Nerys accepted. She needed a mate, though, and Tristan imagined every last male Empyrean falling all over themselves for the job. They managed not to, and he laughed at their decorum. The opposite proved to be true; none felt worthy of the task.

Tristan thought for sure, in the end, it would be Thorvald and his inflated sense of self-worth. Instead, it was quiet, steady Trygve, the ancient wanderer who was ready to surrender his easy freedom for a gilded cage. It didn't make sense to Tristan at all. One look at Nerys said she didn't understand, either, but also revealed a light blush in her pale cheeks.

Someone has a crush! Tristan nearly laughed. At least someone was getting their happy ending.

They decided to set the coronation for a week hence, but that night they would celebrate their victory in the Great Hall, and all were invited. Grand Empress Nerys and Grand Emperor Trygve were the new hope of the Empyreans, and that meant the Brotherhood could be dissembled. Some decided to stay on as counselors to the new royal couple. Others felt pulled to return to their own tribes. But all were united in a vision of a better tomorrow.

The world is saved, hallelujah, amen. Let us all rejoice in this new regime of benevolent rule.

Tristan wanted to hurl.

He should be celebrating with them. His mission was a success. He'd done what he came here to do... he contributed to the salvation of Farjhem and the conclusion of the Prophecy, both of which would have very real impacts on his family back home.

Had there ever been a victory more hollow?

"Tristan."

Anders' low voice sounded behind him, but he couldn't force himself to turn. Some of his anger toward his mentor had faded... even in his paralyzing grief, Tristan knew Anders was not to blame for what happened to Harriett. Harriett made her decision knowing full well what consequences lay ahead. But to face Anders required a level of rationale he didn't possess, and whatever reasonable advice the creature prepared to offer, Tristan was not prepared to hear it.

"I have something for you."

When Tristan failed to respond again, Anders added, "She wanted you to have it, Tristan."

Tristan whipped around so fast he lost his footing. "She? Harriett? What the hell are you talking about?"

Anders' arm outstretched between them. From his fist dropped a circular amulet, which came to an abrupt bounce when it reached the end of the metal chain. The amulet—made of pewter maybe, but the center was clear like glass—spun from the end of the chain.

"That's not Harriett's," Tristan asserted. "I've never seen it before."

"No, it is not hers," Anders said with great patience. "If you must know the origin, it once belonged to my mother. I've carried it with me all my life." He swallowed and released a quick breath. “Harriett came to me, Tristan. Before we left for Farjhem. She wished to know how she could leave a part of herself behind should the worst come to pass.”

“A part of… what the hell are you on about?”

“I don’t know if she had a vision, or if she was being careful in her preparation,” Anders went on, “but she was insistent I show her how this could be accomplished. I knew only what my mother told me.” Anders lifted the amulet high in the air and regarded it with a soft nostalgia. “For a part of her lived here once.” He sighed. “And now, a part of Harriett does.”

Tristan shook his head. “That doesn’t make any sense, what you’re saying. I saw her die. I saw her soul…”

“The soul is many parts, Tristan. And many of her soul’s parts have moved on, to a place of peace. But she left one part of it behind, for you. To give you strength in the knowledge she is with you, always. She knew you would struggle if her death came to pass. But she did not want it to be the end for you, too.”

Anders opened Tristan’s hand and dropped the heavy pendant in his palm. The chain made a soft shimmer as it filtered into a small pile.

“Harriett would not want you to wither away and let the world pass you by,” Anders said. “Nor would she want her physical death to lead to your symbolic one. Our life has many phases, and each lead us from the last to the next. Harriett was your usher.”

“She was more than that. Don’t try—”

Anders held up his hands. “She was more than that. When your trials have ended, she may prove out to be the piece of your journey that meant the most. I cannot say. You cannot say. But as long as a part of her lives in that amulet, which, when worn, rests right against your heart, she will never truly be gone.”

Tristan looked down at the necklace resting in his sweaty palm. “What does it mean, though?”

It was not Anders who answered.

It means I'm here, Tristan. Always. As long as you need me, or you'll have me. I cannot hold you when you have a bad dream, or kiss away your fears, but I am no less real in the ways that matter most.

Tristan closed his eyes to keep the heavy pool of tears from spilling down his cheeks. He had released enough. More than he thought possible after the deaths of so many he had loved.

He found he couldn't look at Anders now for very different reasons than the ones moments ago.

"Thank you," he whispered.

JACOB INSISTED TRISTAN HITCH A RIDE BACK TO LOUISIANA WITH THEM. They waited until Sebastian's body was prepared, and Jonathan secured the transport from Trondheim. Harriett would be prepared on a pyre that night and sent down the River Farvann. They would stay for that, and then be on their way.

The Quinlans, and those Empyreans living outside of Farjhem, planned to stay another day or two for the celebrations. Tristan had no gaiety in him, and neither did the others returning home with him, though they had saved their loved one. But Tristan understood... the Deschanels may have won in the end, but they had suffered dearly along the way... ah, how they had suffered! Unlike the Empyreans, who could measure their lives in millennia, the Deschanels held dearly to the short lives they were given, and they felt each loss to their marrow. A victory here meant their future suffering would soften, but it didn't mute what they'd already lost.

"We leave in the morning," Jacob said as they stood side by side watching Harriett's pyre built. "We should be home in about three days."

"Three? Why so long?"

"We're stopping in Ireland."

Tristan started to ask the question, but the answer came to him. Of *course* Aleksandr would go to where his heart was. Who wouldn't?

He pressed his hand to his own heart, where Harriett's amulet burned warm against his soft flesh.

20
COLLEEN

Colleen had sat many vigils in her lifetime as mother, as magistrate, and as a woman invested in her family beyond what duty called for. But she had never feared more for an outcome. They'd never had so much to lose, and if the fates sang their name with a smile, so much to gain. One way or the other, the news would be borne her way first, which meant she would need to decide what to do with it, for better or worse.

The call came in moments past the deep chimes of the witching hour. Jacob's voice rang like music to her ears. Noah propped against the doorframe with a hopeful look.

"It's done, Colleen. It's done."

She began her peal of questions, but Jacob politely cut her off. This was his story to tell—his and many others', but not hers—and her role now was to listen. Jacob would only tell this story for a first time once, and a gracious recipient would accept this gift for what it was.

Farjhem had been reclaimed. The Prophecy no more. The

Myths of Midwinter overturned with the banishing of Margarethe.

But Colleen did not touch her tea, which now cooled in the saucer. She would not be soothed so easily. For she knew Jacob had come about the victories first.

And ahh, there were losses.

Colleen's arms went slack as he recounted the final moments of the brave Harriett and the tragic Sebastian. The latter was coming home so he could be placed in the family tomb. The former had been given a warrior's funeral in Farjhem.

Noah appeared behind her, her silent strength. His hands fell on her shoulders.

Colleen didn't verbalize her uncomfortable relief that Aleksandr had not been counted among the dead. Or her son-in-law, or Finn. Colleen understood, even if others could not accept this about themselves, that there was little gain in forgetting you were human.

"I'll call a meeting," she said when Jacob had paused for a reasonable amount of time.

The response from Jacob was barely audible, and only readable to one who knew him well.

She corrected herself. "I'll schedule one so that you and the others can tell your story yourself to the family. When can we expect you home?"

"Once we have Aleksandr settled with the Quinlans. A few days, I would guess." Jacob swallowed. She felt him preparing the question he had started the call with, but Colleen had—unfairly, she saw it now—withheld the answer until he had given his report.

"Amelia is resting, just as when you left." She didn't dare suggest what she was thinking. That something had shifted... something fundamental, something huge, with the dissolution of the Prophecy. "When I tell her you're coming home, I know she'll be so happy to hear it, even if she can't tell me."

"Maybe..." Jacob faltered. Was he thinking along the same lines? The same hope? "Never mind. Tell her I'll be home before she knows it. Tell her... tell her I've loved her forever."

Colleen smiled into the dark office. "She knows. And I will."

COLLEEN ORDERED HER CAR AS SOON AS SHE HUNG UP WITH JACOB. THE ride from The Gardens to Magnolia Grace was hardly a mile but felt a hundred.

Anasofiya threw the door open with a wild look. "Aunt C! I was just getting ready to call you... you won't believe... it's crazy..."

"Oh, I will," Colleen replied with a grin and gently nudged past her niece into the foyer. "I have much to tell you both."

Amelia stood at the base of the staircase, gripping the bannister. When she saw her mother, she pulled straighter, one hand pressed to her swollen belly. The color filled her cheeks as she smiled.

"I just woke up," she said sheepishly. "I'm sure the magic was fine, and something—"

"Darling, our dark days are over," Colleen managed before she crushed her daughter to her chest. Ana's arms came around them both as she joined their hug.

"They're coming home, girls." Before either could voice their fears, Colleen assured them. "They're fine. Your men. All of them. All of them! All of us!"

The three women embraced in a blur of laughter, hugs, and so many tears.

PART TWO
THERE'S NO PLACE LIKE HOME

21
COLLEEN

"The Prophecy is no more. Margarethe is extinguished. Farjhem is safe. *We* are safe."

She began with these words, for her loved ones had waited a great long while for them. To draw out the message would be pointless cruelty; the details, for once, not nearly as imminently meaningful as the outcome.

A shared sigh passed through the many gathered at the Deschanel Magi Collective gathering. Their relief was tentative, though, because they saw that Colleen's expression wasn't as happy as they expected. She would not smile when their victory had come at the cost of lives dear to them, and she didn't relish the task ahead of having to share these losses with the family.

Colleen continued with more positive news.

There was a change in Amelia's pregnancy. With the end of the Prophecy, Moira no longer developed at the same rate, but the growth she'd experienced to this point wasn't reversed, either. Amelia would give birth, soon, and she had reason to believe the child would grow from infancy to adulthood at the rate of a normal child.

Colleen secretly believed the normal birth of Amelia's daughter also signaled the healthy rebirth of the Deschanels after a period of great agony. Their House of Dusk becoming a House of Dawn.

But it was too soon to share that sentiment with an understandably superstitious family.

Finn and Jacob perched nervously to her left, awaiting their turn to speak. Colleen gave them the choice of her telling the story on their behalf, but they had both, almost in unison, declared it their responsibility. They were both members now, since she'd sworn them in at the start of the meeting. Not only as extensions of their wives anymore, but as true members of the family in their own right.

Sullivans, too, now had this designation. To make it official, they sent their new elected Council members to attend, Rory and Connor. Colleen had been unable to predict who the Sullivans would nominate to the two seats. She'd expected perhaps Rory. He spoke on behalf of the Sullivans not only in this matter but in others, and had been involved in Deschanel business for several decades.

Chelsea, then was not a surprise, only an alternative to her expectations.

Connor, though... his appointment *did* surprise Colleen. Twice now, Sullivans had married into the Deschanel family, and twice those spouses became more deniers than believers. Connor knew what his late wife, Elizabeth, was capable of. When they were just children, he'd embraced it and protected her from the worst parts, but as they aged, he seemed to shy away from it, as if hoping he could wave away what made her less than normal. When she took her life, that seemed to seal away his desire for any connection with her Deschanel relatives, despite that his son was one of them. Was it Tristan's return, and some encouraging words, that swayed him?

Maybe Colleen would attempt that conversation later, but she was glad to see him there, more so than any other Sullivan. Connor was one of them on many levels, and seeing him come to this acceptance was as important as it was symbolic.

There was another that night who would be given a special designation within the family, but Colleen planned to save that for the end.

She turned to the two men who had been willing to give their lives for this family. This time, she did smile.

"Jacob, Finn. The floor is yours."

Colleen Deschanel, for as long as she had lived, had worn the yoke of leadership. Before she was old enough to have been granted any such thing, the responsibility fell upon her shoulders. Her two older brothers, Charles and Augustus, strong and staid in their own ways, had nonetheless always looked to her for the big decisions. They had built and grown their own empires, but deferred to her on matters of family, both in public and private. When Charles died, Augustus made no move to lead the family. The unspoken assignment fell to Colleen, and there it remained, and would remain, until she passed it along to someone else.

Leadership came with its own set of challenges, as was true in any hierarchy, in any organization, familial or business, but for her the very highest and most challenging had always been knowing when *not* to lead. When to fall back and let others step up. When to let her humanity show, and with it, a glimmer of her weakness.

When Finn and Jacob came to the losses in their narrative, Colleen, for once, chose not to offer words of encouragement and strength. She bowed her head along with the others in the room who had not had the chance to say goodbye in any proper way.

With Jasper, Leander, and Tristan. With Katja, Olivia, and Stella. She didn't search for any of her usual methods to stay her tears. She didn't hide them.

In her mind, a logical speech formed. One about the greatness of sacrifice and how all peace must come with its share. But she was not a president addressing her constituents in a State of the Union. She was a woman who many looked to for guidance in the family, but who, right now, knew they needed her comfort.

For they had all lost. Every last individual in the room. These losses began years ago, centuries even, and had touched everyone. They wore the losses like scars of battle, bravely but damaged.

And now the Deschanels would need to learn, together, how to live again.

WHEN THE GRIEF IN THE ROOM SUBSIDED, COLLEEN SPOKE BRIEFLY OF the future. Of a family who had, amongst their suffering, also learned. Of who they were, and where they came from. Of a world of Empyreans and Quinlans, and of races beyond their comprehension.

"Our archives are among the most comprehensive in the entire world. Witches and wizards all over the globe have come to us for knowledge, and we have always offered what we can. We have an opportunity, now that the greatest of our troubles are over, to shift our focus to expanding that knowledge. To grow our list of allies, and with it, absorb what they know."

The room nodded. They weren't yet ready for grand visions, but she would plant the seed. To move past their grief, they must see a future of hope and promise. "With that, the Council has, for the first time in our history, opened membership to someone who is not of blood or marital relation."

This didn't garner the scandalized reaction she expected, but she chalked it up to the shock still permeating from earlier news.

"Lauren Weatherly, who many of you know, if not personally then through her father, gave up months of her life to help us track down Stella and Quillan. She worked tirelessly, without being asked. She was exposed to many of our greatest secrets and handled them with grace, which has not often been true of outsiders. But mostly I want to recognize Lauren's selflessness, of which I have seen few equal in my years," Colleen continued.

"I can vouch for Lauren's integrity," Rory added. "She may be the hardest worker in our firm, and I do mean above the Sullivans as well."

"She's amazing," Leander whispered in agreement. Several seats down, Nicolas dropped his head and blushed.

"And so, we opened our vaults to Lauren. Not even Rory and Colin, our trusted Sullivan attorneys, have had this access. She has accepted an expanded role within the firm as our special counsel, and this will include helping catalogue and explore our archives in a way that will protect us legally for many years to come. She will partner closely with the Council, particularly with Nicolas, in the coming months and years. I ask that you welcome her with open arms, as we have always welcomed new members of the family."

Nicolas looked ready to say something, but for once, chose silence. Colleen didn't miss his smile as the words faded on his tongue.

"We could have cut her a check, but Lauren isn't interested in money," Luther explained, though the clarification wasn't necessary. No one, not one person, had balked.

Colleen wondered again at how they had all changed. The dynamic of their entire clan shifted with their battles and losses, and choosing when to fight was a side effect.

She went on to explain the Empyrean Lucia had also joined

the Collective as a researcher, though her inclusion was less overtly controversial, as Deschanels shared a deep ancestry with all Empyreans.

For once, Colleen felt no fear in declaring the worst over. They would all have their share of trials and tribulations, but all families did, and all families, in the end, prevailed.

And they would prevail.

Colleen knew that now. She knew it deep in her marrow, where once she had felt nothing but a powerful, aching dread she could only fight, but never defeat.

Colleen Deschanel blew out the candles on the sacred candelabra, an artifact that surfaced only in meetings discussing the direst topics.

She noted to Imogen that she could store it in the vault.

They weren't likely to need it again anytime soon.

22
AMELIA

Any day now.

Those had been Colleen's words during her frantic examination of Amelia's pregnancy, following the call home from Jacob. Amelia's heart wanted to burst clear from her chest at the sight of her mother so frazzled, especially as she repeated the same rigorous inspections three days in a row. Colleen said not a word until she was sure, and once she was, she let Amelia in on her findings.

Colleen had been searching for any sign that the promises of Morrigan had fallen flat. And she had found none.

But while Moira's growth had slowed, as the goddess promised, there was no going back. Amelia could not "un grow" her daughter. She had swelled to full term during her short but intense pregnancy, and Moira was coming, as her mother said, "Any day now."'

Inexplicably, Amelia was more mentally ready to deliver her daughter when she believed Moira would be "abnormal" by most medical standards. Now that she knew Moira would grow as any child grew, Amelia couldn't help how her imagination ran wild with every mistake she would make as a mother. When she thought Moira's childhood would pass in a blink, she was sad, but somehow, relieved. Amelia's dark truth was she feared, despite being raised by one of the best mothers in the world, she was not quite up to the task herself.

"Can I stay with you until Jacob returns?" Amelia had asked.

"You can stay as long as you need," Colleen gently corrected, and, as always, took quick charge of the situation to ensure Amelia didn't have to worry about a single detail.

"I WOULDN'T HAVE LET YOU GO WITH THEM IF I'D BEEN AWAKE," Amelia whispered. She shifted in the large, soft hammock on her mother's back porch, pressing herself tighter against the warm frame of her husband. She left one hand looped over her heavy belly. "And there you have it, Donnelly. You married a selfish, terrible person."

Jacob laughed. With one dangling foot, he pressed his toes into the flagstone to rock them to the rhythm of the fauna's song. "We both know if you weren't pregnant, you would've gone yourself. I would've been the one relegated to house duty, pining into the darkness of the loch like Marie de Guise awaiting the return of King James V at Linlithgow."

Amelia sighed. "Ah, you know what a sucker I am for a Mary Queen of Scots reference."

"I've been waiting for the right moment to use that one."

"Except Marie was pregnant, like, I don't know, *me,* so the reference really applies more in my case. And had I been coherent, I could have easily pined into Lake Pontchartrain."

"Always trying to steal my thunder."

"Selfish *and* a thunder stealer. Where do my atrocities end?"

Jacob checked his watch. "How long do we have?"

Amelia closed her eyes as she laughed. "What was she like? Morrigan?"

Jacob slowed their rocking pace. "Brilliant. Magnificent, *Blanca.* It was like seeing her in the visions but amplified. Almost like the way you see someone in person versus through the lens of a camera, you know?"

"I wish I could have seen her myself."

Jacob ran his hand over the tight, swollen skin of her abdomen, brushing her hand to the side. "I think it's a better sign for all of us if none of us sees her again."

"But you don't really believe what she said, do you?"

"Which part? Where she killed the Prophecy like it was nothing, or where she told us we were going to live forever?"

Amelia didn't know why she had asked the question. She was so used to dissecting and finding the reason in any situation that she couldn't turn it off now. Of course she believed Morrigan. To do otherwise would be to deny...

Well, everything.

"There's really only one way to find out," Jacob said.

"Oh?"

"We just have to live forever, obviously."

Amelia squeezed his inner thigh, where he was most ticklish. She was rewarded for her efforts with a high-pitched giggle and squirm from her husband. "Let's not get ahead of ourselves, Donnelly. I'm more concerned about our immediate future."

He craned forward to press his lips to her belly. "Moira is going to be a very happy, healthy baby. How could she not? She hit the baby lottery to land us as parents."

"I meant it. I would've made you stay."

"That's your fear talking. There's nothing to be afraid of anymore, except normalcy."

Amelia faked a shudder.

"We should give it a go, normalcy," Jacob went on. His words went from casual to practiced, and she guessed he'd been considering them on his long ride back to New Orleans. "Moira is just the first step."

"Did you have something in mind?"

"Remember before when I was thinking I might go back and finish my PhD? And you might start your own practice?"

She pressed her ear to his chest so she could hear the soft beat of his heart. "I remember."

"Nothing to stop us now, is there?"

Amelia had loved this man for over a decade of her life and for the first time, there *wasn't* anything to stop them. No Deschanel Curse. No Prophecy. No imperilment. Victor de Blanchefort promised he would keep his distance, and for the first time, she believed him.

No, there was nothing standing between their future happiness except silly hang-ups and irrational fears, and Amelia would never let them stand in the way of her happiness again.

23
OZ

"Are you *sure* this is what you want?"

Oz raised his head and met his father's eyes. That was what Colin Jr. needed, a show of confidence, to end this. "The Deschanel estate will be fine, Dad. You and Rory still have ultimate oversight, and now Lauren is involved and even has extended privileges at The Gardens, which is something none of us were ever granted."

Colin folded his hands over his desk with a pensive look. "I'm not talking about the health of the estate. We have plenty of competent attorneys the family trusts. Oz, this is the only client you have ever asked me for in your tenure with the firm. We all know the reasons why, and at times, I wondered if I had done the right thing. If I was contributing to your obsession with Adrienne—"

"She was my *wife*!"

"Don't get worked up over words, son. Your mother and I loved her, too. When she disappeared, your focus *did* turn to obsession, though I don't know if I would have handled myself any different in your shoes, if I'd lost your mother..." Colin turned to face the rain pouring outside the double-paned window overlooking Carondelet Street. Beyond, the streetcar came to a shuddering halt, and then rumbled on. "My point is, your whole life has been tethered, in one way or another, to the Deschanels. Attorneys very rarely get an opportunity to take on work that is a true labor of love. Your son is a Deschanel, Oz. You will always be connected to them."

"Maybe that's the problem," Oz said. He looked past his father, at the walls of his own office, upon which hung the degrees and credentials defining this part of his hard-earned life. "I'm too connected. I need to find some distance, for myself, for the kids. My life has been intertwined with the Deschanels for as long as I have memories. From Nicolas, to Gisele, to Nathalie. Anasofiya and Amelia. Adrienne. You said I was obsessed, and I got defensive, but who gets that defensive with no reason?"

Colin said nothing.

"I've never loved anyone the way I loved Adrienne. And it's unlikely I ever will. Lightning like that won't strike twice for me, and that's okay, but I can't wallow in my pain anymore. I have two children who need the best of me. What's sad is, I'm not even sure I know what that looks like."

His father gave him a tight, sad smile. "Your mother and I do. This firm does." He flipped the top folder on the thick stack of closed files. On top was a letter Oz had written and signed. Colin lifted his own pen. His hand hovered above the signature line. "I wasn't trying to talk you out of this because I think it's a bad idea." He met Oz's eyes. "I happen to think this is one of the best decisions you've made for yourself. I just needed to know you felt that way, too. Forget the firm, Oz. Forget the case. I only want you to be happy and healthy."

Oz swallowed hard the wave of emotion that hit him. His relationship with his father had always been complicated, because Oz's sensitivity to the world never gelled well with his father's hard pragmatism. Yet somewhere along the way, they found some middle ground. Colin saw Oz's strong sense of chivalry as a type of strength, and Oz came to appreciate the virtue of choosing what *was* right over what *felt* right.

Colin signed the form releasing Oz's interest and oversight of the Deschanel case. Oz internalized a long sigh. The estate would be in capable hands with Lauren. Plenty of other clients lined Oz's portfolio to keep him busy for years. Clients who did not come with the heavy baggage that tethered him to the person he used to be instead of the one he wanted to.

"Oh, and, Oz," his father said as Oz rose to leave. "Half of the Deschanels you named off have since passed on, God rest their souls." His eyes fluttered closed briefly. "The others have moved on with their lives. But what about Nicolas? You two have been best friends since you were crawling through our garden in diapers."

Oz nodded. "He's my next stop."

"GALATOIRE'S? THIS IS WHERE WE TAKE OUR DATES, NOT EACH OTHER," Nicolas teased as he gestured around the high ceilings and mirrored walls. Overhead, the paddled fans had come to a standstill in the cooler months. He took a swig of water, emptying his glass, and signaled the waiter for a refill. His foot tapped in nervous staccato, an apology for their last ugly encounter hanging over them, unspoken.

"I only have an hour for lunch. I have a client at two. Didn't have time to drive all the way to *Ophélie*, and I figured you were in town anyway."

"Only an hour? Attorneys are such an oppressed bunch. Tell me, who will think of them?"

Oz forced a smile. "Says the man who never worked a day in his life."

"Aunt C is sure putting me to work now," Nicolas said. "And Lauren is a slave driver." He went on to describe something they were working on together, something mundane by the standards of Nicolas Deschanel no doubt, but he was more animated than when he told drunk jokes.

Oz decided to make an observation before breaking his news. "You're into her."

"Lauren?" Nicolas slapped the table and laughed. This was where he would have drained his cognac and ordered another, but there was no cognac. Only his persistently empty water glass. "She's not my type, Ozzy. You know that."

"Which is exactly why I'm perplexed at the way you're talking about her now." Oz set the menu aside. "And you've changed. For her?"

Nicolas stopped his laughter, which had not been genuine to start. "For myself. I don't know, maybe for her, too, but it starts with me."

Oz had never heard such maturity from his old friend. He said so.

Nicolas shrugged. He watched his water glass refill with a distant look. "You never know what the moment will be. What will cause it."

"What about Mercy?"

"What about her?" Nicolas demanded, but diverted his eyes. "That was doomed from the very start, Ozzy. At first, I wasn't good enough for her. I wasn't ready to give her what she deserved. Now, for the first time in my life, I realize the opposite is true. I loved her. You know? I really loved her. But she wants the love of a god, not a man. I can't give her more than I have."

"You're right," Oz said. "I'm glad you see it."

"But don't ask me about Lauren." Nicolas' voice had dropped low. "This is different. She's different. I don't want to make a big deal of it or talk about it. She doesn't want anything to do with me, and I'm not going to harass her or make an ass of myself."

"You've changed," Oz said again.

"Yeah, well." Nicolas swirled the ice in his glass, an old habit. He set it down again.

"Look, the reason I called you here..."

"I'm sorry." Nicolas met his eyes. They filled with glassy tears. "Not just for what happened at *Ophélie*, but for everything. Our whole lives. Everything you said to me in the kitchen was true, Ozzy. I've always looked for ways to push you, because I knew you'd always come back, and you always did. You were the only one in my life I could push and push and push and always came back."

"I know you're sorry," Oz said. "And I'm not coming back."

The color faded from Nicolas' face. "What?"

He tried to smile. He didn't come here to hurt Nicolas. What he was about to say to his oldest friend wasn't retribution. He loved Nicolas and always would. But. "I need to find some distance from the parts of my life that have held me back. I'm not blaming you, Nic, for the things you said, for pushing. The coming back was on me. Just like my incessant pursuit of Adrienne, all those years."

"You *married* my sister. Don't make it sound like you were a stalker."

"Our marriage was tumultuous," Oz said with a soft sigh, an admission he had never spoken out loud, or even explored much in his own head. He feared reducing his time with Adrienne to a mistake. She wasn't a mistake. Never that. But while their love had been electric, their time together had been a current running through water. "And had it not ended with her passing, it might have eventually ended another way." Oz closed his eyes. "Or not. I might have stayed forever. And that's the problem."

"What are you talking about?"

"All the meaning I've found in life came in what I could be for others," Oz said. "All of it. I started as your best friend and support system. You know I used to introduce myself as your best friend? Like that, above everything else I had to offer or be, was most important? And then I found purpose in your sisters, and your cousin, Ana. Adrienne was the one who 'stuck.' She needed me! Not in the way you did, Nic, as someone to do her homework or listen to her ramble on and on about the world. She needed *me*. She was searching for a hero to save her, and boy, was I willing and eager to step up to that. It was like I had been waiting my whole life for it." The words came out like a heave of stuck air forced from his lungs. He had a sharp urge to order a stiff drink, but he wouldn't, for Nicolas' sake.

Nicolas frowned. "Ozzy, that stuff I've said all these years, about you having a hero complex—"

"Is the truest thing anyone has ever said about me," Oz finished. "And now it's time for me to be a hero to myself and my children."

Nicolas flopped back in his chair. His arms fell to his sides. A wave of understanding passed over him. "You came to say goodbye."

"I did."

"Because you don't think you can do those things, be a great dad and a good man to yourself, as long as you're around the things and people who... I don't know... enabled you to those destructive behaviors."

Oz was impressed. "Yeah, that's basically it." He leaned across the table and offered his hand.

Nicolas tightened his lips and looked up, gauging him, formulating questions. Then he dropped his hand on Oz's outstretched palm.

"You're my brother, Nic. You have always been my brother. I'm not blaming you. But I know that until I separate myself from certain parts of my old life, I won't be able to become the man my children and I deserve. It's like a drug addict who works in a heroin store."

"Ozzy, that's not how heroin works."

"You know what I mean."

"So, you're leaving the firm? New Orleans?"

Oz shook his head. "No, but that's mostly for the kids, not myself. If it were just me... but it's not. They need their grandparents, aunts, uncles, cousins. I can't do that to them after they lost their mother." He squeezed and then released his friend's hand. "I took myself off the Deschanel case."

Nicolas smirked. He sniffled. "I'm sure your dad was thrilled."

"He was worried."

"I'm worried."

"Don't be," Oz said. "For the first time in my life I have a clear head. I know what I need to do."

Nicolas turned his head and swiped at his eyes. He looked back. "I guess there's nothing I can say."

"There's nothing you need to say, Nic. I love you. I always will. But I have to find my own way."

Nicolas laughed through his tears. "Family reunions are going to be awkward. Us casting longing glances across the room at each other, like star-crossed lovers."

Oz laughed too. "Will they find us later, both dead as a result of our miscommunication?"

"You think I'm kidding."

"Look, I'm not going to ignore you, or pretend you're dead to me. You're family. And you'll still see Christian, if you want that. He's your blood."

"He's my only nephew. The only one I'll ever have, unless someone decides to put up with Anne," Nicolas said. "And

Naomi... maybe she's not my sister's kid, but it never mattered to Adrienne, and it doesn't to me."

"I know. I'll send them to you for weekends whenever you want. Promise. Send word through Colleen and she'll make the arrangements."

"What about us?" Nicolas asked. The vulnerability in the question made Oz's heart ache.

"You'll always be my brother. My very best friend," Oz said. "But right now, what I need is your understanding."

Nicolas dropped his head. Nodded. "This really is goodbye, then."

Oz's own eyes blurred. "For now."

24
QUILLAN

Quillan stared at the short stack of client files assembled squarely in the center of his neatly organized desk. The tidiness wasn't his doing. It was also unlikely his father had taken the time, so the task had probably been delegated to one of the secretaries. A dirty look in the hallway later would confirm which one.

Only a handful of clients to start. Not because I don't trust you, kiddo, but because... well...

It's okay, Dad. A handful is fine. I need to screw my head back on, anyway.

Quillan was still conflicted over the giant Patrick Sullivan hug that had awaited him on his return to New Orleans. He'd never felt more genuine affection from his father, not even after Riley died and his parents went overboard to restore a sense of normalcy for him. That it had taken Quillan running away for months on end was what made him feel unsettled, as if expecting the moment his father's care would return to an afterthought.

Other members of the firm offered their own enthusiasm for

his return. Clearly, they'd forgotten what a fuck-up Quillan was, how many clients he'd turned away with his lazy indifference. Or maybe this was what it meant to be a Sullivan. *Family before all else* went their motto, and he guessed *all else* equated to decency and blind loyalty. He could open fire on the town from the clock tower and still have a place in the family Christmas card.

He looked up at the sound of a knock on his office door. Lauren peeked her head in.

"Getting adjusted to being back?"

A sigh readied on his tongue, but he stopped it and smiled instead. Lauren didn't want to hear about how difficult this job had always been for him, and after all she'd done for him, she didn't deserve more whining. "A little weird, but I'm glad to be back."

"Good." Lauren nodded and passed her gaze around the room. "This is definitely the best I've seen your office. Who gets credit?"

"All I know is, not me," Quillan said with a laugh. "Congratulations, by the way. On the Deschanel case, and the special access. That's a first for anyone in this firm, ever. You deserve it."

Lauren waved him away. "We'll see if it ends up being anything more than glorified paper pushing."

"I mean it, Lauren, you do deserve it. It must be hard not being a Sullivan in this firm, especially when you see an asshole like me get bailed out of his problems over and over."

"Being a Weatherly comes with its own set of ups and downs," she said. "But I'd always rather be the one in the room with the different name."

Quillan stood. He spent so long comparing Lauren to Estella through the lens of a blind man. Estella's beauty ended the moment her mouth opened, or one got a glimpse into her black heart. Lauren was beauty, through and through. With the curse of hindsight, he could only now appreciate the way her pale hair swept the soft lines of her jaw, or rested in the hollow of her cheek when she tilted her head. He would give anything for the gift of losing himself in her blue gray eyes and listening to her, to anything she said, everything she said. The gift of Lauren's time and affection was offered and turned away, more than once. She wouldn't offer it again. He didn't deserve it then, or now.

He was a fool.

Quillan brushed his hands over his trousers to wipe away the beads of sweat.

Lauren raised a brow. "Everything okay?"

"I wanted to say... needed to say... I really messed up with you. I know it doesn't matter now, but I'm sorry."

Lauren smiled, but it was the kind you offered someone when you no longer had anything more substantial to offer. "Apologies always matter. What happened, happened, and the past is the past."

Quillan heard in the undercurrent of her words the soft but distinct relief she'd not ended up with someone like him. The only way to prove his apology was sincere was to surrender the hope she might change her mind.

Lauren broke the uncomfortable pause that followed. "Well, I need to head to The Gardens. We're kicking off our first project and I need it to start on the right foot."

Quillan said the words before he could stop himself. "Nicolas is a lucky guy."

Her hand hovered over the handle of the door. He couldn't see her face to gauge her reaction, but her body shook with... laughter.

She was *laughing*.

Lauren turned only her head, peering over her shoulder. "He came along on the rescue party because he's a spoiled little prince who insisted. I have more respect for myself than that."

"I'm sorry... I wasn't trying to..." His stumbling ceased when he realized she protested not because he was off base with his assumption, but because he was closer to the truth than she wanted.

Lauren shook her head. "Welcome back, Q. Today is the first day of the rest of your life, so try not to get fired by any clients today, eh?"

Her playful laughter trailed her into the hall, followed by his mournful gaze, and then his regret.

A FLUSTERED SECRETARY THRUST HER HEAD IN AN HOUR LATER, JUST AS Quillan had organized his thoughts around how to attack the day. She wedged her body between the door and the frame with the stern, purposeful look of someone on an important mission.

"What's wrong, Claire?"

"We tried to stop her, Quillan. We all did! It was a team effort." Claire panted the words through desperate gasps for breath.

"Who? Stop who?"

Claire grimaced with a heavy grunt as the door flew open. She stumbled into the room, holding tight to her balance on three-inch heels in a feat of strength that left Quillan awed.

Quillan's smile quickly dissolved. In the door stood Estella Broussard.

Her petite, pinched face flushed heavy with some emotion or another. His guess was frustration. Even after what she did for young Stella, he would never believe her capable of a passion where her needs were not dead center.

"Quillan." Her lower lip quivered. The much put-upon Claire held her ground and shot Quillan a look that seemed to say, *See? She's crazy.* He might have laughed at her unwarranted tenacity if the sight of Estella hadn't stolen his joy.

"I'll call security," Claire said, with a satisfied half-smile at the intruder.

"No, it's fine." Quillan couldn't make himself look at either of them directly, so he kept his eyes on the open folder atop his desk.

Claire shifted her heels in clear exasperation. "We had clear orders from Patrick..."

"You gave orders about me?" Estella's voice was small and vulnerable, no longer the confident trill of the *belle fleur* of the Garden District. Her blue eyes fluttered wide and the effect drew Quillan's gaze to her, despite his reservations. She was such a good actress when she needed to be. If he didn't know better—and he did know better now, he absolutely knew better—he would say she was genuinely hurt.

He shrugged his explanation. "Claire, I'll handle it."

"But—"

Quillan choked out a laugh. "Look at her. What's she gonna do?"

"Your father said—"

Another curious new way Patrick chose to show his love, though it came in the form of another delusion. As long as Estella was to blame for Quillan's strange behavior and defection to the West Coast, he could act as if none of it had ever happened. Problem solved.

Well, Quillan couldn't.

"It's fine, Claire," he insisted, and after a few more hard looks at Estella, she finally left.

"Thanks," Estella said.

Meekly, he added in his head. A word he would not have thought possible to appear in a sentence describing Estella Broussard.

"Don't thank me," he said. "I just didn't want a scene on my first day back to work."

"Oh." Estella bit her lip. A long blond strand, a child's bouncy curl, twirled around her finger. There was a time when these simple gestures sent him completely over the edge.

He could hardly control his disgust.

"Why are you here? I have work to do."

Estella dropped her eyes, starting a slow trip around the small office. He wondered if she chose the light-yellow sundress strategically, a color that screamed of innocence. She had always known which buttons to push.

"I feel terrible that I never thanked you for what you did for Stella," she started, glancing back to assess his reaction. Even the way she did this had a deliberateness, with her coquettish head flip and lips pursed in feigned consternation.

"You don't need to thank me," Quillan said. He pressed his lips together to trap the witty, cruel retort that tried to follow. "I didn't do it for you."

Estella glided back in his direction. He tensed as she approached the desk, but she stopped on the other side and sank with a hard flop into one of the client chairs.

Quillan relaxed but didn't take his own seat. She had a way, one he could hardly explain, of stealing and assuming the shift of power in any room. If standing was his only weapon, he wouldn't relinquish it.

"I lost my sister, Quillan. My Harriett." Estella buried her face in her hands and did what any rational, emotional person would do. She sobbed.

But Estella was neither rational nor emotional. And Quillan had seen firsthand the atrocities Estella committed against her younger sister over the years. She had no rightful claim on the grief that was now consuming Leander and Jasper.

"I know," he managed. "I'm sorry."

She swung her head up and he could have sworn the look she wore was disappointment. That he hadn't rushed to comfort her? That he hadn't properly appreciated the scope of how this affected her, and only her?

Not this time. Not any time. Not anymore.

Estella's tearless eyes narrowed. "Are you?"

"Excuse me?"

"Because the Quillan *I* know would be on his knees, gathering me in his arms, telling me everything would be okay," she charged. "The Quillan I know loves me and can't bear to see me in pain."

Don't laugh, don't laugh, don't laugh. "When did *you* ever really know *me*?" he demanded. "Don't answer that, actually. I know the answer. I don't need to hear whatever bullshit you'll come up with."

"You're not yourself, Quillan."

"Oh, I am." The laugh escaped, and then kept going. "For the first time, actually. He dropped onto his palms, spread across the desk. "You're wrong. I'm very sorry about Harriett. She was like a little sister to me, and it breaks my heart what this is doing to Lee and Jasper. But you can go cry your crocodile tears elsewhere, Estella. Harriett deserved better than what you gave her in life, and she sure as hell deserves better than using her death to manipulate someone."

"How dare you!"

"You came here for a reason, obviously. Let's skip the fake grief, and whatever else you had ready to throw on me, and get to the point."

Estella shot out of her seat. The red blooming in her cheeks, this time, seemed real. She wore her frustration like the first real truth of her life.

"I love you, Quillan! Okay? If you're going to make me say it, I love you, and I'm here to, I don't know, *apologize*, and hope maybe you'll forgive me and love me as you once did."

The dark side of Quillan's heart wished to dissect her words and lay them parallel with every cruel thing she had ever done. To throw them back in her face like a tightly wound softball and make her feel as small and paralyzed by emotion as he had felt, all those years of loving her, following her, becoming whatever he thought she might want, even if it sacrificed a part of his soul to do it.

An even smaller, yet infinitely more terrifying, part of Quillan considered the words he had desired his whole life were here, *finally here*, and maybe he should throw all the lessons of the past months to the wind and follow where they led.

Tell her the truth. That's all you have to give her now.

Estella's chest heaved as she struggled for breath. She looked truly ridiculous to him, and he wondered if she always had been, and how he had never seen it.

"I don't love you anymore," Quillan said. Each word released him of his past and filled him with strength.

"That's not true!" Estella cried. She reached for his hand, but he yanked both off the desk and stood straighter. "You and I both know that's not true. You're just angry, and that's my fault, but—"

"No, Estella. I'm not angry anymore, except with myself." Quillan's voice shook, but the rest of him was steady as steel.

"Is it that lawyer, Lana? Is that it?"

"No, it's not Lauren."

"Some other girl?"

"No, it isn't anyone else."

"Then *what?*"

Quillan shook his head with a sigh she would never understand. For people like Estella, even when they found cause to be better, never really changed. To her, the world and all its reasons centered on her, and anything else only confounded her.

"Sometimes you get what you want, and only then do you realize you should have never wanted it to begin with." He didn't attempt this explanation for her; she would never grasp it. He said the words for himself. "And then what you really needed nearly slapped you in the face, but you couldn't stop wanting what you shouldn't. I did a lot of stupid things, Estella, in the name of loving you. My punishment for that is not getting what I needed because I gave up too much for what I wanted."

"You're not making any sense, Quillan."

He smiled. "That's okay."

Estella rushed around the desk and hurled her tiny body at him, crushing herself into his chest with a powerful awkwardness. The gesture was so strange he nearly held her anyway, to make the moment less uncomfortable.

Quillan gently grasped her arms and peeled her away. "Maybe you should try not getting what you want for a change, too, Estella. You might like it."

"Quillan," she whined, a woman who had never grown beyond a child in the ways that mattered most. Who had never known defeat, and had no capacity for dealing with it.

"I have a ten o'clock. You need to leave."

"You're all I have!"

"Then find more," Quillan said. He nudged her toward the door. She dug her heels in like a toddler, but gave up halfway, surrendering, or maybe weary of the act. "I don't have ill will for you, Estella. I really do hope you find what you're searching for."

"It's you, Quillan, it's always been—"

"But it isn't me," he finished with a sad smile and carefully closed the door behind her. He pressed his back to the oak and drew in a long breath.

I'm proud of you, big brother!

"Yeah, well, you were right all along," Quillan said, breathing out the residual strain from the strange interaction.

I thought you were gonna have to call the police on her. I was thinking about them rushing in with those things in front of them, you know…

"Riot shields?"

Yeah! Riot shields! And big guns and secret code, and everyone hiding under their desks in fear.

"A bit extreme, don't ya think? I had it under control, buddy."

What are you gonna do now, Quillan?

Quillan settled again behind his desk. He ran his hands over the aged mahogany, let the scent of furniture polish and deep heritage pass over him.

"Live," he said finally, to the voice of Riley, who would never really be Riley, not again. For Riley was gone, and that, above all else, was the punishment he would carry for the rest of his days.

But Quillan *would* live.

QUILLAN PULLED OUT HIS YELLOW STENO PAD AND STARTED MAKING notes for his first client.

25
OLIVIA

Olivia dreaded the conversation from the moment Greg returned home. She knew it was unavoidable and would remain a barrier to future progress in their marriage if not addressed. They had lost their way to each other once. This was their chance to prevent it a second time.

She had lost her brother and two of his children. Her mother might never speak to her again. Olivia could see her faults in both losses, enough to know she would fight to the death to protect her marriage.

From a practical standpoint, her relationship with Victor had not technically been *wrong*. Greg was the one who'd left. They were separated, and in a separation, she was free to explore her options, as was he.

In her heart, Olivia knew none of this mattered. These justifications were technicalities, not reassurances. She had never been unfaithful to Greg before Victor; it wasn't who she was or how she was raised. And now she had, even if she could find a million reasons to defend her actions.

To her surprise—and the powerfully sad feeling she didn't

deserve this kindness—Greg wasn't angry, and even went out of his way to make sure she knew it. He couldn't hide from her the hurt in his eyes, though, and she would remember that look for the rest of her life, the great pinnacle of her shame and regret.

Greg's hand cupped the side of her face. At the softness of his lightly calloused hands, she melted, and the tears ran unabated. "I shouldn't have left you, Liv. I knew what I was getting into when I married you, and into this family."

"No one ever knows what they're getting into with the Deschanels. How could you?"

"Still. I understood enough. I suppose I thought over time the idea of being married to a... well, witch, would grow on me. A part of me was glad you didn't embrace that part of yourself. That was wrong, and it was even more wrong of me to turn my back on you when you finally accepted who you really were and your part in that family."

She turned her head and sniffed through a face full of snot and tears. "And then I jumped into the bed of the first man who paid attention to me."

"He gave you something I didn't and should have," Greg said, so understanding. Too understanding. "I wish I had, Liv, but I'm... well, glad that he did because when I think of how I left you alone, after Alain died, after the miscarriage... I can't even face myself."

No, this was all wrong. He wasn't supposed to take her guilt and turn it around on himself. She needed to suffer, to feel this, so she would never, ever do this again. She had to be punished!

And then it hit her.

Greg felt he needed to be punished as well.

Olivia had lived so long under the thumb of her mother's Catholic guilt that her capacity for objectivity was muted.

They could each pile their list of sins and take turns

surpassing one another, or they could accept, forgive, and find a way to move forward.

"I want to be more understanding," Greg went on. He stroked her hair, and as he did, his eyes moved around the room of the home they purchased together. Built their life in together. "Hell, I don't know, maybe I can even go to those... meetings y'all have."

"The Deschanel Magi Collective meetings?"

He chuckled. "Is that seriously what they're called?"

She laughed, too. "Deschanels take themselves very seriously."

Greg kissed her forehead. "I suppose I need to as well then. It might be the oddest family in New Orleans, but it's my family, too, right?

She nodded into his shoulder, where she nestled her head. "I'll try to think more before I speak or act."

"Let's not get crazy, now!"

Olivia lightly pinched the skin on his belly. "I said I would *try*."

"I knew you were a little crazy when I married you. You knew I was a little boring when you married me."

"It doesn't mean we can't both try to be better."

He kissed her again. "And we will, honey."

Olivia remembered something. She reluctantly pulled herself out of his arms and away from the tender moment. "Victor wrote me a letter."

"A letter? Do people still send those?"

She sighed. "I'm trying to be serious, and I don't want secrets between us. He left it in the mail slot yesterday."

Greg leaned back against the couch and nodded at her. "Okay. Do you want me to ask what it said?"

"Don't you want to know?"

"Only if you want me to know."

Olivia's hands flipped to her hips. "If I can be so honest, your insouciant reaction right now is infuriating for me."

He grinned. "I appreciate your use of 'I' statements and five-dollar words in lieu of docile cuss words."

"I don't want to keep things from you," she insisted. "I'm trying to do the right thing."

His eyes closed. He gestured toward the mail pile. "All right, then. Let's see it."

Olivia retrieved the letter and handed it to him. It wasn't long, and she had memorized the words, not from fondness but confusion.

My dearest Olivia.

Dearest. She shivered. How had she ever allowed another man to use those words on her?

I never expected this. You never expected this, either, I know. But I love you. And I am gutted at the loss of you. Let's meet.

Meet. At her store, at Galatoire's. Her bed. Those places felt tainted with her choices.

Love for eternity, your Victor.

Greg's face was blank as he read the note. "You should respond to this."

Olivia double blinked. "I should?"

"How else are you going to tell him to screw off?"

She sagged against the hutch. "I tried that... or not *that*, but something *like* that, and then he sent this."

"Then ignore it," Greg said. He folded the letter and tossed it on the table. "In the end, does it matter what he thinks?"

"No, but... what if..."

"He shows up?" Greg opened his arms. His regarded her hesitation with amusement as she gaped in confusion. She finally relented and folded herself into his lap, one of the few places Olivia Claiborne had ever felt safe.

Olivia nodded into his chest. She had never felt shame in

how she needed to be comforted and cared for, and how she had let Greg assume that role. She found her independence in other ways, but when it came to her emotional well-being, she was every bit the woman who needed her man, and damn anyone who had a word to say about it. Greg was home and that meant, she, too, was home.

"I'll tell him thanks for the help, but I've got it from here," Greg said and kissed her the way he had on their wedding night.

26
LAUREN

Lauren closed her notebook. "I think I'm clear enough to get started. I'll get my new assistants on the task of scrubbing the archives and turning them into something digital and searchable. I should have an estimate on completion for that project by the week's end, if that's all right."

"More than all right," Colleen replied, drawing a dainty sip of her tea. Her all white Vivienne Westwood suit glowed in the light of dusk hitting the glass lining the porch; a formidable angel. Lauren admired this woman enough to want to be her and hoped this time under her wing served to teach her beyond the task she was brought on for.

"From the visual inspection earlier, I don't believe it will be quick. Weeks, if not months, to assemble the whole of the archives, if we want it done right. I'll provide weekly status updates, or daily if you prefer, so you'll stay in the loop of our pace every step of the way. I just want to be clear, upfront."

"Of course. I expect nothing less."

Lauren uncrossed her legs and stood. "Once everything is digital, we can begin the next phase, of building and arming a research team to grow the data bank. My assistant at the firm is already working on an agile travel plan using our connections at the visa offices so we can send anyone, anywhere, as quickly as we might need to."

Colleen nodded. "I've had a few volunteers already. I don't want to lose momentum. Can we begin this program in tandem? I trust you to iterate as we develop better resources."

"I'll do my best to deploy the research teams sooner than plan." Lauren, meticulous to a fault, struggled to get the words out. She would not fail her mentor so early in her tenure, though. Whatever she needed to do to make this happen, and keep Colleen satisfied, she would.

Colleen settled her tea in her saucer and looked away. "Very good, thank you."

"Something else is on your mind," Lauren observed. "Anything I can help with?"

The leader of the Deschanels ran her hands over the soft linen sleeves of her blazer. They stopped at the elbow patches. "I've hesitated for months on this, but perhaps now *is* the time." The words seemed more for herself, but then she looked square at Lauren. "I would like you to investigate something for us. Personally."

"You know I'll help however I can. What is it?"

"There's a branch of our family that has never been involved with us. We didn't know they shared our blood or we would have reached out sooner." Colleen dropped her arms. "We have, in the past come across those of our ancestry who were not interested in what we had to offer, and we let it go. Immersion in the business of our family has never been a requirement for anyone. We have many Deschanels, in fact, who have nothing to do with us outside of the annual family reunions."

Lauren stepped closer. "But?"

Colleen's breath came out in a controlled stream. "This may

come as a shock to you, but then again, maybe not. After weeks in our archives, it's doubtful anything ever will again." Beyond the glass enclosure, fresh rain coated the flagstones. "My daughter, Amelia, and her husband recently traveled back in time to 1861."

Lauren tried not to look predictably surprised. To work for this family meant unwinding most of what she knew to be true in this world and set aside what was left of her doubtful nature. She swallowed. "Go on."

"Her time in that period was revealing for us on several points. The one particular to our conversation now involves the LaViolette family. I assume you know the name."

Lauren laughed. "The senators? Billionaires? Most powerful family in Louisiana?"

Colleen's brow arched. "Don't let other Deschanels hear you stealing their claim to those titles. Yes, those LaViolettes. It seems they descend from the illegitimate sister of our Louisiana patriarch, Charles I, and, what's more, *they* know this. Have always known this. That knowledge was not passed on through Charles' line, so it has lived solely through the line of Charlotte Deschanel-LaViolette."

Lauren didn't know whether she was more taken aback by this familial connection—which perhaps wasn't so surprising, all things considered—or that real people in the real world referred to their relatives the way some cultures referred to kings.

"You want to know why they've kept it to themselves for over a century," Lauren said. She hesitated before adding, "Because you're not convinced their intentions are positive."

Colleen smiled. "There's Deschanel in you yet, Lauren Weatherly. You've hit on my concern precisely. Others might see this as an overreaction on my part, but we have not survived, open in the world, without caution." Colleen stepped forward so they were face-to-face. She reached for Lauren's hands and took them in her own. "It's time to confess I had another reason for bringing in an outsider to the family."

Lauren became consciously aware of the sweat on her palms as the Deschanel matriarch held them.

"You are a remarkable woman in many ways, Lauren. But you are utterly unremarkable in a way that matters to us. You have no special abilities, least not of the supernatural kind. Plainly, you are not a witch."

Lauren managed a laugh. "No, that I am not, though I've been called similar things by certain male members of my firm."

Colleen smiled politely. "Witches can sense other witches. Call it a seventh sense, if you will. If I send a Deschanel into a room with a LaViolette, they will sniff us out a mile away, and it may invite friction where none is needed. I only want to assess the situation so we can decide how to move forward."

"I see." Lauren dropped her hands, which had become an oil slick of nerves, and hid them behind her back. "I'll do whatever I can."

"Please understand," Colleen assured, and in that voice, in that chocolate, soothing tone, Lauren would have believed anything the woman said, "until now, with the exception of those who married into the family, I have not successfully found an outsider I could trust with our secrets. I trust you, Lauren. I hope you understand the weight of such a thing."

Lauren's heart raced. She nodded.

Colleen rested a soft palm against Lauren's cheek. "I will not ever ask anything of you that you are not free to decline. This is a partnership, not indentured servitude. You owe me nothing except your discretion."

"Even if I hadn't signed the non-disclosure agreement, you would have that, Colleen. I'm not the type to look for loopholes, or personal advantage. I only want to help others and do what's right."

"I know that," Colleen said sweetly. "And that, my dear, is why you are here."

COLLEEN ESCORTED HER AS FAR AS THE DOOR TO THE COLLECTIVE chambers. "I'm due for a board meeting at the hospital, but will return by evening. Call if you need anything."

"Thank you, I will."

"For now, familiarize yourself with our files on the LaViolettes. We will partner on a plan, but there's no need to rush on this one."

"Very well. I'll pick it up tonight."

"Oh, and, Lauren?"

Lauren paused in the doorway.

"I don't know what you've done to influence our dear Nicolas, but it encourages me."

Lauren listened to the commanding click of Colleen's heels as she returned down the marble halls, wondering, with more than a hint of dismay, if she had misunderstood the full scope of the expectations the magistrate had for her.

NICOLAS WAITED FOR HER WITH THE EXCITED LOOK SHE USED TO GIVE her father when she expected a cookie for finishing her chores.

"You're early," she noted, the closest to a compliment she was willing to offer the princeling.

"I wanted to get a head start," Nicolas said, beaming as he shuffled through a stack of paperwork that was, not shockingly, upside down.

"What are you doing, exactly? I've got the assistants working on the vault."

Nicolas flashed her a wry, *you got me!* grin. "All right, then, boss. What's up on the schedule for us?"

Lauren set her purse on a nearby desk and leaned against the chair. "There's not much for *us* right now, not until we get everything archived and can set a plan for our field researchers. That could take weeks." She didn't tell him they needed to begin preparing the research teams much sooner.

"But you're here."

"Your aunt has tasked me with something, but I need to do it alone."

Nicolas made an *ahh* sound. "The LaViolettes."

"She told you?"

"I'm on the Collective Council," he explained as if he had offered up a résumé that included a lifetime in the Senate.

"So, then you know why she wants me to do this alone," Lauren said.

"Did you know Aunt C has never had a speeding ticket in her life?"

"What does that—"

"This is a woman who wouldn't know a risk if it cut her town car off in traffic."

"Those are her orders, whether you agree or not. Anyway, I'm only here to look at the file on the family. She's not ready for me to approach them yet."

"I can pull it for you."

"Sure, thank you." As she said it, she wondered if even small favors would come with an expected return.

Nicolas returned from the library with a thick folio. "This is a lot of reading. Definitely not for the faint of heart, or the casual toilet perusal."

Lauren smiled in spite of her long-formed annoyance with the man. "I have time, while the assistants are doing their cataloguing."

Nicolas' eyes twinkled. "I have a better idea. Why don't we read them together? Over dinner?"

Lauren snatched the file from his hands. She pressed it to her chest. "You're relentless."

"I don't mean to be," he said. "I like being around you."

She looked away. "I wish you didn't."

The feel of his slow approach was as heavy as the file in her arms. She didn't want to hurt him, but he seemed determined to make her.

The dark mustiness of the old chambers mixed with the soft, sweet heat of his breath. "I wouldn't say yes to me, either, Lauren," he said. "I haven't earned it yet."

Lauren sighed. "I don't want you to earn anything, Nicolas, you're just not... I'm not..." She couldn't finish. Was he not her type, or was it the other way around?

"You are," he said. His smile lit up the dim room. "I'm just happy to be working with you again, Lauren. For now, let's leave it at that."

Lauren stood alone in the chambers for several more minutes, file pressed to her chest.

27
ANASOFIYA

Aidrik left around midnight.

A piece of Anasofiya had always known this moment was inevitable. She dreamed about it when they were a triad in Europe, facing down an enemy. When she watched him die she thought, well, *this* is how it ends, and was it really so shocking that a radical like Aidrik the Wise would see the end of his road at the hands of another?

And then he came back, and Anasofiya considered that her fears were less prophetic and more human. But Aidrik, no matter how he loved her, how connected they were, was not himself tethered to a mansion with a pretty garden in the middle of a bustling city. He had roamed the earth as a vagabond apostle, where creature comforts stood as reminders of a world he couldn't begin to relate to or understand. Only for Anasofiya, and later Finn and Aleksandr, would he ever desire to try.

"Anasofiya. My *kjære*. My eyes-like-the-sea." He whispered the words against the drone of the winter storm, and she felt them more than she heard them.

"I hate you," she lied through her tears.

She didn't tell Finn what Aidrik intended. Her husband daily toed the line between sadness at Aleksandr's absence in their life, and excitement for this new idea he had budding. *We have to find a way for life to go on,* he said. *A purpose of our own.* He'd found his purpose, he told her, but he wasn't ready to share the details. He wanted to wait until he had something tangible to show her, so she could see his vision as he did.

They both had secrets, she supposed. Aidrik seemed to know that, of his two great loves, only Ana would have the presence of mind to see him off without losing her mind. This is where she and her evigbond were most alike, in their inclination to sever emotion from pragmatism when it mattered most.

If Aidrik was her darkness, Finn was her light.

Finn would forgive her, but she wondered, would he forgive Aidrik?

Aidrik's hands pressed down the side of her damp cheeks. His fingers tangled in her long red hair, his thumbs pressed gently against her throbbing temples. "I will always come back. When the equinox fades to solstice. When the earth finds its way back to the sun. As you have always been two people, so, my *kjære*, have I. I may be called to roam, but I will always be called to return to you. The threads of my life are now intimately tied to yours, even more than before. To you both."

Ana twined her fingers in his. Tears drenched her flesh and his. "Then you can wait to hear me say I love you."

Aidrik pressed his ancient lips to hers. "You just did."

And then he was gone.

28
TRISTAN

Tristan sat across from his father for the first time in many months, on the couch his family acquired long before he was even a twinkle in their eye. They should have tossed the beast years ago. The purple fabric pilled into a design beyond recognition, faded to pink in the spots where the Sullivans sank in to watch television. The cushion Tristan chose had, like the others, long given up any structure and announced a sharp metallic clang unless you eased into it just the right way.

The sofa was completely and utterly a piece of junk, no debate.

But it was also home. A piece of his past, and his self, just like the grandfather clock that had never worked, beyond serving as a terrible hiding place for his mother's Valium stash, and the front bay windows that required a background in heavyweight lifting to open and close. His mother, never one for the domestic side of life despite choosing to stay at home, nor willing to let strangers in her home to do the work for her, had never dusted in Tristan's recollection. Their family photos lining the far wall had a layer of detritus so thick you couldn't make out who was who.

As a child, Tristan used to run his finger over the faces, creating mustaches or horns in the grime. More dust would form over his art, but a thinner layer than the rest of the photos. To this day, his mother was mustached and Danielle was an agent of Satan. He had no reason to believe they wouldn't be immortalized this way, unless his father suddenly became a new man.

Yet, his father *had* become a new man. When Danielle died, he buried himself in his work, and why not? His wife kept his world spinning, even if that world was altered to one they hardly recognized. He could pretend, in a household where an imagination was sometimes the only tool for survival. When Elizabeth decided to end her life, she pulled the rug of illusion out from under Connor Sullivan, and, predictably, his first instinct was to drown. But the man sitting before Tristan now was no longer drowning. Now, he was the one in control and holding the life raft.

"You look good." Connor's hands twisted in his lap. He rubbed his palms on the knees of his trousers, then resumed his wringing.

"I'm numb," Tristan answered. His tongue was sandpaper. When he swallowed, cotton choked him.

"I know." Connor rolled forward and dropped his elbows to his knees. "This will always be your home, Tristan. You can stay here, or wherever else you want to, of course, that's your choice. I thought about selling the house after... well, *after*. But I don't think I can, or that I should. They're gone, but a part of them will always live here, and I'm not so ashamed to admit that gives me comfort."

"I understand." Tristan didn't really know how to, or if he should, tell his father he carried a piece of Harriett around his neck. It seemed like the kind of thing he could tell his father, but at the same time, felt like a secret belonging only to him. He nodded, instead, when Connor studied his response.

"Yeah, kiddo. Maybe you do. Maybe you do."

"I came to tell you, Dad, that I'm not staying home. I'm not running away or doing anything dumb, before you get worked up." Tristan picked at the couch fuzz. "I'm going to offer my services to the Collective. They need researchers, you know."

"I do know. I'm a..." Connor scrunched his forehead as he searched around for the right word. "Council member now."

"Right." If there was a definitive sign his father had changed, it was how eagerly he now embraced the Deschanel Magi Collective and taking on a leadership role within. "Then you know this research is important. Not everyone in the family can just drop everything to travel the world. People have kids. Jobs. Other stuff."

"It is," his father agreed. "Important. I don't really know much about it, to be honest with you, Tristan. I'm trying to wade my way through an ocean at the moment. I grew up in this world, with my Lizzy, but I was never really a part of it."

Tristan laughed. "Aunt Colleen is probably the only one who doesn't feel that way."

Connor smiled. "I doubt that woman is ever at a disadvantage when it comes to knowledge."

"Anyway, I wanted you to know why I'm doing it. It's not a way of avoiding my life here."

"Oh, kiddo, I know that." Connor tapped his fist against the top of his knee. "I know, Tristan. I know a lot of things now that I didn't before, and you don't have to hurt yourself for the next twenty minutes trying to explain yourself to me. We each have our battles. Our baggage. Our own way of finding meaning. Despite what you lost overseas on your last journey, I would say you also found something, right?"

Tristan clutched the amulet around his neck. His heart raced. "What's that?"

"Purpose."

"I thought I did, and then everything was taken from me, like it always is. Harriett said something to me before she died." *Not only before, but also after.* "About the family needing me. Maybe they do, who knows? I'm going to go see Aunt C and offer my help, and if she takes it, I'll give it." *For Harriett,* he added silently.

Connor's nod was slow and thoughtful. He looked at the wall of dusty collages and left himself there for a long pause. "You and I, Tristan, we're survivors, but that's not the badge of pride people make it out to be, is it? It's more of a consolation prize, for losing."

Tristan glanced at his hands and shook his head, but his father was still turned away.

"We're the ones who have to remember," Connor finished. "And I have to tell you something. It's something I've known long before you were born, because your mother told me." He swallowed a breath. "I knew your mother would die. I knew before I ever married her. She saw it in a vision and told me, and I thought I would be okay, with the time she and I were given, but it wasn't enough. The way I loved your mother, when we were young... you wouldn't believe me, if I told you. You'll never see your mother the way I once did, and to know how her visions eventually changed her, how I watched this, day after day, how it killed the youthful hope in me. It made me bitter, and changed me. As a man. A husband. A father."

Tristan was speechless. He didn't know what to do with this confession, which changed so much about the way he'd viewed his father over the years, but at the same time, changed nothing." *We're the ones who have to remember.*

Remember who you are, Harriett's voice echoed from... *somewhere.* From within him, from the amulet... he didn't know, but he knew it was her, and not merely her memory.

"I love you, Tristan. I never said it enough, or showed it enough, but you and Danielle were the best things I ever did."

Tristan's eyes closed when he heard his father's soft steps on the worn carpet. He let his head fall forward as his dad embraced him from above, repeating words Tristan would eventually, when the pain receded, find so comforting.

They were not *it will be okay.* For what comfort could be found in a lie?

"We will both find our way," Connor whispered against Tristan's matted hair, as they both cried, as they both found their way back to one another.

COLLEEN FOLDED HER BONY HANDS OVER THE LEATHER MAT ON HER mahogany desk, smiling a smile Tristan had seen many times but had never been able to read.

At his side, his father cleared his throat. "Tristan's time overseas with Anders is just the experience you need right now, Colleen."

"You don't have to sell me, Connor," Colleen said evenly. Her smile faded to a warmer one, as she turned again to Tristan. "I remember, what now seems a lifetime ago, when you came to me, eager for membership. Your mother was against it, which may have been part of the appeal for you, but you came to us not as someone fulfilling a duty or a birthright, but eyes wide, soul ready. Of course I welcome your services, Tristan. We should be so fortunate as to have someone with your heart."

Tristan clutched the amulet in his fist, where his heart now lived. "I'm not offering my heart."

"I know, darling."

"I left it in Farjhem," he pushed on.

Colleen's eyes dropped to his neck and he knew she knew his secret. *Well now, that's not entirely true, is it?* his aunt sent to him only, privately, before he realized he hadn't bothered to block.

"You honor your family, yourself, and her," Colleen said, with no hint of what she had intimated a moment before. "Your offer is well-timed. The Council is only beginning to organize our field program, but we have unanimously agreed we will send pairs, never individuals alone. We're no strangers to peril, but there's far more to be found outside the bubble of our family, and we will take all precautions. As it is, we have a very eager Lucia, who is ready to take on her first assignment, and now, it seems, she has a partner. You get along with her, I presume?"

Tristan nodded, but liking Lucia was such a minor detail in comparison to reclaiming his usefulness.

"How soon can you leave for Hungary?"

His pulse sped into hyper drive. Colleen hadn't blown him off, or tried to talk him into going back to college, or something equally unfit for the man he was becoming. "When... whenever you need me to," he stammered. *Breathe. Show her you're the man she needs you to be for the task ahead.* "Is two days from now too late?"

Colleen laughed. "Let's say a week from now. Two at most. Lauren and Nicolas are still working out the details."

"You can count on me," Tristan said.

"Of that I have no doubt," Colleen answered. She rose, and the two men followed suit. "Expect to hear from Lauren or Nicolas soon. In the meantime, get your affairs in order. You could be gone for a long period of time."

I would prefer that. "I will."

"Quite so," Colleen said, and Tristan again had the feeling she was responding to his unspoken words. "If you both will excuse me, I have an appointment with Katja and Evangeline." She smiled. "It seems Katja is ready to embrace the healing she was given, and just needs that extra push."

“That’s wonderful news!” Tristan exclaimed. How nice, after all he’d seen and done, to hear some happy news for a change.

“Indeed.” Colleen embraced them both and left.

“One to two weeks, huh?” Connor said. In his face, Tristan witnessed both pride and loss, and he wondered if he had done enough to show his father that leaving wasn’t a way of escaping him.

Tristan looped his arm around his father’s back. “Is our old fishing spot on the river still around?”

“I haven’t been there in years, but I think so.”

“Wanna go?”

Tears appeared in Connor’s eyes as he pulled Tristan closer on their way out. “You bet, kiddo.”

29
NICOLAS

Nicolas searched for the keys to his Aston Martin. He was due at The Gardens in an hour for a Council meeting and wanted to be early for a change. He decided to drive himself this time, much to the bemusement of long-suffering Richard, who merely cancelled the hired car without comment.

He eventually located the keys in the bottom drawer of his nightstand, but the search set him back thirty minutes, and he would have to fly to make it on time. Nicolas cursed under his breath as he slipped on his tweed jacket, wincing at the anticipated disappointment in Aunt Colleen's eyes when he rolled in late, or with a hefty ticket in hand.

Rome wasn't built in a day, Nicolas reminded himself. If he wanted others to see outwardly the changes he experienced inwardly, he had to unwind years of their memories of his shenanigans and indifference.

Lauren wasn't the cause of his change of heart, but she was certainly a catalyst. Nicolas had been building to this moment for most of his life, rolling over a series of bumpy hills toward the finish, never quite finding his footing. In Lauren, he saw life could be fulfilling without seeking unhealthy thrills or giving into his baser self.

Lauren's upbringing had not been so different from his, really. Wealthy, a prominent name, a storybook home hidden behind lush gardens and generations of history. But Lauren let these things become footnotes of her life, where Nicolas allowed them the authority to write the headlines in bright neon lights. The result was a lifetime of searching for happiness in dark places. Lauren's life, by comparison, seemed bland on the surface, but she was more content, more comfortable in her own skin.

Lauren was critical to his new understanding of the life he had led, but she was so much more than a warning sign. Nicolas had never desired a woman for more than how she made him feel. Even Mercy, whom he had loved with the best parts of himself, he had craved for the thrill of her love.

When Nicolas thought of Lauren, he wanted to know everything there was to know. He wanted to talk to her, and more importantly, to listen. To set his own story aside long enough to hear hers.

And Nicolas had listened, both to the words she said and the ones she did not. Her quiet confidence showed him that he first had to look out for himself before he could provide anything for anyone else.

A smile appeared on his face. He would see her soon.

Nicolas flew down the back stairs, the quickest way to the old livery he'd converted to his stable of cars. Richard's voice called out for him no sooner than his hand turned the knob of the back door.

"I'm late!" Nicolas answered over his shoulder.

"Nicolas, you're gonna stay late, I'm afraid." Richard was

now several feet behind him, and when Nicolas turned, his face paled at the sight of his old caretaker.

"What's wrong? What happened?"

"You have a visitor. A very unusual one. I didn't let her in. That's a bigger decision than my job entails," Richard said with a heavy look.

"She?"

"Mercy, Nicolas. Miss Mercy is back."

NICOLAS STOOD BEFORE THE HEAVY OAKEN DOOR OF *OPHÉLIE*, FROZEN IN place. His mind was blank despite the heavy range of emotions that hit him whenever he thought of Mercy. She was on the other side, actually, physically here. What was she thinking? Did he want to know?

No, but he had to. When he left her in Scotland, his deepest regret—not the only one by a long shot, but the biggest—was walking away without any semblance of closure. He had always known this day could come, where she might seek him out. Her intentions would remain a mystery until he let her in, and without resolution on that, closure was still as elusive as it had been that day in Scotland.

Nicolas held his breath and swung the door open.

All doubts Richard might have been confused melted away.

Clementyn.

Mercy.

She had lost weight and cut her hair cropped tight to her scalp like a pixie, which together had the striking effect of making her resemble a Dickensian orphan. Draped over her thin form was an oversized wool sweater too warm for a Louisiana winter, and chunky combat boots.

On second pass, she reminded him of the women of the dystopian future in his favorite video games.

Yet, she was still beautiful. She was still his first true love. Still Mercy.

Her lower lip scrunched into a ball. Fresh tears glistened in her eyes. "I've missed you, Nic."

Nicolas' whole body went rigid. His heart, now an organ he knew how to put to use, felt like a fist held tight to it, constricting blood flow. "You're here," he managed to say.

"I'm here."

"Sorry, I just..." Nicolas pulled his hair through his fingers. "I wasn't expecting this and I don't know what to say."

Mercy stepped forward without invitation and threw herself toward his arms. He didn't remember making the motions, his limbs responding with the instinctual direction of his subconscious, as his palms shot out to stop her. He held her at arm's length, and his heart pinched further as the surprise flooded her face.

"I thought you would welcome this," she whispered. "A second chance."

"A second chance?" He searched for a sign she might be teasing, though that kind of levity was a rare thing with Mercy. He found nothing unusual behind her intense expression.

Mercy stepped past him into the house. Her unlaced boots clopped on the cypress flooring with steps heavier than her. "I'm not mad, Nicolas. I threw a lot on you and gave you no time to think it through. You're only human." She turned. "Did you? Think it through?"

"Did I..." Nicolas licked his lips. He could almost taste the Hennessy. Oh, how he missed it. That amber heaven would give him some much-needed stability in a moment he feared he might fall straight through the floor. He would find the right words, instead of stumbling over his repeating of hers.

She turned from him, but he caught her smile pass by the hall mirror. This was how she had always looked at him, but now he saw it through a new lens: lovingly patronizing. If she was a Southern woman, the undercurrent swimming behind her words would be, *bless your heart.*

"To love you is to love you for who you are," Mercy continued, as if reciting from a practiced speech. "And I do love you, Emyr help me. What is the expression Children of Men favor? Warts and all?"

The words burned in the back of Nicolas' throat, screaming. He opened his mouth to silence.

"I was wrong about the child. The Scottish sorceress couldn't help me after all, and if I've learned anything from my trials, it's that Emyr always has a plan, even if it isn't the one we want." She sighed, another rehearsed move. "So here I am. I waited for you, but I understand why you didn't return. You didn't know if I would take you back, and in our darkest times, all we have is our pride." She reached for one of his hands and squeezed it between hers. "I hope now you can see this for what it is."

Nicolas' skin singed with the words he hadn't been able to say. They pushed at his pores, desperate for escape. He was a prisoner in his own body.

Her lips against his finally broke the spell. He shook off her hand and stumbled into a table. "I do see it for what it is, Mercy. I see so clearly now."

The confused look she wore was as condescending as her earlier words. She eyed him like he was a petulant child, unresponsive to discipline. "Why do you seem angry with *me*?"

Nicolas didn't answer this. Some questions had no right answer. "I didn't come after you because it was *over*." *Say it. Get it out. You don't need a drink. You never did. Find your strength.* "We both want different things, and instead of fooling ourselves into believing we can compromise, or overlook it, we need to accept it."

"What are you saying? I told you my desire for a child was a fool's errand. If that's not a compromise..."

Nicolas shook his head. "It's not as narrow as that, Mercy, and you damn well know it. First it was Emyr, then it was a child. You search for meaning and signs everywhere, and when you don't find any, you keep searching. You say you learned from what happened with your Mark of Emyr, but I'm not so sure."

Mercy scoffed. She went to respond, but Nicolas was on a roll.

"You'll always need some kind of dogma to guide you, but nothing will ever be enough. *I* won't ever be enough. You need something or someone divine to tell you what to do next. Instead of finding a lesson in your Mark killing you, you decided that was yet *another* sign. And another, and another. Each time you come away acting more enlightened, when it's just the same problem with a different flavor."

"Coming from the man with no faith, I'm not sure your words mean much," Mercy spat. She crossed her arms. "I was amenable to overlook your faithlessness, but you seem indisposed to live with my faith. Who has the problem?"

"Mercy, there's faith and there's unwillingness to accept that what happens to us in life is the result of our own actions, not because we've spent all our time currying divine favor." Now that the words were flowing, they wouldn't stop. They were the total culmination of months and months of agonizing over his loss, over his own changes. He expelled them now like a man ridding himself of the poison determined to kill him. "I have no doubt what I felt for you was love. I may have been a bit slow on the uptake, but hey, it was my first time. I still love you, and I think I always will, for whatever that's worth, but that's not enough."

"Will you listen to yourself? You say love isn't enough in the same breath you admit you have no experience. How can you be such an expert?"

Nicolas laughed. "I'm nowhere near an expert in anything except screwing shit up. But I know myself, and what I have to give. I thought I could love you enough to overcome the rest, but I can't. Or maybe I can, who knows, but whatever there is of me to love back, it isn't enough for you. No man or Empyrean will ever be enough for you. Your search for higher purpose never ends, because you don't want to stop looking long enough to realize you might have already found it."

Mercy's face had flushed a deep red. "What would my faith be if I gave up on it?"

Nicolas caught his breath. He still had so much to say, but none of his words were chosen to hurt her. "I would never tell someone to give up their faith. I'm the last person who should be telling others what to believe in. But is that really the hill you want to die on? To be so focused on the signs that you miss living? It happened to you once already, and this was your chance to try and see the world differently." He shook his head. "You don't have to answer that, at least not to me. I used to think I wasn't worthy of you, and there were no doubt times I wasn't. I've spent so long seeing my faults that I didn't see the other problems between us. I did things, felt things, *wanted* things I had never wanted before. I was ready to settle down and make a life with you. I wanted to be a man you could be proud to have at your side."

He no longer thought of the cognac that once rested not ten feet away on the silver tray. He didn't need it anymore. "We want different things, Mercy. I want to be the man my family needs me to be, and I want, maybe, one day, to meet a woman I can settle down with. I want to stop chasing my demons with more demons. I can't use them as an excuse not to *live*."

Mercy pressed her lips into a tight line. Her boot tapped to hold down her rising emotion. She had always done this, held so much back, and where before Nicolas saw this was a way to guard herself, he now wondered if instead it was her decision to share all of herself with Emyr alone. That no one else could be worthy.

"Is that what you think? I use my dogma as an excuse not to live?"

Nicolas shrugged. "That's for you to answer for yourself. What I think shouldn't matter."

"I don't get it. I'm here, ready to take you back, and you're not yourself." Mercy's hands went to her head, where she wound her fingers in her short-cropped hair. "Have you found someone else? Moved on to some other little strumpet awed over the size of your wallet?"

Nicolas sighed. "This isn't about anyone but you and me. I can't be with someone who will always be looking for more, and if you're being honest with yourself, you want far more than what I can give."

"You're threatened by my love of Emyr! You aren't capable of understanding how a woman can be a bride of her god, and her husband," Mercy charged.

He thought of Lauren. A woman of great faith who nevertheless found purpose in the life she had built for herself. "You know that's not what I'm saying. I may not believe in God, but I'm not one of those intolerant assholes who shames others for their beliefs. From the time we spent together, you know that."

"You treat me like this, when I gave you my love? When I gave you, an unworthy Child of Man with so few redeeming qualities, my time? The fortune of my presence was yours! A bride of Emyr is a gift you don't have the capacity to appreciate. How I could have ever thought you were the one who would help me fulfill my destiny, I don't know. I'll never know."

Mercy's sadness turned to rage in an instant, and Nicolas

finally understood why she had given him so much of her time when her heart lay elsewhere. Loving him was yet one more element of her dogma. He was one more test in her arduous list of them as she proved her faith to Emyr. Loving him, a mere Child of Man, was proof of her humility and charitableness.

"That's the thing," Nicolas said, as the sadness settled over him. "I'm just me, Mercy. Just a man, not a demigod or a path to enlightenment. I don't want to be a stepping stone for someone. I want to be the end game."

Her laugh lost all pretense of the loving pandering she showed up with. "But you could have been so much more than an average man with an average life."

"I *will* be so much more," Nicolas said. He checked his watch. "I'm late for a meeting. I have to go."

"You have to *go*?" She nearly choked on her anger, making several disgusted sounds. "After I came all the way here to see you, you *have to go*?"

"I don't know what to say that hasn't already been said." *And you're the one who showed up at my door out of the blue.*

"If I leave, I am never coming back. You will never see me again," Mercy warned.

"I already came to terms with that when you left me standing in the woods of the Highlands."

"Is that what this is? Revenge for hurting your delicate feelings?"

"No." He shook his head slowly. "I don't want revenge. I don't want to hurt you at all. All I want is to move on with my life."

"You're not yourself."

"You say that because you don't really know me," he said. "Only the flawed and broken version that fits your narrative."

"You fault me for wanting you to be more? To be better?"

"I know I can be better," Nicolas said. He moved to the door.

He had somewhere to be. Responsibilities. People who counted on him, and who he now felt a keen disappointment in letting down. And there was someone else, too, but he wouldn't think about her now. He had business with himself to tend to first.

"Then what? What is my crime?" Mercy demanded. She stared at the open door like it was an open threat.

Nicolas glanced past her, to the long drive leading to River Road, to what he couldn't see, the levee beyond, and the river. Maybe tonight he would go fishing, like he and Oz did when they were still in grammar school. He could walk down into Vacherie to the dime store where he took his little sisters for candy on hot summer weekends. Dangle his feet over the Veterans' Memorial Bridge and watch the steamships pass down the Mississippi.

But right now, he had somewhere important to be, and this chapter of his life was closed.

"I mean it, Nicolas. I'm not coming back."

He quickly kissed her on the cheek. "I really hope you find what you're looking for, Mercy."

When she was clear of the door, he gently closed it.

PART THREE
HOUSE OF DUSK, HOUSE OF DAWN
TWO MONTHS LATER

30
COLLEEN

Colleen had always loved tea on the veranda with her sisters. She looked forward to these magical dates more than just about anything, except the precious time with her children. They were always a time of reflection and relaxation in a world where they moved forward without much pause. Where guards came down, and the words and wine flowed in tandem once the sun set over the wide branches of the magnolia tree shading them.

Over the years, Colleen's tribe of sisters had dwindled one by one. First, Madeline died in a car crash, just shy of her eighteenth birthday. Years later, her relationship with Maureen, which had always been one nasty fight away from eternally fractured, finally fell apart at the seams. And then Elizabeth took her own life, and it was only Colleen and Evangeline left to reflect on the family, their lives, their sins.

Her brothers had never joined in their tea parties. Charles and Augustus claimed they had more important work to do, looking after the financial security of the family while the "girls" looked after the heart and soul. But then Charles, too, died. The children of August Deschanel had once been seven, and now they were four.

This changed things.

Augustus hovered across from Colleen and Evangeline with the awkward deportment of one utterly out of place. But he couldn't hide his contented smile conveying his joy to be included.

"Colleen tells me you're staying in New Orleans," Augustus said to Evangeline. He eased into the lounger and released the top button of his sport coat.

Colleen's breath caught. He looked so much like their father in that moment. Augustus had always been the one to resemble the venerable August the most. Now, when their lives had settled and a new quiet blanketed the family, she found herself missing those lost to her even more. If she stopped long enough to tick down the balance of their losses, she would lose herself to the unending grief of the exercise.

"Would you believe I'm finally calling in my entitlement under the Deschanel Trust? You'd think I wasn't committed to the cause or something," Evangeline said with a deep laugh. "I picked a property by the lake. One of the Mandeville homes. There are way too many of us in the Garden District already."

Colleen made a light tsk. "There's something to be said for convenience, sister. Should I take a wager on how often you'll be using one of the guest rooms at The Gardens?"

Evangeline shot her a playful smirk. "Only because you miss me so much."

"And Johan?" Augustus asked.

"I'll divide my time between New Orleans and D.C. I can't ask him to leave his life's work, and he knows he can't ask me to leave my family when we're on the eve of a new, exciting time for the Collective. And with Markus moving out here, Johan finds comfort in knowing I'll be around to keep an eye on both children."

"Are you sure I can't put in a word for him at Tulane?"

Evangeline's eyes rolled. "Most of us wouldn't be halfway where we are without a phone call from Augustus Deschanel. Don't think I've forgotten you calling M.I.T. on my behalf, once. No, brother. His passion is in science and tech. He's worked out a way to do most of his coursework remotely, and we will fly him back and forth to Washington as needed."

Colleen leaned forward and filled each of their cups with the tea Aria left. "Did Evangeline tell you Katja also claimed her inheritance?"

Augustus nodded. "I assumed as much when Rory Sullivan intimated over lunch that he'd gotten the call to work up a new contract with Grace Sullivan. I'm to take that to mean she's pursuing Stella's coursework again?"

"Stella wants to go to college." Evangeline beamed from across the top of her teacup. "Grace will help get her ready to pass the high school equivalency."

"I suppose then you'll want me to—"

"Make a call? Yes, yes, you silly man, we still need you, we always need you." Evangeline smiled and waved him away. "But only as a last resort. Stella wants to prove herself on her own merits, and I, for one, believe she can. She *is* a Deschanel, after all."

"As do I," Colleen agreed. "She's a quick study."

Augustus favored them both with his famously stoic glower. "You both think my only value is calling in favors."

Evangeline wore a mischievous look as she said, "You also have a phenomenal singing voice." She ducked and narrowly missed the throw pillow he sent hurling at her head.

"We also enjoy the pleasure of your company from time to time," Colleen added, always the peacemaker.

"Katja is applying to Loyola," Evangeline said. "Before you ask, no, she doesn't need a connection. My daughter is a genius."

"I said nothing," Augustus said.

"Besides, she made it clear to Leena and me that she'll accept no more help from the family."

Augustus raised a brow. "Aside from accepting a free home from the Trust, you mean."

Evangeline sighed. "It's called an *entitlement* for a *reason*, Aggie."

"She wants to make her own way. No one can fault her," Colleen said reasonably. "As all our children have." She looked at her brother. "Anasofiya seems to be doing well."

Augustus nodded. "I'm very proud of who she's become."

"She and Finn make a perfect match. He's exactly what she needed. He's a good man."

His nod was slower this time. "I've had to... let us say, adjust my expectations for her over the years. A seaman wasn't what I wanted for her, but as always, she knows better than I do. Her happiness was hard-earned." His next words seemed to be for himself. "Finn *is* a good man. My debts to him can never be repaid."

"When does Ashley leave, again?" Evangeline asked Colleen.

"End of the week," Colleen said, with an attempt to veil her torment. It stemmed in part from the danger her son signed himself up for, but also from the agony of a knowledge she could never share, not even with her sister.

As the magistrate, she couldn't show her own children favor over any other in the family. She couldn't aim to shield Ashley from what lay ahead, while offering others into service to the Collective willingly. If he wanted to join the research team, she couldn't stop him.

What was more, she shouldn't. For what Colleen kept from him would be the greatest secret she would ever keep in her life:

Christine and his sons were dead. The details still trickled in, but her investigator believed evidence pointed overwhelmingly to a murder-suicide. Poison. Colleen couldn't fathom the desperation Christine must have felt to take it that far, but she wondered how much culpability the Deschanels should claim in this crime. There were always inherent risks in bringing in outsiders. Some, like Jacob and Finnegan, found their footing. Others, like Christine...

Colleen should tell him. She wanted to, and at times, found the strength to voice the words. But her Ashley had never been the strong one, and she couldn't lose another child. Instead, she let him sign up for a dangerous mission, to save him from himself, and a truth she did not believe him capable of bearing.

"Leena?" Evangeline leaned forward. "Did you hear my question?"

Colleen had not, but she made a logical guess. "Sorry, he'll be assigned to the Ukraine project."

Evangeline whistled through her teeth. "Pripyat," she explained, for Augustus' benefit. "The old, abandoned pre-fab village where Chernobyl employees and their families once lived before... well..." She spread her fingers and made an exploding sound.

"I know of it," he said. "Why are we sending anyone *there*? There's a reason the place remains abandoned."

"Not entirely abandoned," Colleen hedged. "Some have said vampires live there."

"Vampires!" Augustus threw his hands up. "Are there leprechauns as well?"

"Only in your cereal, brother," Evangeline quipped.

"A year ago, I would have shared your skepticism," Colleen said reasonably. "That was before we met Victor de Blanchefort and learned what we know of his family. In the past, I've ignored reports of vampires as the same hysteria we often assign to people claiming to have run-ins with spirits. Now... we can't afford to be so narrow-minded. Not if we want to become more. To grow. To become—"

"*The foremost paranormal familial researchers in the world,*" Evangeline finished in a sing-song imitation of her sister.

"You don't agree with our mission?"

"You know I do."

"Evie, you can't express these doubts, even as humor, in Council meetings. You know how divided we can be, and they look to the two of us to set the tone."

"Always so serious," Evangeline chided. "You know me better than that."

"Ladies." Augustus rose. With two fingers, he re-fastened the button on his sport coat. "I've taken longer away from the office than I intended. If you'll excuse my interruption to your champion bickering session."

Both the sisters joined him on his feet. In unison, they planted kisses on his cheeks, eliciting a blush and an uncomfortable chuckle.

"Don't be a stranger, Aggie," Colleen said as he made for the door back into The Gardens where Aria would show him to his car. The words were as much an admonishment as an invitation. Things were different now, for so many reasons. Could not some of those changes bring happiness? Hope?

"If only you had told me Aria's tea was so agreeable, I might have come by sooner," he rejoined, and if Colleen didn't know better, she would say her brother was being playful.

"Now that the buzzkill is gone, show me that letter!"

Colleen turned to her sister, who slumped in her Adirondack chair with both legs dangling over one arm. She wore a Cheshire cat grin. "It's not scintillating, you know. He's very formal."

"I'll decide for myself," Evangeline declared and snatched it from Colleen's hands after she pulled it from her suit pocket. "Let's see. 'My Dearest Olivia.' Oh, this is already good. You think Greg talks to her like that?"

"I think Greg is a kind man who has a stabilizing effect on Olivia."

"Boring, you mean." Evangeline went back to reading. "'The absence of response from your end leaves me to form my own conclusions. Can I blame you? No, alas, I cannot.'" She laughed. "Alas! Who is this guy?"

Colleen pulled in a deep breath.

"'I have caught myself quite unawares in my love for you, but I will not be false with you any longer. I do love you. Yet I have been a disruption to your life and cannot pretend what you need from me exists beyond what I have already given. Thusly, I am retiring from my courtship of you, but also, the Deschanel family as a whole. You can assure your meddlesome aunt that I have also surrendered my pursuit of Ophélie, for the time being. She will either seek me herself, or she will not, but that is her decision to make. For now, I retire to my home in the countryside to reflect upon my life. Yours in love, Victor.'" Evangeline let the letter flutter to the flagstones. Colleen collected it with a sigh and returned it to her pocket. "Heavy stuff. How is Olivia taking it?"

"She was quite relieved, I should say."

"And Greg should be quite relieved that he doesn't have to figure out how to defend her honor against a dapper immortal."

"You sell him short," Colleen said. "He loves Olivia. Some of us Deschanels can be hard to love. To discover an outsider ready for the challenge is a rare find that can't be overestimated."

"Well," Evangeline said. "Victor was very easy on the eyes. I can't blame Olivia for wanting something a little more exciting than what she was used to. But our family is far better off without him. Good riddance to Victor de Blanchefort, I say." She made a show of wiping her hands in the air.

"And Margarethe," Colleen rejoined.

"Definitely Oriana and the Senetat."

"The Deschanel Curse."

"The Prophecy!"

"Brigitte."

"Don't forget that little shit Jean."

Colleen fell into the playful rhythm as they recited the names of their adversaries, smiting them in a symbolic way, a way that said they could only henceforth be named in academia. Her memory scanned the many injustices done to her loved ones. She did not know where to start, and she understood it would never end. They had come to see the worst of their foes vanquished, but life was never that neat. Their lives were not now magically exempt from pain and suffering. Every last one of them had a season, and only God knew that story from beginning to end.

"Things feel... good," Evangeline said. Her voice carried softly against a gentle, florid breeze. "It seems blasphemous to even suggest it. We have always, always waited for the next set of chips to fall. We've lived looking over our shoulders our whole lives."

"I know. But that's no way to live, Evie."

"No, but can we trust that the worst is over?"

Colleen chose the precise order of her words carefully, for they were ones she needed to take to heart as well. She, like Evangeline, couldn't shake the sense that more dark clouds lay ahead, but that was not her head talking, but the mouth of her fears. "We have seen the epoch of demons haunting our family for many, many generations. Will we see more dark days? How can we not? How can anyone ever not?"

"You're always so wise, Leena." Evangeline dropped her

unruly hair in a cascade down the back of her chair. "That's why I came home, you know. I needed you."

"Then you must have known how I needed you as well."

"Then let me give you some of the wisdom you've always given me, so many times over the years," Evangeline said with a slow smile. "Let's now, and always, remember that dwelling on what the future holds brings us nothing but misery. All we have is the happiness of the day."

Colleen closed her eyes and surrendered to the earthy scent of a storm brewing on the horizon. To the newly budding plants in her endless garden. To the sounds of the many, many species who shared this world with her, this careful, protected world that was more than she'd ever hoped or dreamed for. Her world of awe and loss, of memories no illness, no curse, no malevolence could ever steal from her.

Her hand reached blindly for her sister's. Evangeline wrapped their fingers together in the twined, messy embrace of their childhood.

"Is it wine time yet?" Evangeline asked.

31
ANASOFIYA

Anasofiya's finger hovered over the send button on the email. She'd practiced the same hesitation with her last short story, questioning whether every last one of her words were right, whether the tale she told was worthy of the memory. This was the second installment now in her serial fiction series, *Into the Hinterland,* about a human woman who meets a man of preternatural origins and falls in love, throwing her life into a tailspin as they fight against the challenges their relationship presents in the real world, as well as the geopolitical turmoil brewing between their worlds.

Except it wasn't fiction. She changed details to protect herself and her family; had renamed Farjhem to Terre Padre and relocated the ancient land to an island off Cape Horn. But Anasofiya had a story to tell, and this was not a world ready for the truth. Maybe her words could play a role in preparing the world for that day, or maybe not, but if she didn't get them out into the universe, in some form, she would go mad. Her "therapist," Aunt Evangeline, reaffirmed this.

She never expected anyone to read them. When she sent the

draft of the first installment to her father, looking for his advice as a publisher, the force of his reaction startled her. Augustus removed his glasses, wiped his hands across his eyes, and when they came away, tears glistened in the dark circles. "Ana... you have a gift. You always have. Would you permit me to publish this?"

Anasofiya was dumbfounded. Her father's magazine, his entire empire, catered to lifestyles of the affluent. *Should one summer in the French Riviera or the Amalfi Coast? Top 10 tips for finding the million-dollar home to match your lifestyle. The best dog spas in America.* "I'm not sure this fits, Dad."

"That's exactly why I want it," he said. "I've been thinking for a while, Ana, about the future of our publishing enterprise. Not just Deschanel Magazine, but the smaller publications as well. Our readership grows at a rate of ten to fifteen percent annually, as you may know. This is respectable growth in our industry. But I would not be a Deschanel if I was satisfied with the status quo. To push harder, we need to offer what our competition doesn't. To diversify our audience. I'm not interested in more articles about the woes of choosing an au pair. Are you?"

She laughed. "I never was."

"I want to offer something provocative to our readers. What better than thoughtful, weighty fiction? You know, that was how it was, in the early days. That was my original vision."

"You know it's not really fiction, right?"

A sure sign her relationship with her father had evolved for the better over the past year could be seen in his lack of visible discomfort with the topic at hand. He smoothly said, "Of course I do. It will be our secret."

She started to ask what he meant, but her question was cut short when he made the offer she guessed he'd wanted to make her whole life. He found a way for her to be an integral piece of his business, by offering Anasofiya her own department at

Deschanel Media: Head of Storyville, a new monthly production from the media empire of Augustus Deschanel, filled with the best short fiction from the brightest minds. It was hers to shape, to guide, to mold into her own.

"I know you will never want to run this company, not even when I'm gone," her father said. "Instead, I offer you this, Ana. It's not only your birthright, you were made for this. I would also like to give you a seat on the board. Before you say no, please consider this is how I will ensure my only child is cared for, the rest of her life, no matter what may come of me."

Anasofiya instinctively leaned toward rejecting the offer, but she was a mother now herself and could relate to the desperation he felt at leaving a child behind someday.

She said yes. For him.

"This will give you financial freedom unlike any you've ever known," Augustus said. "More importantly for you personally, you'll have a career you can discern meaning from. That has always meant more to you than money. I'm happy to be in a position to offer you both."

She realized how little she knew about the magazine world —a shame, given who she was—when they were able to produce the first issue within two weeks of their conversation. They were overwhelmed with submissions, and Anasofiya personally read through each one. But it was her first installment of *Into the Hinterland* that sent letter after letter pouring into their mail room. More, people asked. They wanted more about Terre Padre, more about the love story and the story's heroes. Book deals came next, and even an offer to meet with a studio to discuss movie rights. She turned them all down.

In two months, Anasofiya had become the head of her own magazine, a board member for one of the largest media conglomerates in the South, and a woman with an individual purpose beyond wife and mother. She and Finn split their time between Magnolia Grace and *Vivra sa Vie*, and if turmoil lurked around the corner, waiting, she never saw evidence of it.

Her son lived his own life now, and they had to do the same.

"Are you overthinking things again?" Finn came up behind her with a kiss to the back of her neck. "I liked this chapter even better than the last one."

"Oh?"

"Obviously. It's the one where Ana realizes she was way wrong and reunites with Finn. I mean, where Natasha gets back together with Peter."

Anasofiya reached over her head to pat the side of her husband's face. "I'm calling this one 'Bound.' It's when my life first began to feel whole."

Finn pressed his hand to hers, twining their fingers together. "The threads of fate weave slowly, until at last, an unbreakable knot."

She smiled. "Our vows."

"Hit send, silly girl. Time to send this diamond out into the world."

Adjusting to life without Aleksandr didn't take as long as Anasofiya imagined. Aunt Evangeline suggested this was because she had been a mother only a year. But Anasofiya believed it had more to do with the security of knowing he was exactly where he was meant to be. No one hammered him anymore about fulfilling a prophecy, and instead, he followed his heart and was living the life of his choosing. There was nothing more she could ever want for her son than that.

Sleep slowly returned to her life. The smile appeared on her face with greater frequency. She rediscovered joy, in her own life, in the arms of her husband.

She missed Aidrik as well, but like Aleksandr, he was living the life that gave him the most meaning. Like Aleksandr, he would return, from time to time, to the people who meant home. In her heart, she knew they would never stay away long enough for her depression at their absence to set in and sink its tendrils.

Anasofiya double-checked the cargo in the backseat of her car, securing it with the lap belt. Finn wouldn't be expecting her, but that would make delivery of this gift even more special.

Anasofiya, you place so much importance on his reaction, when you have not assessed the most important piece of this equation.

"Good morning, Wraith." Anasofiya grinned. Anyone looking would see only her in the car, but she would always have this passenger wherever she went. Over time, Wraith had learned its presence was not always welcome, so when it chose to show up, she was almost glad for it. "And what is the most important piece of this equation?"

His feelings for you supersede any natural reaction he might have. You could bestow upon him a pile of manure and the man would smile and feel unworthy.

"Well, when you put it *that* way."

She hit the Pontchartrain Causeway shortly after noon. Finn and Jacob's marina was just on the other side, near Fontainebleau State Park. It was still a mess of netting, old equipment, and new construction, but they expected to be open for business by the end of summer.

Finn finding his own purpose in New Orleans came as a great relief to Anasofiya. Despite his many reassurances he was happy here, there was no denying he gave up a part of himself in leaving Maine. When he and Jacob spent a night in their cups throwing around ideas, she watched and listened, smiling. And when they then sobered up and shaped their wild ideas into a real plan, and then put that plan into motion, she encouraged it. Finn called in his references in Maine to help get the information and licenses needed to start his commercial charter fishing business. Jacob brought in his background in environmental science, and they began to build their enterprise in an ecologically conscious way, with a special focus on preservation of the unique wildlife found in South Louisiana. Their vision was fairly simple: Finn would pilot the charter, while Jacob educated their patrons on conservation. A portion of all proceeds would be donated to local conservation groups.

"Think we should be jealous?" Amelia whispered with a half-cocked grin when they had watched their men excitedly cut the ribbon together at their ground-breaking ceremony. They looked like young brothers opening their favorite presents at Christmas.

"Probably," Anasofiya replied. They both laughed. It was the careful laugh of a Deschanel who knows something might still one day prove too good to be true. For now, they both took comfort from knowing they had married men from the outside world, and those men might just make it in the craziness of theirs.

SHE WEDGED THE CAR INTO A CORNER OF THE GRAVEL LOT THAT DIDN'T have materials stacked or scattered. Finn spotted her before she could get out and hopped down from a ladder, shirtless and glistening with the sweat of hard labor. He stole her breath, still, always.

When he kissed her, the musk of his day overwhelmed her. *Easy, girl. That's not why you're here.*

"To what do I owe the pleasure?" Finn asked with a lazy smile spread across his tanned face. He pulled his shirt from where it was hooked into the back pocket of his jeans and used it to mop the sweat from his brow.

"Where's your skipper?"

Finn squinted into the sun and nudged them both into the

shade of a nearby awning. "He's spending lunch with Amelia and Moira. Don't tell me you came here to see another man."

"No, but I definitely didn't bring enough po'boys," she teased. She didn't want to reach into the car for their lunch, not just yet. "And Forbia?"

"In the lake, collecting driftwood. See that stack over there?" He pointed to a pile of several dozen sticks of various sizes. "I told her I was building a structure." He wrinkled his forehead. "This is where the translation between dog and man speak sometimes gets a little fuzzy."

This gift was for Forbia as well. "Call her over."

"Better resign yourself to being tackled by a hundred pounds of sopping wet canine." He sounded a whistle through his fingers and a very excited Forbia came bounding out of the lake. With great enthusiasm, she shook the water from her heavy fur, coating her parents and everything else in near proximity. "Good girl. So helpful," he assured her as he scratched behind her ears.

While Finn was occupied, Anasofiya opened the back door of the car. Carefully, she slid the crate out and settled it on the gravel. She opened the wire door and backed away.

Forbia was the first to notice. She elicited a light, wary growl but then very quickly launched into a full sprint to welcome the newest member of the family. Finn pulled himself back out of the crouch, slowly, as he registered what he was seeing.

"This is Cicero," Anasofiya said with a sheepish grin. She gestured both arms to the wolf pup rolling around on the gravel with Forbia, who was now a muddy mess. "I thought Forbia could use a friend."

"Did you?" Finn approached the two wolves with a growing smile. He gave Forbia a good pat, and then lifted small, wiggly Cicero into his arms. "Where on earth did you even find this little guy? I thought Forbia was one in a million."

"My father, actually," she said. "He located a wolf rescue in

Saskatchewan. Cicero was abandoned by his mother before he could learn to survive on his own. They nursed him to health, but now he's too domesticated to be reintroduced to a life in the wild. The man said he's too 'used to eating from the hand,' and needs a patient owner skilled in raising wolves. Turns out, I knew just the guy."

Finn set Cicero back down to play when Forbia barked at him. "Okay, okay."

Cicero lapped at Forbia's muzzle with eager licks, then rolled to his back in submission. Forbia looked at her two masters, tongue hanging halfway to her chest, with an expression Ana could only describe as animal joy.

Finn crossed his arms, wrapping his fingers around his triceps. "Ana, I don't know what to say."

"I know you've been worried about leaving Forbia alone at *Vivra sa Vie*, and you're right, she draws too much attention to herself at the house in New Orleans. I thought to myself, what if she had a friend? She's a pack animal, but has never had a pack. They can run and play to their heart's content out there. Our neighbors know not to do anything stupid, like shoot at them." She rattled off her list of reasons, but they all led back to one that she was inexplicably afraid to say aloud: *I may not be able to have any more children, but there's more than one way to grow our family.*

Finn pulled her in close. He sank his hands in her long hair and pulled her in for a soft, lingering kiss. "We have always been cut from a different cloth than others in this world, haven't we?" He rested his lips at the right corner of her mouth. "We knew our path would be different, and it has been, at every step. I never thought I wanted a family, but I've been drawn to you since the moment I laid eyes on you on the shore in Maine. I'm drawn to you now. I'll always be drawn to you. I will always need you. Always want you. Don't ever think that's not enough, my silly girl. Because this?" He kissed her once more. "This is love." He tapped his chest twice with his palm. "This right here."

Aleksandr was fine. Aidrik was fine. Their world was no longer spinning off its axis. With the chaos peeled away, there was a life here to be lived.

And there was love.

"It is," she whispered. "Isn't it?"

32
OZ

Oz pulled the roast out of the oven. Through the window above, he watched the kids play in the yard and marveled at their endless energy. They played all day with him and Lucia at City Park, and played hard. Oz was barely still on his feet, and they had launched into a fresh game of soccer.

"I don't even remember being that little," Lucia said over his shoulder. She took the roast from him and settled it on two pot holders. "And I certainly don't remember having that much energy."

"You read my mind," he mumbled. He watched them in a daze, exhausted by proxy. Only thirty-one himself, he wished he could keep up with them, like Adrienne had. Like Lucia still could, despite her protestations that he guessed were more for his benefit, so he didn't feel so bad for tapping out early.

"Should I call them in, Oz?"

Oz leaned on the edge of the stove, propped by the palms of his hands. Naomi squealed with joy when she tricked Christian and managed to send the ball flying past him and into their makeshift goal, which was just a gap between a couple of bushes. She threw her arms up and wide, and launched her little hips into a victory dance with so much sass that Oz wished he had been filming.

"Nah," he said. "Let them play a bit longer. Grab the plates and forks. I'll open the wine, and we can talk about your adventures in Hungary."

"So, you and Tristan?" Oz inquired carefully, barely above a whisper, after listening for almost thirty minutes to Lucia's animated retelling of the past two months overseas.

"Me and Tristan what?" she asked through a mouthful of meat and carrots.

"Nothing."

"Nothing you say is nothing. I know you."

"You seem happy," Oz said. He slid his fork around the remnants of his plate. "That's all. It's good."

Lucia curled her mouth. "You're jealous." When Oz immediately launched into protestation, she laughed and clapped a hand over his. "Here, I can help you with that. Tristan and I are just friends. Good friends. Like you and me, right?"

Oz ignored the obvious sarcasm at the end of her sentence. "I'm saying, if you *were* more than friends, I would be happy for you. I want you to be happy."

"I've never heard anyone say those words and sound less convincing."

Oz regretted not calling the children in sooner. He tossed his napkin on top of his plate. "Anyhow."

She grinned. "Anyhow."

"I actually invited you to dinner for a reason."

"Not because you missed me?"

He had missed her. So had the children. But Lucia was so incorrigible and so cavalier about it, that his pride wouldn't let him make the confession. "It's more practical than that, really."

Lucia made an exaggerated show of submission, folding her napkin into a neat triangle and dropping her hands in her lap. "You're nothing if not practical, Oz. I'm all ears."

"I believe... well, I believe the children's lives are better with you in them. They miss you when you're not here, and while no one could ever replace their mother, I don't know that I realized how important a feminine presence was in their life until you went away."

"I see." Lucia relaxed. "You know how I love the kids, even when they're being impudent brats." She watched, as she always did when saying something provocative, for his scandalized reaction. He decided not to disappoint her. "And you, Oz? What about you?"

"What about me?" He hid his sweaty hands under the table.

Her smile widened. There was a sense of knowing in the slow, lazy gesture. She had always looked at him this way, from the moment they met. As if she knew everything he refused to say, and sometimes, refused to think. "You look like you swallowed a cat. Is it because *you* missed me as well and can't bear to admit it?"

Oz coughed and then regretted it when he saw the look on her face. *Coughing out that cat, are we?* "I can... I can admit our lives are fuller when you're around than when you're not."

"Our," she repeated, bemused. "I will take that to mean you're including yourself."

"I can't give you more than friendship, Lucia." *Can't. Won't. Does it make a difference?*

"So presumptuous." She tsked. "Always acting like everyone wants to jump your bones. Oz, the irresistible."

His face flushed dark as the blood jumped north. "That's not what I meant."

"Believe it or not, I *am* capable of being your friend without having to exercise great sexual restraint," she teased. "But maybe that's because I'm not human and I have some kind of preternatural resistance to your charm." She cocked her head and looked at the ceiling with a thoughtful look. "Poor, poor human girls. You must have a trail of tears as wide as the state."

"That's enough." Oz choked out a sigh. He hid the smile tickling at his lips. "You made your point."

"So, the kids miss me. You can't admit you miss me and have slapped upon me a philosophical chastity belt for when I am gifted with the pleasure of your company." Lucia rubbed her hands together. "I sense a proposition coming!"

"Move in." The words came out before he could continue to let his fears suppress them. "I don't have an extra bedroom for you, but you're going to be gone for long periods anyway. The futon in the library is comfortable enough and should be up for the job. It will give you a place to stay when you're between travels and... it will make the kids happy."

Lucia slid back into her chair. She watched him. "Say you miss me. Just once. Say you miss me, too."

Oz dropped his eyes, an instinctual defense tactic. No, this wasn't a time to hide behind his own awkwardness and uncertainty. He had to look at her. She deserved that. "I miss you, Lucia."

The heaviness his words left was so powerful he had an urge to leave the room. She broke it with a self-satisfied grin. "Sure, Oz. I'll move in."

His body deflated. The pressure dissipated. He shoved his chair out from the table. "Should we break the good news to Naomi and Christian?"

Lucia rose and came to his side of the table. She lowered herself into a crouch. “My life is better with you in it, too, Oz.” He froze as she leaned in, certain she was going to kiss him. Instead, she bit the tip of his nose. “Let’s go grab the rascals.”

33
AMELIA

Moira giggled as Amelia fitted the onesie over her head. Her chubby baby legs kicked up and down without purpose. She gazed up at her mother with her father's green eyes.

It's a bit early for her to be settling into her permanent eye color, Colleen had said, *but I believe we can expect her development to be unusual and unpredictable.*

"Did she pee on you today? Because she peed on me twice." Jacob appeared in the doorway.

Amelia lifted her daughter into her arms. She breathed in her soft baby scent, and a fresh wave of dopamine passed through her. There was nothing else in the world like the blissful calm that came over her with her daughter pressed to her breast. "Maybe she just loves you more, Dad."

"I'm waiting for her to poop on me, and then we can consider that a done deal." Jacob opened his arms wide. His whole face lit up as Amelia placed Moira, and he wrapped her in a gentle embrace. "Was that your mother who called earlier?"

Amelia nodded. "The baptism is set for next Tuesday at St.

Alphonsus, in the evening. Have you heard from Father O'Connor? Or Sister Agnes?"

"They're both coming." Jacob beamed from over the top of Moira's silken swirl of black hair. "Sister Agnes agreed to stay."

Amelia wrapped the dirty diaper and put it in the bin with a sigh of relief. When Jacob proposed the idea of Sister Agnes moving back and becoming their nanny, Amelia's initial reaction was a tense protectiveness. She didn't want anyone else to raising her daughter. Even as she thought it, she knew it was a foolish notion. Amelia missed work. She missed helping people. The paperwork had already been filed to open her own psychiatric practice when she was ready to return.

"You still want that, right?"

Amelia smiled before she turned to face him again. "I do. She was a mother to you, and look how you turned out. We're very fortunate she's willing to devote her life to doing it again."

Jacob shifted Moira to one side and flexed with the other. "It's all true, everything they say about me."

"Especially the part about modesty."

"You don't think anyone in the family will have hard feelings about us choosing Finn and Ana as godparents, do you?"

Amelia tidied up the changing station. "Why would they? Ana and Finn spend almost as much time with Moira as we do. I can't imagine anyone else as godparents."

"Your cousins get wound up about weird stuff sometimes," Jacob said. He cooed in Moira's ear as he bounced her, and she erupted in more giggles. "I wouldn't want Ashley to feel left out."

"He's leaving tomorrow for the Ukraine with Charlotte Fontenot for two months. Even if we wanted to include him, he won't be here." Amelia glanced at the clock. "Speaking of which, if I don't leave now, I'll be late for my coffee date. You sure Finn doesn't need you today?"

"I'm not sure Finn needs me any day, but he's good at

pretending my confusion with a hammer and nails is helping us open faster," Jacob joked. "Go, have a nice time with your brother. Moira and I will be fine, won't we, *a mhuirnín*? We'll just busy ourselves playing with sharp knives and hot stoves."

"If you keep speaking to her in Gaelic, your *little darling* will grow up confused," Amelia teased, though she loved the sound of his soft brogue when he gifted endearments on their daughter.

"But knives and stoves are kosher?"

"She's gotta learn somehow, right?" Amelia kissed Moira on the soft crown of her head and then pressed her forehead to Jacob's. "It's going to be all right, isn't it?"

"What?"

"Everything."

With his free hand, Jacob cupped his palm to her cheek. "I can't see the future, *Blanca*. That's not one of my many, many gifts." They both smiled. "But I'm not afraid. Not anymore. There's nothing the universe can throw at us that we can't handle. This little witch?" He nudged Moira. "She's our secret weapon. She's a badass. She'll slay our mightiest of foes without even breaking a nail."

Amelia looked down and laughed. "It's a little early to be making that kind of pronouncement."

"*Blanca*," he whispered. "Look at me."

She did.

"The Prophecy might be done, but that doesn't erase anything for us. We will always be Cianán and Cerridwen, crossing the stars to find one another. I would cross the galaxy for you, Amelia Donnelly. I would cross ten. But I don't have to, do I? We fought our battles already. And now we get to enjoy the spoils of war."

"I love you, Donnelly."

Jacob kissed her. "Now, go. Go get coffee with Ashley, which is what normal people do. They have coffee dates and run errands. We're suburbanites now." His eyes flew wide. He feigned a chill. "On second thought, maybe we should go back in time and fight off presuming vampires again."

Amelia kissed them both. "Don't forget we have dinner at Ana and Finn's tonight, with Anne and Jon. I'll be back in an hour or two. Try not to get yourselves killed."

ASHLEY WAS ALREADY WAITING FOR HER AT THE CORNER BOOTH OF THEIR favorite coffee shop on Magazine Street. He had an air of anxiousness about him as he whipped around, scanning the shop in a frenzy.

"I'm not even five minutes late," she teased and slid into the booth across from him. "I'd say that's pretty damn good for a new mom."

"His Mia." He had calmed some, but there was still agitation in his face. "I didn't even notice you were late."

She wrapped her hands around the coffee cup he slid her way. "Then what's wrong? Are you nervous about tomorrow?"

"I'm *excited* to leave tomorrow," Ashley said. He twisted the warming sleeve in circles around the cup, sliding the recycled cardboard back and forth. "I know this will be good for me. Even if it does feel foolish walking into the remnants of a nuclear meltdown."

"Mom wouldn't send you if she wasn't confident in the safety precautions she set up for the two of you," Amelia said, though she, too, felt unsteady about her brother's trip to the abandoned Chernobyl village of Pripyat. "And our cousin Charlotte is nice. She'll make a good traveling companion."

"I like Charlotte," Ashley said absently.

"You can talk to me." Amelia pressed her hand over her brother's.

He exhaled. "I don't want you to go back and tell Mom."

"Come on, Ash, do you really think I would?"

"You've always been close to her."

"I can be close with one person without being disloyal to another."

Ashley looked away. "I'm hesitant to leave because what if Christine comes back?"

"We would bring you home right away, you know that. And we would damn well make sure she couldn't run off with the boys again."

Ashley withdrew his hand. Shook his head. "That's the other thing. I don't think she *is* coming back, Mia. And I think Mom knows it, too. She knows something and isn't telling me."

Amelia went silent. He wasn't the only one who thought Colleen Deschanel had kept critical information about the whereabouts of Christine and the boys to herself. She even tried to ask her mother, but Colleen was a fortress. This only fanned Amelia's suspicions, because when her mother was most locked down was when she had the biggest reason to be.

"If that's true," Amelia said. "I'll find out. I promise you."

"Be real. If Mom doesn't want someone to know something, she'll make sure they never do."

Amelia bristled. She pushed her coffee aside. "Well, it's not up to her. If she knows something about your family, you have a right to that information."

Ashley snorted. "You tell her that."

This wasn't helping him. He couldn't leave with this cloud hanging over his head. Amelia needed her baby brother—her only brother, now—to be okay when he embarked on this next phase of his life. "I'll talk to Lauren and Nicolas. They have full, unmonitored access to the archives and data bank. If she has information she isn't sharing, it will be there, and I *will* get my hands on it."

He nodded. "Thank you."

"But you have to promise me something in return."

"Okay."

"I need you to put this out of your head when you step onto that plane. I will tell you if there's something to your fears, but unless you hear from me, your focus should be on moving forward."

Ashley considered this. Several long moments went by before he bowed his head in agreement. "I promise."

Amelia smiled at the brother who could have been her physical twin. She longed for the days when there were three Jameson siblings, instead of two. When Ben made them all play "Red Light, Green Light" in the yard, and even "Red Rover," despite that they never had enough people to play it right. She hadn't been able to protect Ben from the terrible fate that snared him, but if she could protect Ashley from himself, she would.

Her brother was intelligent, kind, and handsome. He had more to offer the world than his caution and skepticism. He still had a whole life ahead of him to live.

Moving forward was as easy, or as hard, as letting go.

Ashley passed a folder across the table. "It's all there. My realtor's info, the home appraisal, the contact for my accountant who can help with the funds transfers, or if repairs are needed. Rory is helping arrange the estate sale, so you shouldn't have to do much there except drop off the keys. Thanks for doing this."

"You don't have to thank me. I think selling the house is a good step forward. I can help you look for a replacement home when you're gone."

He smirked. "Or maybe I'll save some money and move back in with Mom and Dad."

"Trust me, that'll cost you in other ways."

They both laughed. "You'll say goodbye to Jacob for me? And give Moira a kiss from her uncle Ash?"

"You know I will."

Ashley drained his coffee and stood. "I better go. I haven't even packed yet."

Amelia looked whimsical. "What does one even pack for a relaxing getaway to Chernobyl?"

"One does not know," Ashley joked. "But one is about to find out."

It warmed her to hear him being playful again. She pecked his cheek and pulled him in for a quick embrace. "Bring me home something fun."

"'My brother went to Pripyat and all I got was this stupid T-shirt?'"

"Or maybe a vampire!" she called as he disappeared out the door.

34
TRISTAN

Markus steered the car around the bend, going well over a hundred, with the deft precision of a professional race car driver. Tristan gripped the ceiling handle and middle console for dear life, only letting go when Markus shot him some peripheral judgment from the driver's seat.

"You haven't said a word," Markus said.

Tristan fought the wave of motion sickness that rose up when he opened his mouth. "Nothing to say."

"I haven't seen you in months and you have nothing to say?"

No, Tristan had plenty to say. He missed his best friend. He was beside himself that Markus was actually finally moving to New Orleans, so they could hang out together. In his mind, he had already coordinated months of endless video game parties. When Tristan was home, anyway.

But he wouldn't be, not for long. He and Lucia were returning to Hungary in a couple days, and this time, they might be away even longer. They were so close to tracking down the immortal chieftain of the ancient Magyar witches, and that was the easy part. Earning their trust and bringing them into the Deschanel circle as trusted allies—assuming they could be trusted and were not dangerous—could take months, if not years. And they had so many questions! Where had their immortality come from? How had they survived for over a thousand years in the Ural Mountains, unmolested and undetected?

"Ground control to Tristan."

"Huh? Sorry."

"Look, I know what we're about to do isn't going to be easy for you. If you prefer silence, I can do that, too."

Markus was right, but Tristan's behavior, in one way or another, had caused enough worry for his loved ones. He straightened in his seat. "You'll be living with Katja, then?"

"For the time being. To help with Stella."

"I thought Olivia was helping her?"

"She is," Markus said. He hit the gas on the next corner, sending them both leaning to the right. "But she's also trying to get her marriage back on track. Why anyone would put that much effort into the unnatural act of monogamy is beyond my comprehension."

"You seemed to like Lucia an awful lot."

Markus rolled his fist over the wheel. "Is this your way of telling me you're fucking her now?"

"No!"

"I wouldn't blame you. She's a minx in the sack."

"God, no, we're partners." That was only half the equation. The other was more personal, and while he trusted Markus with the knowledge, he also knew Markus wasn't capable of the depth of empathy required for such a confession.

Sorry, Harriett. I know you want me to move on, but I'm just not feeling it.

Tristan felt her silence and her smile.

Markus shrugged. "Your loss."

No, my loss is why we're here today. And I know you know that, too, or you wouldn't have insisted on joining me.

Jacob was the one who had thought of this ceremony to begin with, way back in Farjhem, in another life, but Tristan knew Jacob's time should be with his daughter. He would have come alone, but Markus figured out his plans and never gave him the chance.

"Jasper wanted to come." Tristan pressed his cheek to the glass and watched the endless procession of sugarcane fields fly by.

"Today isn't for him." Markus flipped the gearshift into neutral as they coasted to a stop sign. "Why did you even tell him?"

"I guess I thought he might like to know."

"The Broussards had their funeral for Harriett. This is yours."

Markus was right. Tristan shouldn't have told Jasper. He related to the man, on this if nothing else, as the one person who might understand his deep grief. But this spot was Tristan's. Prior to now, only Harriett knew of it, for she had taken him there and gifted him with a way to release his grief—and his anger—over his mother. Now Markus would know, too, and that made Tristan anxious but also comforted. He trusted few as he trusted his cousin. Markus might not feel things as deeply or meaningfully as most, but he understood how to be there for someone who did.

Markus gestured to the box in Tristan's lap. "Are you sure you want to bury that? Not scatter it?"

I don't need to scatter Harriett. She's with me, always, maybe more than she ever was in life. Burying her isn't a goodbye, it's a step.

"Nah."

"Take a breath. We're here."

. . .

VIVRA SA VIE, PASSED DOWN TO AUGUSTUS DESCHANEL AND THEN TO his daughter, Anasofiya, was more elaborate than the family homestead of *Ophélie*. Built in the Spanish Colonial style, it reminded Tristan of a bigger, more opulent answer to Andrew Jackson's Hermitage. Tristan had always loved the property as a child, because the boundaries couldn't be seen with his young eyes and the world seemed endless, in size and possibility.

His love for the iconic land of his uncle ended when Tristan's mother chose it as the setting for her suicide.

"Hey, look. The wolves are here." Markus pointed to the blur of legs and fur by the property's edge, where the manicured landscape met the crest of cypress and marsh.

"You don't see that every day," Tristan mused. He watched them frolic as he trudged through the lawn and into the heavier grass, in the direction of the tree.

The ghost of Harriett's hand slipped through his. At once, he remembered every last detail of when she took him here to bury the memory of his mother. It was the day he first called her his girlfriend and then worried he had overstepped.

Harriett had squeezed his hand between hers. *Feels like a silly word for what we have. My sister, Estella, went through boyfriends like socks. She probably couldn't even tell you all their names. Not that she ever cared, either.*

Well, what do you want us to be? Hopeful. Anxious. In love.

I don't need a fancy title to love you. Wherever you think you need to go, Tristan Sullivan, I'll follow.

Tristan squeezed the amulet. "Did you know, back then?"

"Sorry?"

Tristan stumbled over the knobby root of an oak. He looked up. "We're here."

Markus hung back out of respect, but his presence loomed large in comfort.

Tristan dropped to his knees in the patchy dirt. He set the

box to the side and closed his eyes. *Show me the spot. You should be with my mother and Danielle. It's the only thing that makes sense.*

His hands fumbled blindly through the dirt. He let Harriett be his guide. He trusted her more than his own memory, and she hadn't steered him wrong yet.

A hot surge passed through his fingers and up, up through the veins of his arm, into his shoulder. *Here.* Tristan opened his eyes and dragged his hands through the dirt, raking and scooping. The start of new growth from the seeds planted not even a year ago hadn't yet crested the surface, but he ignored the soft stalks and kept going. He didn't stop until his fingers struck something.

He pushed the dirt up and to the side, creating piles on either side of the sepulchral hole in the ground that housed, forever, his mother's final words and a sample of his sister's art. Tristan sagged against his palms and hung his head as the tears took hold.

I miss them both so damn much. It isn't just this family that's cursed. It's... it's me. He thought it then. Sometimes, he thought it now.

Harriett hadn't let him surrender to his sorrows that day under the same oak, and her words returned to him to pull him back to his purpose. *You are not cursed! You saved my life! You traveled across the world to help bring your cousin happiness, not knowing if you'd return. You've given up your life to help others. You are the bravest man I know, Tristan Sullivan.*

"Am I, still?"

This time Markus didn't question that he was talking to someone else.

She wasn't there. She *was* there. Sometimes Tristan thought he would go mad with the conflicting nature of these facts. Was she... wasn't she... did it matter when he could literally *feel* her breath hot between his shoulder blades? Her hand tracing the side of his neck?

They haunt you, Tristan, she had said. *We all have our ghosts, but yours eat you alive from the inside out.*

"Maybe before. Now they sustain me. You sustain me." He brought the amulet containing his heart to his lips and let his tears run freely, without shame.

What had she said when he last cried under this tree? *You have to forgive yourself. It's okay to grieve, and you will, for the rest of your life. But you can't hold onto this guilt. I won't let you.*

Tristan looked at the small brown box sitting beside the pile of dirt. When he told Anders he needed to bring something home for her family—they were Catholic, returning without *something* to inter would be almost as bad as her death itself—and Anders had come back from the task with two packages. *One for her family. One for you.*

But she's here. He tapped his chest. *With me. Always.*

You may not think you need them now. You might change your mind later.

Anders couldn't have known about this tree, this place where Tristan could bury his sorrows and rise again, anew. But all creatures had their tree, or something like it. Anders had said Tristan might change his mind, and Anders had been right.

Tristan opened the box. He couldn't look inside. The ash that was once her flesh and bone was not her, only a symbol of her, and he wouldn't let this scar his memories.

He turned the contents upside down. They sifted into the hole like heavy sand, coating his mother's letter and Danielle's drawing. Some caught the wind and drifted, but Tristan didn't follow and did not know which way they ended up.

He should say something. Harriett had, when she brought him here to submerge his grief the last time. *Thank you, Elizabeth, for bringing this wonderful man into my world. And Danielle for being an amazing sister. I promise to love him with all my heart and take care of him for you.*

"Thank you, Harriett, for loving me with all your heart. Thank you for taking care of me."

The soft patter of rain broke his reverie. He looked at the sky, where new clouds had formed. They hadn't been there when they arrived. *Are you reminding me about my tendency to dwell on things longer than I should, Harriett?*

Harriett, or the universe, answered by dropping fatter drops. They mixed with her ash and turned to soft mire. Tristan hurried to fill the hole before the rain could make a bigger mess.

A shadow fell over him. He looked up. Markus dropped down into the dirt next to him and worked to shovel the other pile back into the hole where it belonged.

I want to spend whatever time God gives us, together. Oh, Harriett. Is this time we have now, from God as well?

Until the very last, Tristan had promised then. Promised now.

Wherever fate takes us.

Markus helped Tristan to his feet. They stood side by side, regarding their work. Tristan felt a warm hand come to rest at the center of his back. He turned to his cousin with a tight smile. He was given one in return.

"Thanks for coming," Tristan said.

Markus pulled him to his side with a quick, tight hug. "With Harriett gone, someone has to take care of you, right?"

"You'll look in on my dad when I'm gone? Just every now and then."

"Of course."

Tristan wiped away his tears. The freshly sown ground at his feet would always be here if he needed it, but, as Harriett had taught him, pressing his pain into the earth was his way of giving it back to God.

I won't say goodbye, Harriett. You're here with me. I know you are.

Wherever fate takes us, Tristan.

Tristan sighed to release the last of the emotion trapped in his chest. “So, World of Warcraft?”

Markus smirked. “Now *that’s* commitment I can get behind. Race you to the car!”

35
ALEKSANDR

Aleksandr awoke to the sun breaking through a narrow gap in the overhead trees. He squinted, then shifted to get his bearings. Soft pain in his lower back traveled through him, and he reached behind to feel the heavy knotting of an ancient root.

His arm was asleep. With a glance to his left, he saw the cause. Aleksandr smiled. The sight of her erased any pain and replaced it with his daily reminder that he might be the luckiest man living.

"We fell asleep here again," he said.

"It's our spot," Fiona answered through a yawn. Her eyes were hazy with the remnants of a good sleep. "We're drawn here. We can't help ourselves."

Their spot would always be an integral part of his story. Here the boy in him had traded up to become a man. He discovered his capacity for love and became both in awe of it and afraid of it. He had wished he could tell Fiona then that there would only ever be her. That, despite his inexperience, he nevertheless *knew* he couldn't love anyone else as he loved her. Aleksandr didn't say the words then, for Fiona had known love before him and her experience burned against what he knew, deep within him. He was young, but not naïve. Unfamiliar with the world beyond the limited parts he'd seen, but very well connected to the man he was and would become.

Fiona pushed herself up, but he drew her back to his side. She laid her head against his chest, riding the rise and fall. "Today is Brigid's Day. Or, the first day. For us it lasts a week to a fortnight."

"How do we celebrate that again? Your mom's explanation confused me."

"We honor the flora and fauna emerging from the long winter by blessing and purifying all the dwellings in our tribe and lands to prepare for the coming of Ostara in April. Think of it as opening our doors in welcome."

"Ostara?"

"Spring. When the equinox comes, our homes and land will be ready for new life, thanks to the work we will do now."

"Sounds like meaningful work." Aleksandr could fill a book with all he didn't know, but the promise of knowledge had always thrilled him. Learning alongside the woman he loved made it all the better.

Fiona nuzzled her lips into the curve of his neck. "And then there's Beltane not long after." She nibbled a small pluck of his flesh. "Fertility. Romance. Flowers. Sex."

Fiona gasped in delighted surprise when he rolled atop her.

"I don't need a holiday for any of that." Nor was his heart any longer conflicted between the very grave responsibility of saving his loved ones and saving himself. Aleksandr might never fully understand what he did to cause the goddess Morrigan to rescind her demands of the Prophecy, but he knew better than to question the gift. His family was safe, and he was here, deeply and madly in love with the only woman he ever wanted to be deeply and madly in love with.

Fiona slipped her tongue in his mouth and kissed him so hungrily he lost all sense of himself. She then deftly slid herself out and away and got to her feet. "We're late for the festivities. Winner gets to make the loser do *anything* after supper." Her wink explained the rest.

She bounded away into the forest and Aleksandr shook his head as he watched her. "You're going down, Ona. And I do mean that literally!" he cried as he ran after her, laughing through the crunch of fallen branches and the late winter frost.

ALEKSANDR WAS HAPPY IN THE HIDDEN LAND BEYOND KILLIANSHIRE, Ireland. Other outsiders might have missed the creature comforts of a city, but most of his life had been spent in forests and valleys, under the veil of the hinterland. And he had Fiona, and she made him whole.

He missed his parents something terrible, but he knew they would be okay as long as he was. When he went home at Christmas, any fears at leaving them melted away as he witnessed the meaning they'd discovered in their new lives with Jacob and Amelia, and the newborn Moira. *All we need is for you to be happy and healthy. Don't worry about your mora and me. We can adapt to anything,* Far had said.

Aleksandr was happy, and he was healthy. He felt capable of anything when Fiona was at his side. They talked about what their future should look like. Marriage? Children? Should they move out into the real world and get jobs, and live normal lives? Were they safer and happier here in the forest?

Fiona's urgency to solve these questions superseded his, but he understood. Aleksandr was immortal, and she was not. She approached the end of the first third of her life, while he had no such considerations to make for his own. When she spoke of this, desperation crept into her voice. She knew how this would end, and she didn't want to wait to decide the rest of their lives.

But Aleksandr saw the future, too. He saw her skin lose its elasticity, and the silver spread through her hair. He saw himself love her more every day as her body failed her, and he felt the moment he would hold her as she breathed her last breath, ending that season of his own life with it.

When that inevitable day arrived, Aleksandr would show up at the gates of Farjhem and devote the remainder of his days to the service of Emyr. The Scryers had already made him this offer, before he left. His place awaited him.

Many years yet separated Aleksandr from this future and he would think of nothing and no one but Fiona for whatever remained of their time on this earth together.

Aleksandr pressed his lips to Fiona's forehead. It didn't wake her. Her snores from the long day of toiling and chores were earnest ones. He liked to think he contributed to her exhaustion, too, for he had won their little race in the woods...

He slipped away, beyond the protective veil of their tribe, to the meeting place chosen by his unexpected visitor.

"Aleksei."

"Aidrik."

Aleksandr's second father had never placed much importance on physical connection, but the embrace he pulled his son into lifted Aleksandr's feet off the ground.

"I missed you at Christmas," Aleksandr said. The shock of seeing Aidrik alive in Farjhem had been indescribable, and he'd replayed that moment in his head so many times he thought he could think of it without the urge to sob like a child.

But he was wrong, he wasn't there yet. He might never be.

"Yule, you mean. Christmas is naught more than a pagan celebration appropriated by insecure Children of Men to discover new methods of power extortion."

Aleksandr arched a brow. "Really, Aidrik?"

Aidrik dropped his eyes to the forest floor and grinned. "A creature as old as I cannot change. Christmas is not our holiday, my son. We will have reunions of our own making. You have my word."

"What are you doing out here?"

"Stopping for a brief sojourn on my way to palaver with Birger and Astrid. They have need of me. It is too much to resist the chance to be useful once more."

"You're useful to us," Aleksandr said and was immediately ashamed at how young he sounded... how out of touch with the complexities of the world he seemed.

Aidrik reached out and gripped his son's face in his calloused palm. "We are, all of us, connected. There is no thing on Earth sharp enough to sever the bond that ties us. But we must each forge our own paths. Your mora and far require the pull of routine. I am called to service in the field. You... my son... you are precisely where you are meant to be. You are home."

Aleksandr looked at his feet. "Do you miss them?" *Do you miss me?*

"Every second of every day. From the first whisper of sunrise to the final sigh of sunset."

Tears sprung to Aleksandr's eyes, then, but they didn't hold the same sadness anymore. Instead, they felt to Aleksandr as if he was expelling a well of emotion that had been trapped deep within him, waiting for the right moment, when he was ready, to be released. To finally free him of the last of his crippling grief.

"Will you come see me again?"

Aidrik wiped his son's tears with his thumbs. "And again, and again."

ALEKSANDR CURLED INTO FIONA'S BACK. HE PRESSED HIS FACE BETWEEN her warm shoulder blades, closed his eyes, and fell into a happy, restful sleep.

36
FINNEGAN

Ana bounced a giggly Moira on her lap. She sang a song Finn recognized from their brief time in the Highlands, when Anasofiya was too sick from childbed to play with Aleksandr, and Fiona St. Andrews took over. Fiona had been a woman of many songs, as Finn recalled, but he didn't realize Ana retained the words and tunes from her fever daze.

"We can take her tonight, right?" Ana asked Amelia, who, with Anne's help, brought the food dishes to the table.

"She's been fussy," Amelia warned. "I haven't slept in three nights."

"You can't scare me away from this precious little Hobbit!" Ana cooed with her nose pressed to Moira's.

"Do you need anything, or are you still all set? I have two days' worth of breastmilk in the fridge you can take."

"All set," Finn answered. No one said anything to make it official, but the four had become a village raising the young Moira. Within two weeks of her birth, he and Ana had set up their own nursery at Magnolia Grace. Between dinners together four or five nights a week, and their shared joy in raising the baby, their households had all but merged into one.

"I think that's it." Anne looked around at the table full of food, hands on hips. "Jon, honey, did you remember the wine?"

Ana and Finn exchanged an amused look as everyone settled into their seats. *Jon, honey?*

"Yes, dear." A happily subjugated Jon emerged from the kitchen with an open bottle of cabernet sauvignon in one hand and sparkling cider in the other. "I brought something for you as well."

"Don't want to get langered with the rest of us heathens, Anne?" Jacob teased.

"So thoughtful," Anne charged and rewarded Jon with a kiss as she took her chair. "I'll presume that to mean *drunk* from where you come from, Jacob, and no, I'm going to refrain today."

Ana buckled Moira into her rocker nestled between her and Amelia. "What are you, pregnant?"

They all laughed except Anne and Jon. The amusement died. Looks were exchanged. Questions sat unsaid.

"Jon, darling, pass the green beans," Anne said with the practiced control of the recently scandalized.

"Anne." Jon passed her the beans when she shot him a scathing look. "I know we wanted to wait until later, but we may as well make the announcement now."

"We had a *plan*," she huffed.

Finn marveled at his brother's patience as Jon smiled and took her hand. He brought it to his mouth with a kiss. Who was this man? Had he always been there, waiting for the right person to share this side of himself?

"Plans change, darling. Right?"

Anne hung her head. "You're right, of course. You go on."

Jon nodded. "Finn, will you make sure everyone has a glass of wine?" He put his hand over Anne's glass. "I'll take care of hers."

As Finn emptied the remainder of the red wine into glasses around the table, Jon stood. He held his hand out to Anne. "We have an announcement to make to you, our loved ones."

Amelia tapped her fork against her wine glass.

Jon cleared his throat. He looked at Anne, and they shared a smile. "We won't hold you in suspense. I've asked Anne to marry me, and she's accepted."

"Jon, that's incredible," Finn cried. "I'm so happy for you, brother." He slipped around the table and drew his older brother into a hug. "Who knew we would both find our futures here? You're staying in New Orleans, I take it?"

Anne held out her hand like stoic royalty as Ana and Amelia dissolved into squeals of admiration.

"We are," Jon said. "I'm looking at my own practice. Anne wants to stay at home with—" His eyes widened. His hand flew to his mouth. "Sorry."

"The rest of the news is that I'm pregnant, as I'm sure you've guessed," Anne said. "Due in the fall. I want to be a stay-at-home mother. It might not be as exciting as the careers you ladies lead, but it feels like the right one for me."

"Anne, being a mother is a career unlike any other," Amelia said. "Everyone has their path. This is yours."

"That's what I told her," Jon said. "But she thinks women in this day and age are expected to have jobs outside the home."

Ana raised her glass. "Screw that. Deschanels spend way too much time worrying about what others think. Here's to your wedding, your new family, and choosing the life *you* want."

Anne blushed. "Thank you, Ana."

"We're sisters now, Anne."

"All three of us," Anne said, clinking glasses with Ana and Amelia. "In the ways that matter most."

"We would like all of you to be in the wedding party, of course," Jon said. "Finn, you'll be my best man?"

Finn lifted his glass. "You bet."

"Ana, you once let me help you marry your soul mate, despite... despite that maybe I didn't deserve it so much at the time," Anne said. Her fingers gripped the flute of her glass. "Will you let me say thank you by standing at my side this time, as my matron of honor?"

Ana smiled. "I would be honored, Anne. Thank you."

"Amelia and Jacob, please say you'll also stand up with us?" Anne said. "We don't want a big ceremony, but we do want those closest to us to be there. My brother, Nicolas. Aunt Colleen, Uncle Noah, and a few others."

"We wouldn't miss it," Jacob said. "And I certainly wouldn't miss the chance to see Amelia in an embarrassingly awful bridesmaid dress."

"I would never do that to my girls!" Anne protested.

"Paisley with a side of magenta," Jacob mused.

"Have you set a date?" Amelia asked.

"Christmas, perhaps," Anne said. She watched Jon with stars in her eyes. "After the baby is born. I can't imagine a greater gift than Jonathan St. Andrews and his child."

Finn laughed and almost snorted his wine. "All right, Jon. Fess up. How much are you paying her?"

"Not funny," Jon said, but he was laughing, too.

"The house in Maine is yours," Finn said. He looked at Ana. "We have the one her mother left her, for when we want to go home. You're the oldest... Mom and Dad would want you to have it, especially now that you're starting a family."

Jon nodded. "I would have given it to you, Finn."

"I know. But that was before."

The conversation broke into segments. Ana and Amelia swapped places with the men so they could talk wedding planning with Anne. Jacob, Jon, and Finn conversed about their respective business ventures. Ana slipped out without ceremony at some point and came back with a hefty raid from their wine rack. One by one, the dark red wines flowed into glasses, and one by one, the empty bottles were stashed on the server.

More than a little drunk, Finn fell back in his chair and watched the end of the night unfold like a hazy, wonderful old film. This was the part in the movie where all the bad stuff was behind them and ahead lay the promise of hope. Hope was an endless font, and Finn didn't mind not knowing what the future might bring, as long as these were the people he shared it with.

"I WANT TO TELL YOU SOMETHING."

The effects of the alcohol had worn off earlier, but his head was still heavy with all the red wine consumed. Ana had a history of using these words when she was about to drop difficult news in his lap. "Okay."

"I went to see Aunt Colleen and Aunt Evie today." She ran her fingers along his torso scar, tracing soft lines. Even now, this act of trust and intimacy sent a thrill through him. "I had something to ask them. I didn't know if it was possible, but I had to know, either way."

He couldn't guess where this was going, so he said nothing. The lightness of her touch relaxed him, stripping away his nerves.

"I asked if they could heal me." Her hand stopped at the center of his chest. "My womb."

Finn lit up inside but didn't dare show his hopefulness visibly, for fear of what she might say. He would never let her know how badly he wanted another child, because she nearly lost her life delivering the first one to the world. She was enough and would always be enough. "Didn't they already try that with Mercy?"

"Mercy couldn't be healed because she died and was resurrected," Ana explained. Her words were slow and careful against his racing thoughts. "She wasn't the same when I brought her back."

"And?" Finn swallowed. "What did they say?"

Ana rolled her face into his neck. Her face was damp with tears. "They won't know for sure if the healing worked until we try, but... they said we *should* try. If we want to."

"Want to..." Finn said the words into the dark room. He was afraid to fully say them, to answer her statement that was really a question. What if he said yes, and she didn't share that desire? What if she was only doing this for him? She would wonder for the rest of their lives if she was keeping him from happiness, just as she wrongly believed she had taken him from what he loved in Maine.

But Ana had sought her aunts out on her own. He hadn't asked, or even insinuated. He'd guarded his secret desire for another child deeper than anything else. She must want this, too, maybe as badly as he did.

"I want to." Finn spoke the words into being. He tossed them into the universe, come what may. "Ana, I would love to have another child with you."

He felt her mouth spread into a grin against his flesh.

"Let's do it," he said. "What's the worst that happens?"

"We have the best son in the world already in Aleksei. We have our godchild Moira. And soon Jon and Anne's baby."

Finn pressed her tight. "And we have each other, Ana, and *that* is more than enough."

He waited for her to ask the question often at the center of her mind in conversations like this: *Is it enough?* But they had come too far together for insecurities to have any place in their household.

"More than enough," she repeated. Her chest pressed into his side. Her heartbeat soared through her skin.

"My cup runneth over," Finn whispered and wrapped himself into the arms of his first and only safe place.

EPILOGUE

Nicolas and Lauren stood in the doorway at The Gardens and watched the car pull away down Jackson. They waved at Ashley and Charlotte, but beyond the tinted windows of the town car, he couldn't see if the gesture was reciprocated. It didn't matter. They'd offered their goodbyes and delivered their final instructions to the duo. There was no more to be said.

He leaned into the frame. "When we first kicked off this research program, did you see us where we are now, sending our third pair into the field?"

Lauren uncrossed her arms. "It was a tall order to be sure, with all the hours we both put in to pore over the materials in the vault, and then organize them, and—"

"Come on, answer honestly."

Lauren nudged him out of the way and eased the door closed. "No, I guess I didn't."

"We don't make a terrible team," Nicolas ventured. "You might even say we make a good one."

Lauren eyed him with wariness, a look he had come to recognize almost anytime he opened his mouth. He waited for phase two of her reaction, the inevitable sharp comeback.

The tension fell away from her cheeks and eyes instead. To Nicolas' great surprise, she laughed. "We accomplished a lot more than I ever expected, so, sure. I'll give you that. I would have wagered a month's salary that something would go sideways, but amazingly, nothing did."

"There's a compliment somewhere in there, Lauren, and I'll take it."

The entire contents of the Council's vault—once a handwritten mess of folders and notebooks—was now digitized and completely searchable. From that database, Nicolas and Lauren had identified sixty-two separate missions that could bring value to the Collective's data bank, and were already working on a new project, mapping the genealogy of other prominent Louisiana families who had come up in various stories of the peculiar. Like the LaViolettes, there were other links to the Deschanels they had yet to uncover. Nicolas and Lauren were on the brink of discoveries that would change the way the family operated forever.

"What a day." Lauren stretched her arms over her head with a heavy inhale. She released the breath with her eyes closed. "I'm thinking a long bath, a bottle of chardonnay, and a bedtime early enough to continue earning my reputation for being an old spinster."

Nicolas lifted her cardigan from the hanger in the closet. He held it out. "I had another idea."

"You and your ideas," Lauren chided. She took the sweater, but didn't bolt for the door. Nicolas took that as a positive sign.

"Let me take you to dinner," he said. "Before you turn me down, I'm not asking you on a date."

"Why am I skeptical?"

"Because I'm a rotten rapscallion and secretly you believe my superpower is making panties disappear with the sheer will of my depraved desires."

Lauren wrinkled her lips in bland bemusement. "Who knew you had such a command of the English language?"

"It's not a date. We should celebrate," he went on. "We did this, Lauren. I don't know about you, but these have been the most productive months of my life and I've more than earned myself a rib-eye at K-Paul's."

Lauren glanced at the clock. "It's a Saturday night. We'll never get a table."

Nicolas blushed. "Here's where I confess I already made the reservation."

Here it was, the moment of truth. He was almost certain Lauren would turn him down in spite of the first great reason he'd had to spend time with her outside of work. She tolerated him, but didn't trust him. Before, this would have inspired Nicolas to work harder at what he would have perceived as a very drawn-out game of hard to get. Lauren wasn't playing hard to get, though, and he didn't want to play games anymore. Not with her.

Nicolas watched her debate with herself. Talk herself into it and then out of it, and around and around.

"Why not?"

Nicolas started to thank her anyway, to suggest they do it another time. He froze, mouth gaping.

She'd said yes. Now what?

What would a gentleman do? Nicolas Deschanel asked himself. He had no experience in the role, so he guessed.

He took her cardigan and draped it over her shoulders. "After you," he said and held the door.

As he pulled it shut behind him, Nicolas realized his hands were shaking.

• • •

"To our success," Nicolas said after the waiter had delivered their drinks. A glass of chardonnay for Lauren; mineral water for him.

Lauren raised her glass. "May we have more."

Nicolas observed her over his water as she wrapped her slender fingers around the stem of her fluted glass. She pretended to be relaxed, but the tension in her knuckles gave her away. He didn't know what to do to put her at ease. His only real skill with women was getting them into his bed.

"Colleen gave us a whole month break. What are you going to do with your time?" she asked with an upturned brow, as if anticipating an answer that would scandalize her.

"I decided to decline the break," he said. He brushed his fingers over the condensation coating his glass. "I like being busy. Who knew?"

Lauren declined over her usual inclination to point out his privileged upbringing. "Good for you. You'll be ready when we start back up, then, when Colleen has us begin earnest work on researching the LaViolette women."

"You'll go back to work at the firm during the break, I take it?"

She nodded. "They're not giving me new clients. I think they've accepted I'm a permanent resource of Colleen's, so they'll find something to keep me busy, most likely."

"When was the last time you took a vacation, Lauren?"

Lauren shifted in discomfort. "Who has the time?"

"You have a month right now to do whatever you want."

"Whatever I want." Lauren drained the last of the wine and rolled it around in her mouth. "You know what that feels like. I don't."

"Not everything in life has to be in the extremes," Nicolas said. "You think I play too hard, and I think you work too hard.

Why can't we find middle ground? Be hard workers and enjoy the spoils?"

"What happened to you?" Lauren studied him the way a scientist regards a rare specimen. "Why do you sound so reasonable?"

"Mercy came back," Nicolas blurted. The words popped into his head before he could think to stop them. Only after they were out, did he realize they were also the answer to her question.

Lauren looked taken aback. "Oh? Congratulations."

"I told her it was over." He looked past her, at the kitchen. Where was their food? He needed something to do with his hands. "I spent my whole life being completely averse to commitment, and then I loved her and..." And what? "And I thought when things didn't work out it was because I was right all along about myself."

Lauren let go of her glass. "What do you mean, right about yourself?"

The words flowed easier than he expected, but they didn't sound like him. Turning his feelings into anger or humor came so naturally. Emotional honesty didn't. "That all I was good for was a night of fun."

Lauren propped her chin on her folded hands. "That's really sad, Nicolas."

He shrugged. Her sympathy burned worse than her apathy. "Maybe it's true, maybe it's not, but it isn't why my relationship with Mercy didn't work out. I know that now. And when she came to see me, I told her a truth I don't think she was ready to hear."

"Hard truths are never easy," Lauren said, cautious. "What was it? That you told her?" She laughed and waved her hands. "Forget it, that's none of my business."

Nicolas met her eyes. "I told her I was finally ready to give myself to someone, and she wasn't."

"Wow." Lauren signaled for another glass of wine. "How did she take it?"

"Let's just say her reaction removed any doubt I had left about it."

"I'm sorry things didn't work out for you two," Lauren said.

"I thought I was, too, but I'm not anymore. So many of the things I thought were important to me just don't seem so important anymore." To the left, the bar glittered with beautiful bottles. His mouth watered, but this time it wasn't for alcohol. He craved a clear head. To see, and hear, and feel his life and the world around him. The pleasure and, yes, the pain. "I have you to thank."

Her suspicion returned. "Me?"

"Don't look so ready to punch me, even though you might enjoy it," he retorted. With a playful wink, he added, "Hell, *I* might enjoy it."

"Don't tempt me."

"It's not a line. You really helped me, first on our trip west and then over the last two months. Most of the people in my life threw their hands up years ago. *He is who he is.* But not you. You don't let me eat my own bullshit. You have no time for it."

"I'm shocked your family had time for it."

"I don't know if I realized how they saw me until now. Incorrigible, I would have thought. Fragile is what I think they really saw. They saw through the layers of womanizing and drinking and playing to something deeper and a lot less fun. Was I really that fragile all along? My ego says no." He grinned. "Doesn't matter. What matters is, it took you to help me see. So, thank you, Lauren. For not putting up with me so I could learn to put up with myself."

"That might be the weirdest thanks I've ever received," Lauren said. Her brows furrowed. "You've said things like this more than once now, and I'm afraid you've put me on a pedestal I don't deserve."

He shook his head. "You've got it wrong. I don't see you on a pedestal at all. I just see someone who is real and flawed and, through all that, a good person." He swirled the last of the melted ice in his glass. "And I think, hey, I've got the real and flawed part down. Maybe I could be a good person, too."

"You *are* a good person, but..." Lauren twisted at her napkin in her lap. A high flush rose into the apples of her cheeks. "You're confused when it comes to me. You've been through a lot lately and it's causing you to feel a lot of tangled things that you've somehow projected onto *me,* of all people. I'm the last person on earth who should be at the center of your spiritual awakening, or whatever this is, and I have to think it's just the coincidence of proximity."

"I have no idea what you just said, Lauren, but I know you're wrong. You don't see what I see, and that's okay."

Lauren's eyes had a film of tears. "What is it with you bad boys using me as your life lesson? What is it about me? Do I have something written on my forehead? A magnet?"

"I can't speak for anyone but me," Nicolas said. "And for me, you're not a glass of water after a month in the desert, or however other men have chosen to see you. For me, you're just... you're Lauren, and I'm Nicolas, and all I want is to know you, and for you to know me. The *real* me, or what I hope is the real me. The me I'm becoming."

Tears slid down her cheeks. She wiped at them with the napkin. Before either could say another word, the food arrived, breaking the heavy fugue of emotion hovering between them.

"Thank you," Lauren managed. The waiter asked if they needed anything else, and she told him no. She lifted her fork, but it hung, suspended in midair, with her thoughts.

"I can't give you what you want."

"I only want to be your friend." *I think I'm in love with you. Real love, not dressed with diamonds and caviar but stripped down to the center of everything where it's only you and me.*

"That's not the message you've been sending." Her chest quivered as she choked back her tears.

"I'm sorry, I never meant to upset you," Nicolas said. He reached over to steady her hand that held the fork. She looked down at his hand then back at him. He released her. "I'm not confused, Lauren. Not anymore."

"Nicolas..."

"Your friendship is what helped save me. I won't ask for anything more." He tipped his glass at her. "I still have a long way to go before I could ever be worthy of someone like you. First, I need to be worthy of myself."

Lauren dropped her fork. She folded her hands in her lap. "I want to trust you. Even when everything inside me screams to walk away, I find myself drawn to you. Having dinner with you. Making jokes with you in the dark rooms of The Gardens at two in the morning."

"Friendship, Lauren. It's all I ask."

"You're sure."

"I'm sure."

Lauren reached across the table. Squeezed his hand. Her smile lit up the whole room. "Friendship."

Not quite two years ago, he had gassed up his Porsche and made for Deschanel Island with the intention of ending years of hard living and broken dreams with his father's gun.

Living no longer interested me. The first words of his unwritten memoir, words personifying the indifference he invited into his life in place of grief, in place of assuming the yolk of responsibility.

That was hardly two years ago, and that was a lifetime ago.

Now?

Now, Nicolas Deschanel could not *wait* to live.

LOOKING FOR MORE *CRIMSON & CLOVER* TO SOOTHE THE BOOK hangover? Try one of these series:

Midnight Dynasty: Nicolas and Lauren continue their work —and awkward tension. One of their projects leads them down a path they'll never return from, in ***A Tempest of Discovery.***

The Seven Series: Go back to the beginning, and watch the lives of the seven siblings who mothered and fathered the heroes and heroines of The House of Crimson & Clover. You think you know this story, but you're wrong. The heartbreak, treachery, and unfailing love begins in ***1970***.

Vampires of the Merovingi: Etienne de Blanchefort knows he's being watched. Worse, he knows his specter isn't human. Let this historical fantasy, set initially in the tropics of Saint-Domingue, whisk you away in ***The Island.***

AFTERWORD

"In my end is my beginning." Mary Queen of Scots adopted these words and had them embroidered into her cloth of state, while a political prisoner of her cousin, Queen Elizabeth I. Mary, always strong of faith—a faith that would inevitably be the foundation of her demise—began to realize she would not again rule her country as queen and would die in custody. She saw that her earthly life—all its riches and poverty, the bitter and the sweet—was only a stepping stone into what came next for her, in the afterlife.

This quote has always resonated with me. I have believed, always, that life is a series of journeys. Some are long, some are short, but all lead to the next. The end of *The House of Crimson & Clover* is one such journey of my life—and yours, if you are reading this, Dear Reader—and the end is bittersweet. These are not characters across the space of a page, they are my family. They are part of me. And, wherever they go next, they always will be.

If you read the Author's Note, you know the end of *The House of Crimson & Clover* is the beginning of many more stories within the same world. The Saga of Crimson & Clover has many more adventures in the future that will be thrilling for existing fans and great starting points for new ones.

Some of the stories presented in The House of Crimson & Clover have come to their natural end. I like to think I've given some their happily-ever-afters, both because they deserve them and because I don't know if I'll drop in on them again or not. They don't need me peering into their business all the time. They've earned a break.

Others? Nicolas' story continues. We watched him through one leg of his life's journey and now the next begins. We will learn more about Colleen and her siblings and how they became the pillars of the family they are today. And lest you think I forgot about Monsieur de Blanchefort... a series on that family and their vampiric origins is quickly on the horizon.

So, thank you, Dear Reader, for taking this journey with me. For trusting me until the very bitter(sweet) end. I hope you'll continue with me on to the next journey.

Want more Saga of Crimson & Clover? Below are the starting points for four other series within the same secretive, ancient, powerful world...

Midnight Dynasty Series: A Tempest of Discovery

The Seven Series: 1970

Vampires of the Merovingi Series: The Island

The Dusk Trilogy: St. Charles at Dusk: The Story of Oz and Adrienne

ALSO BY SARAH M. CRADIT

KINGDOM OF THE WHITE SEA

Kingdom of the White Sea Trilogy

The Kingless Crown

The Broken Realm

The Hidden Kingdom

The Book of All Things

The Raven and the Rush

The Sylvan and the Sand

The Altruist and the Assassin

The Melody and the Master

The Claw and the Crowned

THE SAGA OF CRIMSON & CLOVER

The House of Crimson and Clover Series

The Storm and the Darkness

Shattered

The Illusions of Eventide

Bound

Midnight Dynasty

Asunder

Empire of Shadows

Myths of Midwinter

The Hinterland Veil

The Secrets Amongst the Cypress

Within the Garden of Twilight

House of Dusk, House of Dawn

Midnight Dynasty Series

A Tempest of Discovery

A Storm of Revelations

A Torrent of Deceit

The Seven Series

1970

1972

1973

1974

1975

1976

1980

Vampires of the Merovingi Series

The Island

and more

The Dusk Trilogy

St. Charles at Dusk: The Story of Oz and Adrienne

Flourish: The Story of Anne Fontaine

Banshee: The Story of Giselle Deschanel

Crimson & Clover Stories

Surrender: The Story of Oz and Ana

Shame: The Story of Jonathan St. Andrews

Fire & Ice: The Story of Remy & Fleur

Dark Blessing: The Landry Triplets

Pandora's Box: The Story of Jasper & Pandora

The Menagerie: Oriana's Den of Iniquities

A Band of Heather: The Story of Colleen and Noah

The Ephemeral: The Story of Autumn & Gabriel

Bayou's Edge: The Landry Triplets

For more information, and exciting bonus material, visit www. sarahmcradit.com

ABOUT THE AUTHOR

Sarah is the USA Today and International Bestselling Author of over forty contemporary and epic fantasy stories, and the creator of the Kingdom of the White Sea and Saga of Crimson & Clover universes.

Born a geek, Sarah spends her time crafting rich and multi-layered worlds, obsessing over history, playing her retribution paladin (and sometimes destruction warlock), and settling provocative Tolkien debates, such as why the Great Eagles are not Gandalf's personal taxi service. Passionate about travel, she's been to over twenty countries collecting sparks of inspiration, and is always planning her next adventure.

Sarah and her husband live in a beautiful corner of SE Pennsylvania with their three tiny benevolent pug dictators.

www.sarahmcradit.com

www.ingramcontent.com/pod-product-compliance
Lightning Source LLC
Chambersburg PA
CBHW020337310726
48979CB00015B/2410/J

9781958744116